BETWEEN WORLDS

BETWEEN WORLDS

Sandra Billington

The Book Guild Ltd
Sussex, England

First published in Great Britain in 2005 by
The Book Guild Ltd
25 High Street
Lewes, East Sussex
BN7 2LU

Typesetting in Baskerville by
Keyboard Services, Luton, Bedfordshire

Printed in Great Britain by
Antony Rowe Ltd, Chippenham, Wiltshire

A catalogue record for this book is available from
The British Library

ISBN 1 85776 854 X

To Med. and Lit., Glasgow

1

'Zut!' Jean-Claude slammed on the brakes and 'zut-zut' replied a bird woken as he skidded towards its hedge. Jean had left the torch in the barn. He had to go back. It was paint stained, anyone finding it would connect it with him. He made a despairing three point turn. He must get back to the gallery before Bertrand, yet here he was headed in the opposite direction – and the sky was no longer black. Dawn hovered like a bird of prey. Soon there would be other cars on the road. Pretending this was not real only some nightmarish dream, he put his foot down on the accelerator and sped manically back through the twisting lanes, his modest engine straining under the effort. The barn was on the further outskirts of Ivrez. Approaching from the other side he dropped into a quieter speed – no point trumpeting his presence to the whole village – and soon he was scrambling through the dew-damp grass to the barn's musty interior. The torch lay on a ledge by the open door; put there while they indulged a last kiss. He grasped it and paused. The morning star was fading into dawn's blue wash, but there were still no human sounds. Venus must be smiling on him. He slithered down the bank to the Citroen and the engine, thankfully, sparked back into life.

He would not do this again. Bertrand would not take kindly to the knowledge that he shared Jean with a girl. Not that he did, thought Jean. They were two quite separate worlds which must not be brought together. That spark would ignite their whole way of life. But with his luck holding he had to laugh as he drove away. He could look into the shrewd brown eyes of his partner and keep his secret.

At the time of the infidelity Bertrand's imposing figure was leaving Alain Degré's Paris flat after returning a cargo of paintings. The ancient lift down to the streets, with its gates as treacherous as a prison's, could barely contain them both but Alain did not joke about the confined space. Bertrand was acutely sensitive and would read into it a comment on his bulk even though Alain, too, was homosexual. Both men breathed the night air with relief as they emerged onto Avenue Kléber. A group of glimmering nocturnals, radiant in evening dress, spilled out of the Hôtel l'Empereur, mixing improbably with a few cinemagoers heading for the Metro. Alain and Bertrand made their way through the assertive voices and scent of face powder and found Bertrand's car sitting quietly in a side street.

'That was one of our most successful exhibitions, Alain. I hope it won't be too long before you need another.'

'You have sold so many,' Alain smiled, 'it will take time.'

Bertrand smiled too. The percentage from such good sales would keep the gallery afloat for the next six months, even though Alain had the more substantial cheque in his own pocket.

'I have some ideas,' Alain went on.

'Splendid.'

'And I appreciate the prompt return of these canvases.'

'A million francs worth of anything is too much to trifle with,' Bertrand joked as he opened the door of his new Renault. In appreciation, Alain gave him a brotherly pat on the shoulder then turned back towards the Avenue.

The end of the sixties was a good time to be an artist. Post-war affluence had arrived; life had regained its exuberance and ideas had cash value. Painting and sculpture were to Paris what theatre was to London or opera to Berlin. The dynamic arts minister had done wonders. Pity he was gone, but his influence was still there. Any new building in Paris now had to have one per cent of its budget spent on a commission from a live artist. The fact that success was more than a fantasy encouraged many who might not have taken to the life otherwise, and Bertrand was conscious of being part of this good fortune as he edged himself gently into the driving seat ready for the hundred kilometres back to the gallery deep in the countryside, in the château of Ivrez.

The gallery's privacy was part of its success. The setting itself was exclusive, famous for being hard to find and well worth a visit without necessarily buying anything. The château was a twelfth-century fortification, still possessing its central iron portcullis. The wing which was home to the two artists had been a ruin, the corner crumbled to the earth like a page torn out of a history book. With their own blood, sweat, tears and a substantial bank loan Bertrand and Jean had rebuilt everything, using the original method of small, chipped stones in rough cement, and retiling the red roof, including the tapering points which sat like rosettes on the two towers. If the two men's lives were to be remembered for nothing else, they would be for this rebuilding. Once the gallery opened other artists came to live in the area, able to exhibit closer to Paris and away from the increased tourism of Provence. When a local restaurateur edged his cuisine up a notch or two Ivrez became the ideal retreat for Paris lawyers, bankers and doctors to spend a relaxing weekend while placing expensive rosettes on their chosen pieces. Bertrand and Jean had been taken by surprise, too involved with the day-to-day effort to notice much change until they realised they had achieved their goal: without compromise they could now finance their own work. And now painters who prized an exhibition at Ivrez included the very successful, such as Alain Degré.

The road was an unwinding ribbon of dark. With nothing to distract him Bertrand's musings continued to unroll with it. He had come a long way in the last fifteen years. In fact, he could no longer imagine himself as the insurance clerk with the Paris firm that he had once been – unhappy in his job and in his life. Meeting Jean was the turning point. The ambitions of both of them, which had seemed impossible to achieve before, became inevitable afterwards. Or, that was how it seemed now. Bertrand was the greater celebrity: a few critics thought his own work was showing signs of mastery and he couldn't help but be pleased that Jean was intensely private, leaving all the limelight to him.

Thinking of his partner stirred up less happy thoughts: Jean's tendency these days to philander with the opposite sex. It was not something Bertrand wished to dwell on since it revived memories more painful even than those of Jean's lapses. But he must not return home too soon. Jean, he was sure, would have taken advantage of his absence to meet that trollop from the Post Office. Nearing Ivrez he noticed it was still only five o' clock, and he was not expected until breakfast. Well, he could do with a nap. He drew into a leafy space to doze until the treachery was covered by the clear light of day.

Jean was still winding down the narrow road leading home. The scrubby trees on his left came to an end and there the château sat, modestly impressive, long and low, with its red-topped towers no higher than the trees which framed it, and an expanse of lawn brightened by well-tended beds of geraniums between the building and the lane. Despite the anxiety, Jean felt that moment of immense pleasure that always came to him seeing the place again. He turned left down the bumpy track that led to the rear courtyard. The rough area outside the gate where they parked the two cars was empty. Jean pulled up and relaxed, beginning once again to see Monique in a totally attractive light.

The overgrown moat was busy with foraging hens – five thirty and the summer morning well begun. But Jean had always been able to do without sleep. Instead of heading indoors he checked for jobs that were always waiting. The rain, promised yesterday, had not arrived and the vegetable garden needed watering. This done, he headed in to make some coffee. Would his mother be up? No matter if she were. She was a little deaf and would assume his entering from outside meant nothing more than that he had made an early start. He walked across the cobbles towards the cavernous stone kitchen and entered its cool, dark interior. Madame Estienne was not yet at her place by the hearth, so he filled the kettle for the three of them and placed it on the range. He cleaned his shoes and dusted a few traces of grass from his trousers. Promptly at six, the latch of the door over the stairs clicked and the old lady in black appeared. They exchanged habitual brief greetings and she took control of the kitchen. Although only sixty-five her dress, aged face, and self-sufficiency gave her the air of some medieval prophetess. Similarly, she sometimes began conversations half way through:

'That's what she said.'

'Who?'

'Marcia.'

'Said what?'

'That the Laroques are up to no good.'

He paused. Monique was one of the Laroques.

'What have they done?'

'He's opened a betting shop.'

Her father. Jean went on drinking, but his mother's silence asked for more:

'He hasn't much else to do.'

'At his age,' his mother went on. 'He was an intelligent man when his wife was alive. Fancy turning to such a seedy business.'

'Mmmm. What does his daughter think about it?'

'I wouldn't know – never see her.'

So that was all right. They went on with their breakfast: hunk of bread, homemade jam.

'Bertrand's a long time,' he commented. 'Perhaps Alain had company.'

'You both like to drive through the night.'

He looked up and saw that she was not referring to last night. Jean thought of the two quite separate journeys and smiled with satisfaction. Sensations of Monique's plump, ingenious body moving supply and rhythmically with his own came back to him, while Madame Estienne's mind strayed to her love, the vegetable garden.

'The beans are ready for picking.'

'Mmmm.'

'Casserole this evening. Is Bertrand bringing meat?'

'Mmmm.' It was an affirmative noise, disguising the fact that his hands were still exploring the crevices of Monique's body.

'He's a good boy.'

'Mmmm.'

Footsteps could be heard on the cobbles and Monique fled in terror from Jean's mind as Bertrand plunged into the Rembrandt-like dark. It was a moment before their eyes connected and Bertrand's unanswerable question leapt across the space. For a second Jean suspected that Bertrand suspected. Casually, he picked up the everyday threads.

6

'Was Alain pleased?'

'Very pleased. The money, the reviews – it couldn't have been better.'

'And for us.'

'A good start to the summer.'

'Yes.'

Madame Estienne brought Bertrand's coffee.

'Did you solve the problem?' Bertrand couldn't resist throwing Jean the question as he placed the bundle Madame Estienne was hoping for by the side of the sink. Jean shrugged, giving himself time to drag the relevant information back into his mind.

'Well, I tried a few ideas.'

'You got it working then? I didn't think it would be so easy.'

'Yes, it's tricky.' He was working on a decomposing sculpture. 'There's still a problem of getting the arms to detach without catching on the wires. You might have some ideas about it.'

'Right, I'll look later.'

The subject, though, was irrelevant to Bertrand. More important was this world which he suspected had excluded him. Homosexuality was not illegal, but such an eagerly heterosexual society could not help but view those unable to join in as missing something essential. Fine in these hedonistic days to love either sex, as long as you were capable of loving both. The word 'gay' had not yet been invented – and gay culture was even further off. Instead, the phrase 'man of wood' was current for those such as Bertrand. Some of their close friends did not even suspect that he and Jean had any relationship at all other than a brotherly one. René knew. Jacques did not. Jacques was an innocent. It was especially painful to Bertrand when he was excluded by his own partner, and the bonnet of Jean's car had been warm when Bertrand had touched it a few minutes ago. There was no point, though, in driving him into a direct lie. While Bertrand mused into his coffee, an English bulldog careered across the courtyard, hurling itself at him through the door in welcome.

'Édipe, chien!' Bertrand roughed the beast up affectionately. Oedipus was a perfect example of undisciplined procreation and had been named for that by his ironic master. The dog had been restless this morning; trips to Paris were the only ones from which it was excluded. But the unreserved welcome lifted some of Bertrand's gloom.

'We have the cheque!' Smiling, he produced the slip of paper with a showman's flourish. 'No need to worry about money for the rest of the summer. Everything else we do this year can be for love.'

Jean smiled back. He did love him and understood why Bertrand had not mentioned the next exhibition. He needed to savour a good moment to remove a sense of impotence.

'We'll take this to the bank tomorrow,' Bertrand went on, 'and pick up that cutting equipment.'

'Next week might be better.'

'Why?'

Monique had told Jean that a roof fault had been found in the newly-built bank. It was closed for a week for a safety inspection. Still, he thought, the information could have come from anyone, so he gave it.

'How do you know?' This was not something either of them had known yesterday and Jean had not mentioned going into Montargis. Perhaps this was where the meeting had taken place.

'From the post office here,' was Jean's reply. It was close to the truth and he defied Bertrand to read anything into it by looking candidly at him with the blue eyes which always looked truthful.

8

Jean, too, was genetically constructed for cat and mouse games. Both his parents had been abandoned as babies during the First World War. Their blonde hair told the reason. They had grown up together in an orphange and since no one in the world save each other had any affection for them, it was only natural that, when they left it, they married. Jean-Claude was born just before the second war and also grew up in an environment all but devoid of safety. Although a generous man, his actions were habitually furtive and he rarely spoke unless he knew the company well. His lack of family hung over him as punishment for his unknown grandparents' crime. He never really belonged in the world until meeting Bertrand and now life was good in their shared commitment. But with success Jean had discovered something else. His unease with women was shyness only; a feeling which he discovered in the barn with Monique was the foreplay to passion. The double life gave him excitement. He felt less guilty having something to be guilty about and there was power in controlling his secrets. Bertrand understood this. He allowed the candid gaze to win.

'Well, I'll enter it in.' he said, moving towards their bedroom off the kitchen that doubled as an office. Jean felt a pang of regret.

'Let me show you "action man".' He exited from the kitchen to his studio in one of the old stables off the courtyard and returned to their office bearing a gnomish metal figure: head all nose, low forehead, bald metal pate, spiky beard and spiky eyebrows.

'Neanderthal, 2000,' Bertrand commented.

'A good name. I'll call it that.'

The limbs looked rigid but in their trelliswork lay rods that could lift the body off at the knees.

'It is important to conceal the mains connection. It must look like an ordinary metal sculpture and once you switch it on, like so, the rods extend upwards and deposit the body on the ground. The more bizarre it looks the better. The form becomes more interesting once broken.'

'And this is where the rods stick.' Bertrand studied the angles. Their hands touched. Their smiles were no longer estranged.

'I've missed you,' said Bertrand and Jean, for the second time that night, gave himself.

Often Bertrand's physicality needed rousing, but not this morning. The thought of Jean's woman provoked him. He was passionate, intense. He must not lose him, and Jean responded. He did not want to break his ties. He wanted to be repossessed.

2

The time was 11.30 a.m. so, after replacing the telephone receiver, Jacques lifted it again and let it sit unconnected on the desk. Several callers had already talked their way round the secretary and he had work to do before lunch. The new Minister for Arts had been on, of course, so duty was done. The burglary had been a shock but the running of the Orangerie and the Jeu de Paume had to continue. Jacques dropped the pile of newspapers into the bin and picked up the documents which he had intended to work on that morning – the first a routine transfer of items by Corot from the Louvre to the Jeu de Paume. Jacques' practised eye ran through the paper work and noted it was in order; he and Bernard had been setting up these regular shows for ten years now. Good, he could sign and hand it on. The second task was rather more substantial. For twenty years now Jacques had had the dream of bringing to Paris work of the sculptor, Henry Moore. An exhibition was now agreed for June of next year. The British sculptor was up with the top three in Europe, but his work was not popular in France. All that there was of his in Paris was a commission for UNESCO. 'He isn't modern, and he isn't original,' was quite a common opinion; 'He's just a romantic borrowing from romantics of the past.' Jacques could not let this robbery distract him.

He was negotiating the use of the ground floor at the old Gare d'Orsay for temporary conversion into a gallery. It would be ideal – an open, hangar-like space, which could take the largest of the sculptures, and deep in tourist territory on the left bank of the Seine. Jacques' practised hand quickly framed a persuasive reply to the private company's objections. He also needed to write personally to Ernst Braunmüller in Geneva to be sure of "Mother and Child Number 4", and he needed confirmation about the level of insurance. Where were the insurance papers? He was sure he had left them at the side of the desk here. Had Paul taken them? No, the papers were there. He must not demonise his second in command just because he found him a touch abrasive. He read through the insurance figures as assessed for each work. Large sums had been created to value the invaluable. Did the calculations look high enough, Jacques wondered, but not so high as to jeopardise the Minister's approving them?

The door opened and Paul came in.

'Amazing, Jacques! You're working away at this routine stuff when Paris is buzzing with the Neuilly affair.' Paul was not altogether displeased at being able to rub in the bad news.

'You're asked to speak on Canal tonight, but your phone has been extraordinarily busy,' he said, noticing the unhooked receiver.

The robbed building was not strictly speaking a gallery, but it housed rare treasures and now two million francs' worth of them were swilling around the underworld. The house was owned by Le Chevalier Jean-Pierre d'Andervilliers who had an arrangement for France's National Galleries to run limited opening hours for the public. The state provided the staff but security was a joint responsibility. No doubt there would be many quarrels before liability was decided.

'Better not to say too much at this point, wouldn't you agree? Has Jean-Pierre said anything yet?'

'He's licking his wounds.'

'And I, mine.'

'But we are the ones accountable. And you are our public voice.'

It was an odd phrase and Jacques looked at him. Yes, Paul's face revealed that he aimed to be rather more of a public voice than he was at present. Curator in Chief of the National Museum of Modern Art was a cumbersome title, but Paul may well get there. Better give him a run for his money.

'Take the details. I can be available any time after 8 p.m.'

Since 1945 Jacques had been one of a group of curators who had worked with a passion to help rebuild the peace through art. The twentieth century was, they believed, as rich with diversity as the Renaissance and provided a means to create a European rather than a national identity. The two outposts of the Louvre, the Jeu de Paume and the Orangerie, built in the Tuileries, had become the home for this twentieth-century avant-garde. With the recognition and support of the Louvre, which dominated the opposite end of the gardens, they had brought many new talents to the public. Thanks to Jacques and his colleagues, these modest twin galleries had become the most popular in Paris.

But times were changing – their freewheeling style of curatorship was under pressure. The gallery that had been robbed had no official status and several of the up-and-coming staff disapproved of the arrangement. It was, Jacques thought, nearly time for him to retire, to do some serious writing and to let Paul and René fight for his job. He turned back to the accounts but Paul went on.

'Did you know that Tonsin had reduced the patrols during the night?'

'Tonsin. A man with a name like that might be capable of any stupidity,' Jacques thought, and 'No,' he did not know.

'The police are down in Marseille, checking cargoes out of France for a change.'

'Quite – much easier to use the back door.'

'A door which is guarded more by robbers than by cops.'

'The Modigliani is a very large canvas. Would it roll up?'

'Robbery to order – can't see them bothering with anything other than small canvases, otherwise.'

'Mmm.'

It seemed to Paul that Jacques was oblivious of Tonsin's defence that he had reduced the patrols on Jacques' orders. It was not reported in the papers, but would be sprung on Jacques tonight, unless someone warned him. Paul decided not to. Jacques infuriated him. He would have ideas – to renovate a building, to set up exhibitions, make this disastrous joint arrangement – but he had no understanding of the detail involved. Often, there were hitches. Even now he was having difficulty finding an exhibition space for the Moore. Jacques was from a generation that expected organisation to function by kinetic energy and Paul's own attempts to shape events were constantly frustrated. Not that his ideas weren't good. An English exhibition at a time of raging Carnaby St/Beatles anglophilia would catch the public mood. And few people had Jacques' range of international contacts. But, after that absurd event two years' ago – Maurice Chevalier celebrated in the Louvre – and now this lapse in security, Jacques would have to join his colleagues kicked out last year, and Paul would need to think up

14

more decisive methods than the minor public embarrassment he would have this evening. So thinking, Paul left and Jacques made use of his phone.

'Kirsten, could you phone Albert's and let Mathilde know I am on my way?'

'Oh, they're here, Monsieur Duclos.'

'Papa, we've been to the zoo – we've seen all the giant animals.' Lucien's voice came clear down the line and, almost immediately, Mathilde opened the adjoining door. She was still good-looking in the well kept way that money provides, genial and slightly plump.

'I'm remembering all the ways we used to keep the children amused in July. It's so long ago, I hardly recognised the lay-out at the zoo.'

Their first two children were now in their twenties. Ten-year old Lucien was a late treasure.

'Must have been warm, though?'

'Mmmm.'

'Soon we'll be out of Paris ourselves.'

They went in single file down the stairs from his office – the Orangerie was a functional building – then along the right bank of the Seine and across the Tuileries, a walk which often struck him as surreal since he was so familiar with works in the Louvre which featured this part of Paris. And, among the summer crowds this July was a lone painter continuing the tradition. Then across the Rue de Rivoli and into Albert Chapu's for lunch. It was a very amiable two hours and would keep Jacques going until 10 pm. Lunch was often the only time during the week when he saw his son. But, despite burglaries and competitive colleagues, it was still possible to relax and simply enjoy being alive, as his slightly expanding stomach revealed.

At the television studios that evening Jacques picked up an evening paper. The Neuilly affair was on page four he saw to his relief. He read the report, noting possible questions that would face him. Had there been collusion, were they understaffed? He could answer those. Other more pressing items drew his attention: the horrors of Vietnam, Ted Kennedy and Chappaquiddick. More interestingly, there was an account of the growing passion for sailing solo round the world. Jean Matessier had just put into Tahiti for repairs. The strong, lined face smiled thoughtfully out of its garland of flowers. He was asked why he had undertaken the trip. 'It's a way of discovering reality,' he had said. 'In France we worship false gods.' Jacques mused on the idea of the quest. Was it optimism in reaching out or just bravado? Donald Crowhurst had been missing for some months now. Would we ever know what had happened to him alone on the sea? Western society has largely solved the problem of poverty, Jacques thought, a trifle complacently. We have become too comfortable, he thought, though he acknowledged he himself could not do without his creature comforts. And facing chosen difficulties is not the same thing as facing difficulties thrust on you from birth, like poverty. Choosing your own problems to solve could be described as another kind of luxury. The luxury for these men is to discover who they are by facing a chosen unknown. The challenge and the risk of disaster, defines them, gives them their reality. Jacques' theory was more than a little influenced by News Item number 1 that evening which was the return of Aldrin, Collins and Armstrong from the moon. Neuilly, thankfully, would be a mere afterthought for the studio was electric with excitement. It was not just that the moon was more fully discovered but that the earth was rediscovered – its uniqueness as a living planet: its vulnerability as a living planet. There were such wonderful photographs. There is either great optimism or great restlessness in our society, Jacques thought, with

16

men and sometimes women rejecting the cosy world they find themselves in, but trusting it not to reject them. All the current artistic activity, too, is a combination of restlessness and confidence – rejecting art forms used in the West up until 1914; putting the two last wars firmly in the past and starting afresh with new forms, clean primitive images, ideas taken from simpler societies. The book he was planning would set post-war art movements in this wider context. His philosophising, however, did not remove the fact that the Neuilly robbery was News Item number 5 and, at 8.30 pm Jacques faced the cameras.

3

St John's, Blackheath – evening. The church clock struck 8.30. Sarah and Stephen were late. Not in itself so terrible – the run down to Dover only took two hours – but there was always the possibility that something had gone wrong. About to go in, Amy stopped on hearing the deep-throated engine that was so different from those of other cars. Then, around the corner came the bold snout of a once magnificent vintage Alvis. The car's six-foot width dominated the street and, under Stephen's care, the green bodywork and copper trimmings glowed proudly. The polish on the car's frame, though, revealed ridges and bumps from years of repairs. Eventually, it ended its stately progress by pulling up in front of the Victorian house where Amy lived. This too had once seen better days.

Sarah got out, carrying Alexander, and looked relieved at the size of Amy's bag.

'I knew you wouldn't bring much luggage.'

Ali-ba grinned a chubby welcome. He had inherited his mother's ability to radiate security in the most unlikely circumstances. Stephen, too, got out and opened the boot, moving with quiet nervousness, the way people do who persist in aims against the odds. Five-year old James, who was both like and unlike his father, stayed in the car and ignored them all.

'I can only paint properly in France,' Stephen had often said. 'The whole way of life is right; painting is treated as normal, not some freakish sign of instability.'

As a character in a recent novel delicately expressed it: '...if you put artists down t'pit they'd be less sickening.' France was clearly the place to head for. Not only did it hold the promise of a living but houses there were cheaper too. This move had to end the poverty and the bickering. They had deposited half the proceeds of their own house sale with the Banque de France, which left them with a reasonable sum to live on until they could start earning. As part of the surge of optimism, Sarah had included her old friend from secretarial college in the first stages of the voyage, as a form of therapy.

Amy, Sarah thought, should have been an actress – slim and leggy like Audrey Hepburn. But, attracted by the turn in Sarah's life, Amy had, instead, become administrative assistant in an art gallery, working for the young art historian, John Barton. His lack of stuffiness made everyone warm to him and Amy had adored his ease with people more than she did his good looks. She had worshipped him even before they became engaged and she'd still worshipped him after they became lovers. Then he had been killed in a car crash. One moment life was perfect on cloud nine, the next his absence ended her life too. A tendency to daydream had taken her over and she was losing interest in the work at the Greenwich Gallery. The men she met now, it seemed to her, treated her as a 'dolly bird', perhaps because her mind was elsewhere when she talked to them. She began by treating other men as though they were John and lost interest in them when she discovered they were not. This trip was a godsend. She had spent time in France as a child and could act as interpreter. It would also be useful for the exam she was half-heartedly studying for. But what she was really looking forward to was the prospect of dropping into a family routine ruled by combined needs, instead of having to create artificial ones for herself.

However, when the car stopped, Amy could see that the noble old lady was badly abused; the exhaust pipe skated an inch above the road.

'Sarah, this car will collapse. I don't mind not going.'

Sarah laughed. It could not be denied that they were taking everything the car could impossibly carry.

'Don't be silly,' said Stephen, kindly, 'the car'll be fine.' Her backing out seemed to him another example of what was wrong with her. However, the world Stephen inhabited was also governed by personal logic. He worked on the principle that if he stuck with a fantasy long enough it would become reality. It was sometimes hard to tell who was the more unrealistic of the two.

Persuaded, Amy edged her way into the back and James made room among the packages. The boys knew her well and, despite his lack of obvious welcome, James was pleased. He demanded order because of the chaos which surrounded his father's way of life. Everything about him had to be tidy – if a sandwich he was handed fell apart he had a tantrum. He welcomed Amy's appearance because she came from a world untouched by his father's disorder and so would help his mother keep it at bay. Now, as they drove towards Dover for the midnight boat, what he was most conscious of was that they no longer owned a roof over their heads.

'Where is our home now?' he asked his parents over and over again with bell-like insistence. He had watched them sell their precious little house in Southwold with a trepidation confirmed by this drive into the night. Not even his mother's reassurances had worked and it helped him to cope when he punctured their optimistic talk, forcing them to share his anxieties.

It was about ten o'clock, and they were on the new motorway to Dover – about to pass Faversham – when there was a dull thud from under the bonnet and they drifted gently to a halt. Fortunately, the hard shoulder was a refuge they could reach – they could not compete in any but the nearside lane. Missiles with fierce white eyes flashed past; the car rocked with every near miss. They sat for a moment taking this in then, still in silence, Stephen stepped onto the highway, risking his life to wave at the speeding shapes. In the car the two women shared a silent realisation: there was no possibility of reaching the midnight ferry. It was ludicrous even to hope that anyone would tow them off the motorway. This task would fall to the police who would demand a full inspection of the vehicle with all the delay that that would involve. Their venture was ruined before it was begun. Why hadn't Stephen shown the same love for the interior as he had for the exterior of the car? Only silence kept the lid on their frustration.

But an angel of mercy did stop. It took the form of a very unangelic-looking burly, hairy man in a bright red jacket.

'Hi! Magnificent car! Wonderful pub story.'

A rope was fixed and they rolled, regally absurd, into Faversham: out of high-speed noise and danger and into the vacuum of dark, deserted streets. At 10.30 p.m. the devilish-looking saint drove back to his normal way of life, leaving behind a mute crew who envied him. Stephen went on a fruitless search for an open garage.

'There's one which will open at seven a.m.,' he said hopefully on his return.

Tired Ali-ba, missing the comforting movement of the car and sensing the mood around him, was howling. Sally rocked him in her arms. The jar of baby food had had little effect. The rest of them had relied on getting fed on the boat, so had to make do with biscuits and a bottle of water before settling down to sleep. James had gone very quiet. Sarah did not dare even to look at him, now that his grievances against them were so fully justified. As they feared, eventually his decisive treble piped up.

'This is our home now ... Because it isn't moving any more.'

With the success of their laughter in his ears, James curled up and slept. All followed suit until about 5 a.m., when Ali-ba woke to discover he was just as unhappy as he had been the night before. His fierce cries cut through them all and Sarah, absent-minded through concern, said to Stephen, 'If you drive round for a few minutes he'll drop off again.'

At seven Stephen returned to the garage. The problem was a broken fan belt; the repair would not take long. They also found a lorry drivers' café and, at 9 a.m. set off again, a little sleepy, but full of that extra surge of confidence which follows a rescue from near disaster. That afternoon they arrived in Calais.

Next, they needed to call at the gallery at Ivrez to pick up a promised wad of money: – more than Stephen had ever received before in one go. It had been Bertrand's sale of four of his pictures which had motivated their move, drawn by this proof that it *was* possible to earn a living as an artist. Stephen looked forward eagerly to this business meeting and the rebuilding of his confidence.

Instead of the direct route to the south-east through Paris, with all its urban hazards, they took the road round to Rouen through the Pas de Calais. After about twenty miles eager noises came from Ali-ba and a pulling towards the window:

'Flowers,' agreed James.

They had passed the entrance to a side road generously decorated with summer blooms. Sarah and Stephen exchanged glances and Stephen reversed to take a better look.

'The flowers go all the way to the village.'

The children's enthusiasm decided them:

'Well, we could take a look.'

The road round the village green was deserted that Sunday afternoon; there were only multi-coloured flowers and flags, evidence of cheerful human activity which supported their expectations of this country where quality of life 'ruled OK'. They finished their tour and were heading back to the main road when there was yet another explosion from under the bonnet, and they slid to their elegant and now practised halt on the grassy common, where the signpost read 'Étrée-Wamin'. Hoots of laughter rose.

'Well, we're on the right side of the channel!'

'Just!'

'Sounded like a gasket,' said Stephen casually, for a problem identified is a problem half-solved. He got out of the car and looked under the bonnet once more. He was right: a gasket had blown. All that was needed was another garage. He stood up and looked round, bemused, searching vainly across the deserted green.

'Well,' said Sarah. 'We might as well *all* have a look.'

They were about twenty yards from the car when, apparently from nowhere, dishevelled urchins materialised and began clambering all over it. Fearing the instant trashing of their only means of transport, Amy tried out her French in a desperately playful voice:

'Careful – she's going to bite you.'

And they changed instantly to cherubim. A girl of about ten took her hand and led them all home, where after coffee, cognac and fruit, her father organised a rescue.

This time the Alvis's humiliation involved being hitched

to a tractor and towed in procession through the decorated lanes as an unexpected addition to the fête. Cheers and toasts were followed by a visit to the home of the local garage owner who, of course, did not have a gasket to fit a 1930s British car. But he was optimistic and the party retired for further hospitality from Marie-Louise's family, after which the large and cheerful owner of the tractor showed them a suitable field to camp in.

It took two days to trace a gasket, a boy from the village heading out on his bike each day to scour the garages in the Pas de Calais. A dedicated figure, undeterred by the rain that poured down on him incessantly. Sarah, Stephen, Amy and the two boys shared the one tent, and managed well enough not to lose their cool, though layers of dirt seeped up from the earth and came down with the wet. The farmer's wife showed storybook kindness, bringing them fresh bread, milk and eggs each morning. At the garage Stephen communicated quite well; technical terms were much the same in either language, and the engine was there to be pointed at. Stephen knew a great deal about engines. It was because of this that he had not dared look inside the Alvis before leaving, dreading what he might find. Three mornings later, when the gasket job was nearly done and Amy was putting in her pennyworth of translation, the garage hands exchanged meaningful smiles and comments about Stephen and his ménage of women.

'Vieilles amies,' Amy said firmly, stressing the feminine endings.

'Ah, vieilles amies,' they repeated, disappointed. The English must be really mad then.

Once the car was fixed the farmer's wife invited them all in to get thoroughly dry on the outside, and thoroughly wet on the inside. 'One for the road,' was a legitimate cry. It was, therefore, in very good spirits that the project took to the road again, waved off by their adoptive daughter, Marie-Louise.

They started in the evening so that, by driving all night, they should reach Montargis next day. There was a tense moment when, in the darkness, the car drove onto a dug-up section of road. She bounced and clanged like the tin man and they waited for something else to snap, but this time she held firm and they emerged at dawn in Chartres – under clear blue skies. An hour's nap was followed by a bite to eat and a discussion on what to do on arrival.

'We look such a mess,' said Sarah, but Stephen had returned to optimism.

'They'll let us clean up there, and perhaps give us a bed for a night.'

'Bertrand?' said Sarah incredulously. 'Jean-Claude perhaps, but not Bertrand?'

'Why, what's he like?' Amy asked.

'I'm very grateful to him. He's been a great help, but he's not an easy person and he likes things to be – tidy.'

They laughed and James flinched. 'Tidy' was a word he used, and he had discovered a new betrayal of the order to which he clung. These adults, with whom he was forced to live, had expected him to nibble biscuits during the night and stop for drinks, but there had been no real beginning to the day. Since dawn he had wearied them with his new repeat question, asked each time with the same cool innocence:

'When are we going to have breakfast?'

'This is breakfast,' they said as they grabbed their fourth snack at 3 p.m.

'No, it's not,' he said politely rudely, 'I have cornflakes for my breakfast.'

The couple of kilometres down the lane to Ivrez in

their wide car were taken slowly, in expectation of some impossible confrontation. Then the overhanging trees parted with theatrical effect to reveal the squat, sandy-grey stone memorial of the past, with its turrets and freshly cut lawn. About a dozen national flags fluttered along the side of the gallery wing – a United Nations of artists.

'The centre of the building and the far wing belong to Paul du Chambrai, the local squire. He's not often here though,' Stephen explained. 'The gallery is in this first part. He almost gave it to Bertrand because it was a heap of rubble – so they say. Hard to believe though.'

'Mmm.' A mythical tubular beast rose from out of the lawn. It was one of Jean-Claude's, permanently on display. They absorbed the combination of ancient and modern.

Jean-Claude looked into Bertrand's studio.

'Stephen Bradley is here,' he said non-commitally.

Bertrand sighed.

'He should have written. How can I leave this? Oh well, I'll go and speak to him. He can come back this evening.'

As they crossed the cobbled yard, Jean-Claude thought it best to prepare him further.

'He has his family with him. They wondered if they could clean up.'

'Clean up?' Bertrand could not even make sense of the suggestion.

From the car James saw a giant approach them, about seven feet tall he seemed – though Bertrand was only six feet two. Impressively rotund yet not a Father Christmas, James decided, since sombre, dark eyes loomed out from under thick black eyebrows. Ahead of him was the slighter built, wiry Jean-Claude. For his part, Bertrand saw a tangled mass of grimy gypsies in a filthy old car that was obviously about to fall to pieces and, instinctively, he kept his distance. Jean-Claude came nearer: his intense blue eyes communicated through the open window.

'A kilometre back – good hotel.'

'Hotel?' Sarah winced under her breath for their savings. 'Could we camp in the field here tomorrow?'

'Oh...' Jean was uncertain.

'Till we've settled up with the money – we're going south then.' A business arrangement improved their standing and Jean went back to consult with Bertrand whose glance looked inflexibly hostile. But Jean returned smiling.

'Right.'

'Right – see you tomorrow.'

They backed out and returned down the lane.

'True to form,' said Sarah, accepting Bertrand's snub with laughter.

Unbeknown to them, the washing facility at Ivrez was primitive and the five of them unloaded into it would have upset a delicate ecological balance. But the enforced night under a roof was infinitely welcome: hot water, comfortable beds and wonderful local food. To be clean and warm after days of discomfort was paradise. Except for James, who was not going to let go of his grievance against their persistent and wanton failure in duty towards him. When the waiter put before them a variety of irresistibly succulent dishes whose smell made their guts expand in expectation James bawled into the man's astonished face.

'I want my breakfast!'

And then became sweetness itself.

Returning to Ivrez next day, their reception there was,

27

also, quite different. Bertrand had had time to adjust. Their encampment would be picturesque – for a short while. The sun shone; the travellers were rested, they looked presentable. They could be classed as a group of English hippies. But they were not hippies. They were not into drugs, nor were they demonstrating freedom by dropping out of society. Stephen's serious and impractical attitude to life simply excluded him from English society.

Bertrand proceeded to business with Amy as interpreter. It was a delicate task since the franc had recently been devalued and Bertrand had a habit of dealing in old figures. It was essential to avoid misunderstandings and their carefulness over the details became confidential, even intimate, no doubt aided by the fact that this business was carried out in the sculptors' bedroom-cum-office. Amy strove for detachment. It seemed that, from both men, there came an invitation to know them better – a sub-text of kinship. Perhaps she was too gamine for her own good – slim like an adolescent boy, with soft auburn hair and a lost look in her eyes. And how could she help but warm to their approval. Delighted by the treasures of the place, she bubbled like a newly opened bottle of champagne. Bertrand relaxed and came out to watch with a wistful smile as she romped with Ali-ba. He even lowered himself down with difficulty onto the grass to join them, but Ali-ba burst into tears when his giant's features loomed into the toddler's view. With a sigh of resignation and an intimate glance at Amy, which told her he was used to this kind of rejection, Bertrand heaved himself up again. She reassured him that it was the 'inconnu' disturbing Ali-ba, but his essential loneliness communicated itself and she was moved that he trusted her with the knowledge of it. He escorted her, lumberingly courteous, round their medieval gallery. It was extraordinarily exquisite, once you'd learned how not to hit your head on the beams nor impale yourself on the exhibits. Bertrand took her through the gallery and into his holy of holies, his own studio, and watched her reaction to one metal sculpture there. It was a Don Quixote, whose body was constructed as an armour of welded keys, except for its penis, which was a padlock. Release of the figure's sexuality would be frustrated for as long as the bronze lasted. Unlike mortality, released by death, the face of this bronze anticipated an eternity of metal anguish. It was tragi-comedy and Bertrand's ironic smile suggested to Amy an autobiography.

Jean-Claude was usually in the background. Amy would glance up, hoping for some comment – a few words – and with them a torrent of meaning from those intensely smiling eyes. Their total acceptance of her lulled her; their artistic talent impressed her; her French improved and intelligent observations sprang effortlessly from her lips. She found herself falling in love with their way of life; wary of Oedipus, who was also rather keen on her, but seduced by other touches of exotica, like the talking myna bird on permanent duty outside the kitchen door. In this Lethean situation the time to leave overtook her. She thought it was Saturday, found it was Sunday, and had to be in London on the Monday. Hurriedly, Stephen was to drive her to the station. As a farewell Bertrand, with a curious gallant bow, presented her with postcards of their work:

'You will come back,' he said, 'soon.'

Jean-Claude added his support. Immensely pleased, she agreed, not letting her glance into Jean's eyes stay for too long. She refocused on Bertrand, aware of his personal isolation, and wanting no sourness in this friendship.

'I will if I can,' she promised.

29

'Ali-ba wants to pee!' The tryst was broken by James's distant cry, followed by his mother's encouragement:

'Well, you know how to help him.'

'How can I help him? You can only pee by yourself!'

'One day,' Sarah thought, 'James will be a lawyer.'

Amy got into the car.

'Next time,' Sarah enthused, 'come and see us in our French cottage.'

'I look forward to it.'

The return journey was immensely sobering. The last francs spent on a good meal in Paris landed in the channel when the boat unexpectedly sailed over a cliff outside Dieppe harbour. Retching over the rail at least deterred the persistent Romeo who had dogged her from the train. Back in Greenwich, writing to Sally c/o Bertrand, Amy thought of her promise to the two men. She realised in the grey light of London that to go back alone to that exotic château in the silence of the French countryside, with the large brooding Bertrand and the retiring Jean-Claude with the crystal clear eyes, was too bizarre an idea even to contemplate: a positively pornographic fairytale – no matter how beautiful their palace. So she sent them a note.

'Your invitation was very kind, but I regret it won't be possible.'

By return came a hand-drawn card from Bertrand, with the message:

'Nous vous attendons: Vive l'amitié.'

'Oh well, if it's 'l'amitié' we're talking about...' She was intrigued and flattered by the fact that they were intrigued by her. They were a profound mystery, more interesting than anything which had happened since John's death. In the non-sexual state she was in these days she accepted what the card said. They were soul mates; she could whole-heartedly return their spiritual affection. And their world was one of talent and creation where she, too, might find a new direction in life. She replied that she would after all come and, posting the letter, looked into Jean-Claude's blue eyes in the post box mouth.

A few days later Bertrand sat at the table, filled with tenderness. Jean, looking at his beaming face, guessed what was in Amy's reply before it was handed to him. Little was said, just the need to write the time and date in the diary. For Bertrand, her sympathy illuminated the barrenness that surrounded him, and Jean, he could see, was equally pleased that she was coming back. Well, that would be all right; this time they would be equal. Bertrand would not object to sharing her. The bed was large enough for three. His smile communicated these generous intentions but a slightly different scenario came to Jean's own mind.

4

The best thing about travelling, Amy thought, was that you put your life into the care of timetables and ticket collectors. There were simple problems: where to eat, how to communicate – all more fundamental to life than earning a daily living. This time she was going a stage beyond the family venture; this was stepping clean and pure into the unknown and, once on the train, all worldly worries would disappear. She looked back at her empty flat. The milk was cancelled. Mrs Miles below was looking after Butch, the cat. Everything else would now be left to the care of the household gods. Increasingly, she could not bear the routines that reminded her of John; they gave her the sensation of floating uselessly in existence. Cutting loose and really floating, paradoxically, gave her a sense of purpose. Once travelling, nothing was impossible to overcome. The underground connected with the railway, which connected with the ferry, which connected with the train to Orleans. And if you missed one train there would always be another.

At Orleans she left the main-line train for a rickety, slow one into the wilderness. It was only here that Amy began to wonder about what she was doing. The light was fading and gone were the city travellers with their newspapers and comfortable small talk. Now she was surrounded by a breed of weather-beaten, silent, wiry people with 'ancient glittering eyes'. They looked at her, exchanged glances and smiled shrewdly. It seemed they read into her and thought her appearance on their train

– a foreign woman at dusk, a young woman alone with a suitcase – most odd. It even began to seem that they knew where she was going.

The train jerked to a halt again. Peering through the window, Amy now saw a sign which read 'Ivrez'. She quickly picked up her case and went to the carriage door – all eyes swivelling. Opening it, she saw, some feet below, a grassy plateau which had once been a platform. Only the impossibility of going anywhere else that night made her step down onto its weedy tarmac. There was not a soul around and the train chugged away into the twilight leaving her the only person in the universe. What would she do if no one were here to meet her? Then a man waved from a path between the bushes. It was Jean-Claude and Bertrand was behind him. She turned to them in relief, instantly followed by horror. Who were these rough strangers? Had she really come to stay with such dirty men? The weirdness was confirmed. It was almost dark now. As they came towards her, her hosts did not see the thoughts in her face, only its pale oval. She called out tentatively:

'Bonjour.' Her voice floated out, very clear in the still evening air.

'Bonsoir!' Bertrand's correction rang back rather more confidently as he came up and graciously took her case.

'Ah oui.'

She had very little to say as they got into the car. Its smell repelled her. It was a physical smell, of soil and oil-paint, very male, and with more than a hint of dog. She sat in the back and Jean Claude kept turning round to smile at her encouragingly. She did her best to respond, but her doubts showed and she was thankful that Bertrand kept up a constant stream of information to which she had only to reply, 'oh yes' and 'oh really' from time to time. As darkness settled they arrived at the château.

The irritable cluck of disturbed hens produced in her an overwhelming sympathy: like them she wanted life to go back to its familiar routines. But at least Madame Estienne's down-to-earth lack of welcome, and the homely supper, provided some semblance of these. Amy looked round again at the medieval kitchen in which everything was made of stone, iron or wood: the huge open hearth where the cooking was done, stone slabs for the floor and, sitting on them, the venerable and battered oak table. In the corner, under the window, was their capacious old sink. She slotted herself back into her memories and began to relax, recovering the earlier sense of comradeship. Because of the isolation of the place their identities expanded to fill the space, taking on a uniqueness lacking in crowded city life.

'There's nowhere like Ivrez,' she was able to say at last. Her nature was one which looked for empathy. It was almost as though she lacked a layer of skin. Mentally, though, she was undeveloped.

After supper Bertrand prepared her for a surprise. He seized a lever in the wall by the door. Bowing like a circus artist, he pressed on it and a curtain covering the wall further along chugged slowly back, revealing a recess in the eight hundred year old stone. Out of it swung a slightly less ancient television set.

'We're not completely in the dark ages, you know,' Jean said proudly.

Amy was amused and a fraction disappointed. This did not fit with the old world she was looking for.

'I didn't expect you to want one.'

'Why not?' Bertrand challenged.

'I'm glad to escape from all that.'

'We're not.'

The next surprise was the discovery of the guest room. It was a circular space at the top of the central tower;

surprisingly airy – well supplied with windows. In it were a large bed, an old-fashioned wash-stand and an antique cupboard with a good many canvases propped up against it.

'You don't mind sharing the room with a few million francs worth of paintings do you?' Bertrand asked, gallantly.

'Not at all,' she replied, taking the hint not to put her foot through any of them. She responded in the same playful tone, although alone and in a bedroom with a stranger. It was as though she had known him for years, for he was a homosexual, a brother. She smiled glowingly.

'This is a room fit for a maiden in a fairy tale.'

He registered the compliment, bowed again and left her. After washing from the jug, she sank down onto the deep feather mattress and went instantly to sleep.

Next morning she was woken by the silver chimes of an elegant clock. She washed again in the cold water and went down the circular tower steps. It was 6.30 a.m. and she was the last up. Madame Estienne, clearing away the breakfast things, said 'bonjour' and returned to her duties. Left to make discoveries for herself, like Goldilocks, Amy found one clean bowl which must be for her. She helped herself to coffee, bread and jam. The morning air pouring in through the open door was fresh and invigorating.

'Jean is in the vegetable garden.' Madame Estienne did not turn round as she spoke, but it seemed likely that it was Amy, rather than the window frame that was being addressed. False politeness was not a part of life here and Amy, too, replied as she felt.

'Ah.'

'And Bertrand is writing letters.'

'Ah.'

Jean's mother was content that the replies did not wrest the initiative from her. She had something further to say and this time she half turned round.

'They're such good friends,' she said emphatically, 'like brothers. Good friends.' After nodding the point home to her guest, she returned to the pots. 'Madame Estienne was reassuring her,' Amy thought, 'and also reassuring herself, pretending that her son had only a chaste relationship.' But Amy was wrong. Madame Estienne's harsh life had taught her to accept realities. Her son's sexual life worked. Their life here had worked for fifteen years and Amy must not be a threat to it. That was the message she intended.

The working day began, with Amy helping transfer more of the million francs' worth of paintings out of the gallery and into the room where she slept.

'This man is one of the most famous painters in France,' Bertrand told her proudly. 'He can get 100,000 francs for any little daub.' Amy let herself be as impressed as Bertrand expected.

'But he's rubbish,' Jean whispered to her with a twinkle, as they moved a canvas together. She smiled, finding, as she had hoped she would, that there was more to Jean than being Bertrand's side-kick. He was humorous and thoughtful, and had this touch of subversion. Sometimes it seemed he could read her mind as he passed her the sauce at table. Carrying a canvas along the passage, she glanced, interested, at a group of pieces gathered in a side room. He read the glance.

'For our own next exhibition,' he said casually.

That afternoon René Védrine called, so they left the gallery and went down to the men's bedroom to talk business. This time Amy had no role to play so there were no introductions and she was happy with that. Feeling completely at home, she perched on a high stool and studied the works on the walls, occasionally listening to the exhibition arrangements the men were making. René, though, was amazed by the presence of a woman – a beautiful woman at that – and he showed it. In return, she viewed him with mild contempt. His conversation epitomised sixties' attitudes. He was superficially engaging and trivial, constantly joking whether a joke was appropriate or not. He was certainly different from the medieval, angst-ridden group he was among and his view of why Amy was there was almost English, she thought, as he tried to bring her into the conversation with voyeuristic glances. Bertrand gave him a few non-committal facts, not wanting to offend either of them. René turned to her, testing his assumptions.

'Why not come away with me then?' – flashing what he assumed was an inviting smile. He would indeed like to get closer to those long limbs and mysterious green eyes. She looked back from her superior perch. 'He doesn't understand friendship at all,' she thought, far too confidently.

'No,' she said, just drily enough to make it tell without offence. 'I'm staying here.'

He laughed. Bertrand and Jean smiled. She remained impassive. It was a relief when he left, but he had helped consolidate her closeness to the other men and she warmed to them even more that evening when they brought out the photographs of the rebuilding, and confided to her the effort it had taken getting suppliers to find the right materials and told of moments of near disaster, such as the fall of masonry on Jean which had broken several of his ribs and sliced off the first finger of his right hand.

'Just after I'd begun to learn the piano,' he said wryly,

shrugging his shoulders. It was gesture she was becoming familiar with. The tales and recollections brought her into their past lives and they responded warmly to her interested questions with answers which fired more conversation that evening at dinner. She sat between them like Queen Victoria. Jean was on the near corner, able to catch her eye, while on her right Bertrand, unlike Gladstone, fed the cat on the table from his plate.

On his way back from Ivrez René found his car heading for that wonderful restaurant at Meaux. If he stayed overnight he could easily reach the House of Arts and Leisure at Laon in time to start work the next day. The fact that an old flame ran the restaurant was, of course, quite irrelevant. He would ring Madeleine about 11 p.m. with a suitable excuse if all went well. However, all did not go well. Geneviève was no longer running the restaurant alone and appeared to be quite happy with a mouse of a man, René thought, as he was introduced. So he rang Madeleine about 10 p.m. with his plan to rush home to her. She had no idea of the network of alliances René had built up for himself during his travels. He was always so eager to return, and indeed he was. She was his goddess with whom he always behaved angelically. That afternoon he had bought her some perfume, to calm his conscience had he ended up in bed with Geneviève. But he now thought of it, as he continued his northward drive, as the evidence of single-minded devotion. 'Anyway,' he thought, 'I wouldn't be distracted like this had I a more demanding post.' Completely at ease with his self-delusions René approached his Picardy home.

Laon had been a great medieval city. The rock it was built on was four hundred feet high, a natural fortress rising out of the plain. By the tenth century a small town at its top served the needs of a cluster of churches. The present Arts Centre sat comfortably inside a fourteenth-century market and the once open spaces between its pillars were now filled with glass. From the interior visitors commanded a view on one side of the vastness of the plain below and, on the other, the vastness of the cathedral above. But René was not overwhelmed by archaic charm. It was easy to run and Paris beckoned. Turning this impatience into a wish to be home, he drove up the steep winding road to where their house also hung precariously overlooking the plain.

Madeleine had had a full day's work of her own. Her atelier, where she designed jewellery, now received more commissions than she could accept. She too had had close early connections with the Church. Her first leanings towards her profession came from years in the convent school, contemplating the chapel's mosaics of stained glass as she wondered how to escape its walls. The strict upbringing had made her a rebel – but within her class, since there was no point discarding your advantages along with your shackles. René was amusing and sexy – no one was quite so much fun as René. He took life easily, with style, and he adored her – but design was her first love. Her work was the gateway to freedom. She'd seen to it, too, that their home had a liberated interior, bedrooms downstairs, upstairs for entertaining, to make the most of their spectacular view. A spiral stair between floors increased the room space so the dining area could comfortably seat a dozen, serviced by a space-age cooking system half hidden in an alcove. Visitors could not help but respond to its adventure-playground feel, but its design did rather exclude the possibility of children. These lovely old houses were not very large anyway. However, it did not matter. They would not be here much longer. Soon they would be moving back to Paris.

At 11.30 Madeleine took a bath, timing it so that, with luck, she would be still be in it when René returned. She heard the main door close and congratulated herself that yet another of her designs had worked.

'Hello darling.'

His eager, slightly plump face appeared in the doorway glowing with delight at the sight of her reclining among the bubbles. Her face, with its elegant bone structure, was truly aristocratic and her hair, even here, was caught up on the top of her head with a mixture of care and abandon. One long arm and hand, slightly too large and capable for fashion, rested on the bath rim.

'You're just in time, darling.' She rose – like Venus, René thought – the white bubbly water shining on her collar-bone and sliding off her shoulder. He envied the way it slowed down in an intimate passage round the curve of her breasts and lingered in the tangle of her pubic hair, and he blessed the mousy man in Meaux for sending him straight home. She was clean and he dusty. This did not meet their impeccable standards. As he held the towel round her, luxuriating in her fresh warmth and scent, she started to undress him.

'Would you like me to run you clean water?'

'Take too long,' he said, his nose caressing her neck as he relaxed into her hands so expertly undoing his buttons. There were limits, though, to how long he could take even this most delightful foreplay. With a casualness designed to conceal his urgency he sank into the water. She dropped the towel and joined him in a slithery union.

5

Amy found herself increasingly alone with Bertrand in the days after René's visit. He began to confide in her, hinting at terrible things in his life. She could not help but sympathise – moved that this formidable, large, successful and awe-inspiringly formal person should continue to make himself so vulnerable to her. In response to her tenderness he said he would like to give her a story as a present. It was in the form of a book, which he had had printed. She looked at the modest brown cover, now with a dedication to her on the front, and launched into its contents.

Emile was about eighteen and employed as a tutor in a well-to-do household; privately educating the children. Their mother was impressed by his drawings, and he offered to paint her portrait. Like a character out of Stendhal, Emile fell in love with her; he worshipped her and, the way these things fall out, she responded. Now his story reached the point which should pulsate with sex, but Emile discovered impotence – he was 'homme de bois', and Madame Savigny realised it too. He rushed from the room. His humiliation and grief were over-whelming. Never had he anticipated this. The personal revelation was so sudden and so devastating that in despair he grabbed the tumbler from the washstand in his room and downed the entire contents of a bottle of sleeping pills. His thoughts as he lay down were clear and fixed whole-heartedly on death. But life wanted a comedy. He was young and his large body absorbed the narcotic. Next morning he came to, late and a little drowsy, woken by the children knocking on the door. Here was the real despair – a life, no life, but one he was tied to. No remission, no forgetting. Death in life was completed by Emile burying himself behind the ledgers of a dusty Paris office. The story was written simply, with no sub-plot, no light relief and Emile could well be Bertrand, Amy thought. His recent key and padlock sculpture showed he was someone not reconciled to his biology. The revelation was surprising as well as sad. Bertrand's success, his comparative fame, had not obliterated this one fact.

Amy was musing, sitting on the chair in the curve of the window, when Bertrand appeared in the door way.

'You've finished it.'

'Mmm.' Touched that he had trusted her she smiled gently at him, at a loss as to what to say. He stood watching her. She was so sympathetic. More importantly – so sexy. He knew he could make it with her. He moved forwards without speaking and her smile became a question. Why was he staring? It was as though he expected something more. As he came nearer she realised in horror what that 'something' was. She was to make him respond, sexually. She was to put her hands all over his body looking for the key. He saw that she understood and came purposefully on to her. The understanding was a suffocation. She couldn't let him believe it for an instant. Like something from a bad movie, she pushed him away and ran down the stairs. Friendship indeed! The holiday was over. She would have to go home. Needing an ally, she fled to Jean-Claude.

Bertrand did not come after her. He stood gripping the bed rail until his anger at life subsided once more into proportions which could be masked by a polite exterior. Recent public success had gone to his head he realised. There was no magical change. He had been so sure she was the one finally to make his life whole and now he knew that this would never happen.

Jean-Claude was in the forge putting casts into the fire. Just seeing him put everything to rights. He straightened up and gave Amy a glowing smile, like oxygen – dangerous near the open fire. Needing the real intimacy of that smile, she went to him and kissed him chastely on the cheek, remembering he too was homosexual. But his body felt warm and, to her surprise, he kissed her back with a hungry generosity. His response was so passionate that her knees gave way. He held her completely. Passionate, tender, warm: love not known since John died flooded back into her. As their thighs touched orgasm took them over. The floor of the forge was dirty but in seconds clothing was away and he was entering her, so wonderfully, such total sensation she wanted him right in her belly. Their first orgasm was mutual.

'I've loved you so much,' Jean was saying. 'From that first moment you arrived – wet, dirty, bedraggled – I've longed to see you again, longed. And here you are.'

She did not know what to say. Her body had surprised her. He had surprised her. He was meant to be homosexual! She got up, saw that her clothes were filthy, and wondered how to hide this from Bertrand.

'What are we going to say?'

Jean's face went rigid. 'Nothing. Be nice to Bertrand, very nice. Ask him about his work. He needs to be appreciated. At dinner tonight, we must keep thinking of him. But tomorrow we will be together again.'

'Here?' With her mind back in the driving seat, this didn't seem such a brilliant idea.

'Couldn't I come to your room tonight?'

He was silent. Despite the furnace she froze.

'Where is your room?' she demanded.

He remained silent.

He had been so passionate, her mind had instantly concluded that he no longer had ties with Bertrand, but tonight ... she could not complete the thought.

'But you're a famous sculptor,' she exaggerated his success. 'You can do what you want.'

He smiled ruefully. 'It's not so easy.'

She needed to think. She needed to wash! And she needed to avoid Bertrand.

'I wonder where Bertrand is,' she said, thinking how much he must already hate her.

'He was working upstairs in his studio.'

'Let's hope he's still there. What about your mother?'

'She'll be having a nap.'

Emerging once more, the outside world had changed yet again. Instead of being drained it was over-full of life. To recover a little ordinariness, she went out of the gate and onto the path at the back, walking for the sake of quieting her pounding blood, reducing the glow in her eyes. A little calmer, she went back. The myna bird in his cage outside the kitchen was in full throttle. His voice, like Mr Punch's, accused her. Bertrand's other guard was slumped in the shade; she would have to pass him, but it was a hot afternoon and Oedipus slumbered on. The worst moment was re-entering the dark of the kitchen, where it took a moment for eyes to adjust. Had Bertrand been sitting inside, that moment of blindness would have revealed her fear. Thankfully, he was not there. The kitchen was deserted, save for the wonderful smell of one of Madame Estienne's stews. Amy went over to the sink and picked up a jug. The giant kettle on the range was, as usual, full and hot. She poured its contents into the jug, refilled the kettle and put this back on the fire. Now she needed to get up the steep, winding stairs to the privacy of her bedroom. As she opened the door she heard a clatter from the gallery. Was he listening for her? Was he going to jump on her again, this time with a knife? She tensed but there were no more noises. She began to climb, gritting her teeth each time a stair creaked, and creaked again – behind her it seemed. Was it an echo or Bertrand following her? When she stopped the noises stopped. But stopping only increased her panic so she hurried on up the tower. Then came the voice she dreaded.

'What happened to you then?'

She gasped and turned to see Bertrand filling the stairway below: hostile, as he had never been before. He was eyeing her dirty dress with distaste. She hoped there was no semen on it:

'What do you mean?' she gasped.

'You look a mess.'

He knew. The way she'd run out of the room. He'd given her an excuse to go to Jean. But the surprise of his rudeness gave her something to strike against.

'Yes, I went for a walk and fell off a fence. Silly really.' Then she remembered Jean's advice. 'Have *you* had a good afternoon?'

It worked. There must have been real interest in her voice. Talking about his afternoon as though she had not been a part of it reshaped it in his mind. Bertrand surfaced from a private nightmare to a safer level of communication.

'Oh, yes, I did. I have the plinth ready for my new work.'

'That's good.'

'I shall be able to mount it tomorrow.'

Wondering whether French contained the same double meaning, Amy decided not to risk any more.

45

'That's very good,' she repeated and went into her room, firmly shutting the door.

The best thing about that evening meal was Madame Estienne's casserole. Amy and Jean barely looked at each other but even the occasional glance flared into the urge for another roll together, at which they earnestly turned their attention to Bertrand. Watching them, all his suspicions were confirmed. He remembered, jealously, the quiet and easy way Jean-Claude could communicate with her while he was always forced into formal gestures. Even letting her read his most painful, private life had turned into another empty gesture. He was angry, and coldly amused by their antics, their childish attempts to deceive him. He despised what he could not have. He hated love.

'There was a phone call, Bertrand,' Jean aimed at him, 'from René. It's OK for September.'

'We should be ready by then.'

'It'll mean our both going up to Laon.'

'That will be all right.'

'Laon,' said Amy. 'Isn't that the city which used to be the capital of France – perched on a rock overlooking miles of plain?'

'You are very good at geography,' Bertrand commented coldly.

'And history,' she quipped, but there was no smile in his reply.

'Where did you go for your walk?'

'Just here and there – along the track at the back.'

Bertrand was tearing up meat for Oedipus, ostentatiously turning it into a mess to drop into the dog's jaws. He wanted to revolt her even more than he had that afternoon.

'Did you see the quarry?'

46

'No,' she said firmly, not letting him intimidate her.

'Strange, it's hardly a kilometre away. It's very interesting. Suicides' Leap it's called. You know, grieving lovers?'

He looked at her bitterly, recalling his mistaken trust in her. And was he threatening her? The haunted intensity of his eyes was disturbing. It was best to ignore this line of conversation.

'Is it the exhibition in Laon that you're working for now?'

'Yes,' Jean offered. 'We need to put together a lot of new work. René has colleagues with a Paris gallery. We have to keep impressing them.'

He smiled at her, openly confiding this time. The two of them could out-maneouvre Bertrand he was implying. After all, Jean thought, a touch exultantly, he had been doing that for years. Bertrand also read Jean's meaning. As they drank their coffee he said with immense politeness, 'If you don't mind, Amy, this evening Jean and I have some very private business.'

She saw their exchanged glance and realised what he meant. Bertrand's hands would be exploring Jean's body, stroking his thighs, the hair around his genitals, his buttocks. The image she could not prevent leaped to her mind: Bertrand's penis would penetrate Jean-Claude's anus. Bertrand saw with satisfaction that he had made her sick. Another woman she could cope with but this annihilated her entirely, as much as if that afternoon she had gone along with Bertrand's experiment. Now he was getting his pleasure. She looked at Jean. His exultation had evaporated. He did not challenge Bertrand. He did not even look up. The man she had given herself to that afternoon was quite another person. She stayed at the table for a few minutes waiting for a sign. But Jean was locked off. He was Bertrand's. Amy rose and stumbled out of the room.

47

6

Bertrand could not be more destroyed. Jean had taken his place with Amy, and she had taken the one he had with Jean. When she left the room, his whole self focused caringly on Jean, recalling former times. When they eventually left dinner for the bedroom, he was almost the young lover and cajoler he had been when they first met. He caressed Jean, relaxed his body into his own; wanting to create a new life for them.

'We could visit the Marcellines when this work in Laon is finished – spend some time away.'

Jean's feelings were so complex he did not dare stop to consider them. One part of his brain felt Amy's humiliation and knew Bertrand was taking revenge for something, but this was not a message he could listen to. How could Bertrand have known what had happened that afternoon? Jean had to attribute Bertrand's crude behaviour to something less threatening – his unpredictable moodiness. Jean's life had taught him not to question what was essential to his survival. And Bertrand was essential to his survival. Ivrez was his home. So he divided his mind, and played for time.

'Mmmm, after Laon?'

'Yes, best to wait till then.'

'Mmm.'

His mind double-tracked along other possibilities.

Shaking, Amy went up to the privacy of her room and vomited emptily over the washbowl. Her carcass laid itself down on the bed. How stupid of her to have come back.

Why had she been flattered by Bertrand's card and its lie. How unutterably stupid to think she was a match for either of these practised men. Time passed and she became aware of the sounds of birds outside settling for the night. The silver chime of the clock striking nine was indomitably cheerful. Absorption in misery faded. This was not love. It was a terrible mistake! To get free of it she would write a letter to someone – anyone. There was, after all, an outside world. She didn't have to be ruled by this madhouse. She could not write to Sarah as they were still without an address. 'I wonder where they are,' she thought for a moment. Anyway, Sarah did not know she had come back for this tryst and would not approve if she did. Instead, Amy would write a conventional, holiday letter to Mrs Miles who was expecting to hear. She would be back before it arrived in London but putting pen to paper would focus her thoughts. She wrote with still shaking hand and conscious irony.

Dear Doreen,
    The countryside here is so quiet and restful, you'd think nothing ever happens. There's not another building in sight and instead of traffic jams, not a single car has passed by on the lane here since I arrived. (This suddenly seemed a bit ominous.) This afternoon I watched (dare she put his name, or would Doreen instantly surmise?) Jean-Claude cast bronzes in the forge. (She did not add, 'our private parts entwined, and at this moment he's doing the same with Bertrand.') I've been helping them change the exhibition in their exquisite gallery; it has been very exciting to be involved with modern paintings. I'm even sleeping with them – the paintings that is. 'Outside the château remains unknown so, tomorrow, I shall explore further.'

49

Tomorrow she would avoid seeing either of them. She would, instead, walk the couple of kilometres into the village to post this letter. From now on it would be best to keep a respectful distance from them both until, in a couple of days, she could return to dull but sane London.

She knew she could easily miss them in the morning by keeping to the lazy time of 7.30 a.m. and was glad to find the kitchen empty when she went down. The table was clear. If a third bowl had been set it had now been removed. But she took what was needed from around the room, and there was plenty of coffee. It was made to keep the men supplied through the morning and she was pleased to steal it. They could not destroy her existence totally. She decided to try to reach the village along the track which meandered round the back of the château to the ill-omened quarry. It must continue past there to the village. If the doomed had to take a three-kilometre detour via the château any desperate impulse might wear off. And the walk would be a good thing – it was a way of controlling her environment.

The myna bird shrieked at her when she ventured outside and the sickness at her stomach returned. But no one emerged from any of the rooms around the yard. No Oedipus either, which suggested that Bertrand was not there. She was struck by a momentary longing to recover Jean. Should she go and see if he were in his studio? Could she look at him dispassionately? Did she detest him or would she throw her arms round him? Even thinking of it was madness. Instead, she crossed the cobbles, pushed open the wide wooden gate and stepped onto the stony track. Bertrand's car was gone. She was right – he must be on his way to Montargis. The danger was gone. Normality returned more strongly once the sunburnt track turned a corner and Ivrez was out of sight. From there on the countryside assumed a wholly innocent look. Like a mouse that has resisted the cheese Amy escaped unharmed from the trap.

She crossed the Ivrez brook. It was only a trickle on the surface since most of the water sank below, keeping the valley green and lush despite the scorching sun. The path headed out to the opposite side and soon she was walking by the last of the fields lined with trees where cattle, back from milking, grazed and crunched, greedily refilling their sagging udders. Past this field barrenness opened up and the track began to climb. There were no more trees to shade her but, since it was only 9 a.m., the heat had a kindly feel. The landscape could have been painted by Cézanne: there were harsh rocks, which in few hours time would glow red with the sun, and scrubby thorn bushes defying both winter frosts and desert heat. There was nothing beautiful or ostentatious about this landscape. Like Madame Estienne it simply survived as best it could. Then Amy came upon the quarry. There was one steep drop, but the other sides had dried and crumbled into slopes covered in scrub. Since people were leaving the village, there was no more need for stone cutting and, gradually, the hole was filling in. There was nothing dramatic about it, at all. So Bertrand had just wanted to sound frightening. 'He's all bluster,' she thought. 'Had it been a place for jilted lovers at all?' she wondered, and peered ghoulishly down for traces of skulls or other bones. All she saw was a young rabbit on its morning forage. It saw her and scutted away up the opposite slope. What absurd fancies grew at Ivrez.

It was now ten o'clock. There was no urgency so she sat in the scrubland, mentally painting the scene. A buzzard drifted overhead, searching out some prey. How wide the countryside was – open rolling landscape, going on and on, burnt into reddish streaks on its southern

51

sides. The blue of the sky above was growing more intense; it would soon be hot once more. The buzzard plummeted and rose again with the rabbit screaming in its claws. For a moment Amy felt the panic of Bertrand's appearance on the stairs. Then reason returned. There was nothing sinister in a bird catching a rabbit. It was simply part of the cycle of the natural world. In her turn, she plunged into her bag to munch on that inspired fruit hybrid, a nectarine, stolen from the kitchen.

7

Monique called from the Post Office shop to her father, who she could hear moving about in the kitchen.

'Dad, you're not to go out till evening.'

'Stuff and nonsense.'

'You know the doctor said the heat's not good for you any more.'

'Heat! What does he know about it.'

The latch lifted and Monsieur Laroque left as usual for Pierre's bar. The heat was not the sole concern raised by the doctor. But, having done her duty, Monique gave in and her father made his leisurely way to the village square reflecting, as he often did, on the irony that his energetic wife, the pleasures of whose bed he remembered every day, should have developed cancer. He had always expected to go first. Why shouldn't he have a few drinks with cronies to fill an unfillable gap?

Monique had had a long morning: up at five to prepare the post, then tending the hens and the goat, before the shop itself opened. Now the delivery of wool Madame Ernoul had asked for had again failed to arrive. On the phone, the supplier had been unrepentant.

'Who wants wool when the temperature's thirty degrees?'

Monique might agree but her interest lay in maintaining a quiet life. Were it not for her father she would sell up and move south again. Four years ago, before her mother died, she had opened a florist's shop in Cavaillon where her boyfriend, now ex-boyfriend, lived. She longed to regain her independence. And there were no men round here – not to take seriously. She must do something about her life before she withered away in the dark shop.

Avoiding the crumbling edge of the quarry, Amy picked up the track again further on. As she hoped, it kept curving gently to the left, which meant it was turning back to the valley where the village of Ivrez would be found, a couple of kilometres east of the gallery. The cackle of hens heralded the first habitation at a place where rock gave way to grass and a field gate led into another narrow lane. Houses appeared sporadically along the road – set down there, one by one, centuries before. Everywhere was deserted. At ten in the morning everyone had things to do. Painstakingly, Amy eliminated all the houses which did not contain the bureau de poste until, finally, she found it up a small incline. Inside were the groceries and children's goods of a general store. Behind the counter was a striking young woman with black hair, and blue eyes that radiated a strong personality.

'Whatever keeps her buried in such a job?' thought Amy as she bought her stamps.

Monique made the usual enquiries.

'Are you camping round here?'

'No I'm staying with people for a few days?' The query remained in the Post Mistress's eyes. No news had reached her of a guest in the village. So Amy continued,

'At Ivrez – the gallery.'

The sudden change to hostility in the eyes facing her gave Amy some idea of what it might be keeping this young woman in such an unrewarding job. Monique always told herself that she did not take her furtive meetings with Jean-Claude Estienne seriously, but at least he kept her alive, and no one suspected anything because they all thought his inclinations lay in quite another direction. He was the only aspect of Ivrez that held any charm for her and here was a good-looking English girl staying under his roof – a thing Monique could never do. At the thought of losing him he became more important. Amy instinctively seized on a suitable reason.

'I work in a Gallery in London.'

This did not improve things.

'Ah.' So the stranger also had work in common with Jean.

As the atmosphere froze around her yet again and another human being she could have felt sympathy for became antagonistic, Amy silently protested against the injustice. This walk was to recapture her innocence not to entangle her further in the web. But, ultimately, it did not matter. She would be leaving soon. And now she would have lunch before going back to face up to the realities this young woman had reminded her of.

The bar was the same one that Monsieur Laroque was now chatting in and, thankfully, everyone here was much more interested in the Tour de France than in her. Amy's order for salad and a glass of wine, which she injected through the men's discussions, was received without a second glance, putting her in the pigeon-hole she wanted: that of visitor with a home to go back to. Her flat in London beckoned invitingly and for the next half hour she worked out how to be impartial this evening back at the château. Sympathy for Bertrand revived. She would be especially nice to him, and genuinely so. She had no intention of trying to break up his home. It was unthinkable – all for an accidental passion. The girl in the Post Office had cured her. Amy was not central to Jean's life, just another adventure. Tomorrow she would continue to avoid him; she could help his mother, and the day after that she was leaving. It had all just been a rather unusual holiday.

All morning Jean-Claude had been involved with the final stage of three bronze figures, re-melting the now solid surfaces with a narrow jet of flame until they were pliable enough to manipulate into a less perfect roundness. People and life were neither smooth nor round; rough, jagged surfaces satisfied him more. Not that he questioned his bisexuality. It was a fact. Events must be met one at a time. He could be happy with Bertrand or Amy and, preferably, both; there was no use wasting his energy on self-examination. The work took all his concentration and for several hours no lingering thoughts of the previous day came to distract him.

Bertrand returned from Montargis with the extra piece of timber and became equally engrossed in his work on the Crab, which was an abstract metamorphosis: part reptile, part animal, part human. He had now reached the prosaic stage of fixing this to its base, though for the work to be complete the base had to reflect the sculpture. The morning might have been any of their past fifteen years together, continuing – with a break for coffee – for a full six hours. Towards noon basic needs returned, and with them the anticipation of seeing Amy. It occurred to Jean that she had not looked in all morning. This meant he would have to signal to her behind Bertrand's back which was a nuisance. Bertrand, feeling secure once more and not expecting to see her until the meal, planned a more relaxed hospitality.

Her unexpected absence from lunch was disconcerting. It forced the men to speak about her, and Jean's disappointment provoked a wish in Bertrand to hurt him.

56

'Yes, she's out. Didn't she tell you?'

Glancing up, Jean could see that Bertrand was still angry with her and at last realised why she had run into his arms the day before. She was no longer a subject they could discuss casually but it was safe enough to ask Bertrand what he meant. In return came the curt reply:

'She'll be back.'

The pettiness broke their recent tie, giving Jean's feelings space to regroup around the woman. She was outside somewhere; independent, a separate being rejecting him. The thought produced a strong physical urge to see her again. After lunch he could not concentrate. The memory of her sweetness floated through his veins. Time went by and, still, she did not appear. The only place she could be was the village. He would look for her. He would go on foot, he'd have a better chance of seeing her if she were walking off the road. Leaving the château, he automatically concealed himself under trees, out of sight of Bertrand's studio windows. Then he started on the unaccustomed walk.

Amy had started back a few minutes before, sauntering through the shade by the side of the lane. After twenty minutes he glimpsed her through the undergrowth and knew instinctively that she was not thinking of him. It made her even more desirable. In her mind was the clarity of her plan to start a new life in London, cured of her misery over John. At least this adventure had done that. She was strong and whole again; she would leave the gallery at Greenwich and go to University. She had seen articles encouraging women to aim for real careers. She would first need to finish some school exams – a bit of a bind – but she would do it. The past was completely behind her. She noticed how the sun dappled through the trees making ripples and shades of colour;

white where the light reflected, pale yellow through to greens as the branches swayed slightly in the afternoon breeze. Her eyes lingered on the visual effect; it reminded her of an impressionist painting, or a film by Jean Renoir. The colour, the light and the movement created an art form of their own. She surrendered control of her vision to their effect and, behind, slipped in another image. The sight of Jean dropped into her disarmed consciousness and her new plans disappeared like fancy wrapping. This person filled her entire being. She could not explain it. As they approached they could see in each other's eyes the same overwhelming longing. There was no need for words. An hour passed while they fed and satisfied an intense need for mutual possession.

'I can't live without you,' Jean-Claude said eventually.

'I wish it were true.'

'It is. I need you.'

'How can you say that?'

'Impossible here.'

'Somewhere else?'

He'd spoken without thinking. 'I don't know.'

'But we could. You could have your own studio anywhere. You're well known.'

'Yes.' He paused as his insecurities got the better of him. 'But I have no other home.'

How weak it sounded. It put up a barrier she could not argue against.

'Well ... we'd better go.'

'We can't arrive back together.'

'Of course not,' she replied trying to sound sympathetic, but making it clear just how unreasonable the whole situation was. 'I'll stay here. Or rather, I'll go back to the village. There are ceps under these trees. I'll get a bag and collect a few. I'm sure your mother would be pleased to have them.'

He was stung by the easy way she changed the subject. 'You hate the situation here.'

'I'm involved.'

'I hate it too. I have never felt for any woman what I feel for you. I will find a way.'

'I would come and live with you. I came back to see you. I want to spend the rest of my life with you.'

Bertrand did see Jean walking back, wrestling with his thoughts. Why did he feel this urge to stay with Amy? Something which he did not feel for Monique. Maybe Monique was too available. But more than that, there was no real kinship. They were both just passing time with each other. This passion for Amy had a claim on his happiness – something he had not felt before. He would make the Laon plan work.

The unusual self-examination made him appear so dejected that Bertrand jumped to the conclusion he wanted. Jean had not found Amy. Or, if he had, she had been blunt about last night. He preferred the latter; it was more final. When she came back a couple of hours later with the bag of nutty-flavoured fungi, he almost welcomed her. Her gift was added to the evening meal, which became a celebration on all sides. Bertrand was at his most gracious, glad that something had intervened to keep the two of them apart; increasingly, it seemed she did not know Jean had left his work to look for her. His optimistic domination of the conversation meant it was easy for them to deceive him further. If the third person isn't suspicious then there is no need to look guilty. And since they had exhausted all their own desire for the time being it was easy to behave distantly with one another. To a third person it really did look as though it were all over.

They debated the direction that painting should be going in. Were body artists, like the English George and

Gilbert, con men or making a real contribution? Perhaps they were both. Perhaps it did not matter. Perhaps the conviction and the originality with which they presented themselves were all that was necessary for it to be good work.

'After all,' Bertrand pointed out. 'Picasso says what an artist *is* matters more than what he *does*.'

'No!' Jean argued, 'an artist can only be an artist if he consciously presents what he *does* as art.'

'I suppose, though...' Amy could not resist siding with Bertrand, '...what he *does* depends on what he *is*.

As the ideas and even laughs flowed, Amy contrasted this with the misery of the evening before when the raw truth had gutted them. How curious it was that an ability to deceive was all that was needed to transform their small society into one which enjoyed each other's company. Bertrand still cursed the moment he had invited her inside their fortress, yet he consoled himself with the thought that there was only one more day to go. The worst was over.

8

'Good morning, Bertrand.' Secure in the thought of what lay ahead, Amy was very happy. But Bertrand's 'Good morning' was also jovial. In the sun, in the courtyard, stood his "Metamorphosis: the Crab". She watched as the surface of the monster received a final burnish. From some angles, the roundness of the shell gave it a surprisingly appealing look.

'I know you said this was a transition towards the inhuman but, depending on where you see it from, the opposite could be happening.'

He was pleased.

'A perpetual alternation.'

'Is that how you meant it?'

'No, no, I meant what I said. But afterwards, of course, you see other possibilities.' He returned to cleaning the joints, resisting the impulse to be friendly. Obviously Amy could not expect trust and she returned to more practical things.

'Would Madame Estienne let me help in the garden?'

'Good idea. Jean and I will be busy in the gallery all day.' He was concentrated on his statue: there was no glance at her, no ironic touch. Only the powerless descend to sarcasm and Bertrand was in control.

'Ah, but…,' Amy thought, as she moved towards the little gate into the vegetable garden, Jean had promised her he would get away in the afternoon. Madame Estienne had her back to her. Amy called out and the old lady turned round, alarmed as she realised her space was about to be invaded.

'I'd like to do some work,' Amy shouted in explanation. It was a business-like proposition. Madame Estienne thought for a moment and nodded.

'Can you tell the difference between peas and weeds?' she asked as the girl came towards her.

'Yes, that's easy.' Seeing where young peas were struggling to reach the canes through wild flowers she went closer, then glanced back at Madame Estienne who nodded again and, although it was against her present instincts, Amy quickly destroyed the forget-me-nots. The vegetable garden was large. One old lady could not possibly keep it under full control, and Amy could see another patch where grasses were making stubborn inroads.

'May I...?' with a nod in their direction.

'If you like,' came the laconic reply. Amy mused for a moment on those complex furrows in her face, which only a life of outdoor work can produce. And Madame Estienne never complained. She reminded Amy of an old and venerable tree. As they worked on the silence became unnatural and Amy had to break it.

'This is work which never changes.'

'No. If you want to eat you have to grow something.'

'As a child I used to work in the family allotment...,' she searched for the French equivalent, '...gardens where you grow vegetables, like this one.'

'Jardin ouvrier.'

'Yes. They were started in England during the last war. We hadn't enough to eat. "Dig for Victory" was the saying.'

'It was a hard time, the war.'

Amy waited, holding her breath. Was she going to learn something about Jean's background? But no, Madame Estienne did not say any more. She kept to herself the memories of how close they had sometimes come to starvation. Jean's little sister, Marie, had caught influenza and had died. Malnutrition, they said.

'You must be proud of Jean now.'

'Yes.'

So they worked on, the atmosphere between them not greatly changed. Occasionally, Amy glanced up towards the house. Bertrand had gone inside now.

Jean was keeping his head down. In his studio in the courtyard, he could see little through the old glass windows. They admitted a Rembrandt quality of light and little else. Usually he worked with the door open, but he needed to keep apart from Bertrand until some clear plan of action came to him. After the good feeling they had all shared the previous evening Jean had achieved a few hours of amiable distance which could not go on much longer. He would either have to collapse into his old self or risk open antagonism. On the bench in front of him stood the three bronze figures: "Repose", "Anticipation", and "Action". He noticed a flaw in the second. With a small chisel he gently improved the proportions, strengthening the line between shoulder and ribs. He then needed the blowtorch, lightly. It was satisfying, painstaking work and he was glad of the need to concentrate on it.

"Metamorphosis: the Crab" was finished. Bertrand stood back and considered it with satisfaction. It did express a paradox, a tension between creation and decay. It was good work, less careful and more assured than some of his earlier pieces. This would give Jacques Duclos something worth seeing at the Laon exhibition. "Metamorphosis" was also larger, which made getting it into the Ivrez gallery tricky. Before disturbing Jean, Bertrand went to the privy – their only loo – over by the moat. A long way to go in winter, but pleasant enough now. As he passed Jean's studio he interpreted the closed door. Jean was not happy. There was still a situation to be contained then and it gave Bertrand satisfaction to realise that his working out of doors had been doubly useful. Jean was no nearer a plan of his own when his cell was breached and an expansive Bertrand came in to ask for help. Jean's own work was finished too and he was reasonably satisfied – not surprised to find, though, that Bertrand did not break out in praise. Bertrand's own piece was far better, Jean realised, as he helped carry it up the narrow winding stair. 'Well,' he thought, 'we have our different highs and lows. I'm going through a bit of a metamorphosis of my own.' Negotiating the stairs needed cooperation between them; just the level of communication Jean had been looking for. Working together was purposeful but not intimate. It enabled him to retain his sense of being apart from Bertrand without hostility. Maybe this detachment would become habitual – and Bertrand accustomed to it.

The gallery was mostly roof space. Windowless, five-foot high walls were topped by a tapering, ten-foot high point. Large, rough-hewn beams ran at shoulder level between the walls and slotted into an A-frame of ceiling beams. The white plasterwork behind this skeleton of dark wood completed a mood of Quaker simplicity. One wall shone clean under the subtle lighting, but there were still shadows on the other, the ghosts of previous hangings. More whitewashing was to be done.

'Later. We haven't thought of the lay-out.'

At the far end was Bertrand's studio in the outer

round tower, full of their pieces, and a few canvases unsold from previous showings.

'We both have new sculptures,' said Jean. 'Don't we need the whole space?' He was looking at the display dais in the centre. Bertrand agreed it might be better to move this to an end wall and the discussion continued, Jean thought, on a more equal basis than usual. "Metamorphosis" looked good close to the centre of the room.

'How do you think the rest will look in relation to it?' Bertrand asked.

'Hard to say ... I'd better bring the last of my own up,' Jean replied and headed to the door before Bertrand could think of a reason to stop him.

Amy glanced up at the house. Bertrand had gone inside now. Where Jean was she had no idea – in the gallery with him probably. She looked at her watch – 11 a.m. Though the sun had slipped behind clouds, it was getting hot.

'I need a hat,' she called to Madame Estienne.

Jean was not using the forge so his studio next to it would be cool. It was the obvious place to go.

When Jean came in, she was putting her blouse back on, feeling the relief of unimpeded cool air on her skin. She saw him, a dark shadow in the doorway, and paused, holding her breath against that rush of emotion he always brought with him. He came forward to help her, slipping his hand up between her breasts, touching her nipples. There was no help for it. Back against the wall, she unzipped his trousers.

'We haven't long.'

His penis nudged its way in as smoothly as though it had found a long-lost home, and orgasm took them over.

'I go tomorrow. It'll be over.'

'No. Leave your phone number in my coat pocket.'

His old jacket hung on a peg. She nodded. Swiftly, they made their clothes conform to the expected arrangement and turned to Jean's work. "Anticipation" had cooled, but together with "Repose" and "Action" the group was more than Jean could carry.

'I'll bring one of them,' said Amy, 'it's easier than running away.'

They climbed the stairs, their guilt dictating that they left enough space between them to suggest chastity. The arrival of Amy put a strain on Bertrand's good humour but Jean had not been long away and it would be best to have them both under his eye. It was striking, too, how Jean's bronze trio set off his own work. Though not professionally greedy, it was impossible not to respond to the innovation in his own piece by comparison. Artistically, Bertrand had achieved a more advanced perception and Jean was glad to give him this satisfaction.

'One of your best pieces.'

Eyes met, they nodded – brothers again. Amy looked on, amazed at the easy discussion which followed despite Jean's infidelity fifteen minutes earlier. Had their union just been some sort of animal coupling? But this was no time for cynicism. Obviously, Jean must not give himself away. She tried to concentrate instead on the men's conversation, despite her heart palpitating with dread of one and unfinished desire for the other. They had now decided on the lay-out. Each sculptor would have a focal point at either end of the gallery while, in the centre, the rest of their work would be integrated on the dais, which was returned to its usual place. That decided, artistic planning was replaced by the artisan work of white-washing, and uncomfortable realities surfaced in their minds emptied of other thoughts. Jean, working hard up a ladder, had the advantage of distance. Amy was still struggling against her lust so, after the men had taken their starting positions, she chose to work alongside Bertrand.

'Someone should hold the ladder,' he said, abruptly. Gladly, she obeyed.

Bertrand could not blot Amy out of his own feelings. There she was; a spectre, a ghost of what might have been and existing now only as a violent emotion he would rather not feel. The cleansing of the wall was satisfying though. It had ritualistic purpose and everyone's thoughts were calmer by the time it was finished.

Normally, on such a hot day, the two men would strip off outside and run a hose-pipe over each other. Today, their expressions registered the obvious impasse. Fortunately, Amy's instinctive antennae were on high alert.

'You must clean up before lunch!' The thought of leaving a naked Jean alone with Bertrand was hard to contemplate but she added decisively. 'And while you do, I shall go and admire the rest of the work in the studio.'

Bertrand nodded and, once her gaze was removed, they stripped while she, in Jean's workroom, found a scrap of paper, wrote her phone number on it and slipped it into Jean's jacket pocket.

By the time she had cleaned up too the men were well advanced through the bread, cold meat, salad and cheese that lay on the table. After a hurried meal, and a trip to the privy, Bertrand was soon back up the stairs. Jean automatically followed, while Amy tentatively began to help Madame Estienne clear. She was not rebuffed and by the time she too went up to the gallery another transformation was under way. Dry walls glowed white. The covers were off the floor and off the sculptures. More items were brought in and a world of images, ideas, elegance and even visual humour was taking over.

Bertrand noticed her pleasure and spoke thoughtfully. 'You've seen how rough our lives are, but here there is luxury, don't you think? Beauty is a kind of luxury and we have it more than most people.' He looked straight at her, clearly telling her that the beauty he could achieve was far more substantial than the one that was denied him.

'Artists do have the luxury of escaping from the ordinary world. And the result is beautiful. That's true,' she conceded. 'But was it an ordinary world,' she thought, 'when couples found a different form of escape?' A world which she would like to share with Jean? 'That was not likely,' she thought now, watching him play with his inanimate children. He had hardly spoken to her after asking her to leave her telephone number. Did he even care to know whether she had? He was definitely an enigma. His double life made it impossible for anyone to possess him fully. And, like Bertrand, what he cared most about was his work. She would have to be sensible so, neutering her feelings, she helped with the finishing touches.

'Sixteen Orchard Hill' – an easy address to remember. It ran through Jean's mind like a mantra. This was it. He was taking his own decisions – making his own future. His blood pounded through him and he hardly dared look at Amy. Even a glance would tell Bertrand the treacherous thoughts. Dinner that night was torment to him. Bertrand, feeling good about the important things in life, brought out the Reserve Sauvignon and toasted Madame Estienne, who had joined them. His second toast to them all had a touch of irony.

'To the surprises that life brings.'

Jean responded with a suppressed grunt and Amy replied with an equally transparent message.

'To our very last evening.'

'Ah, yes, the very last evening.' Bertrand drank with pleasure.

Jean raised his glass but did not drink.

'Jean, have you tested the camera recently?'

'Not for several months.'

Photography, catalogues, leaflets, publicity – these were on Bertrand's mind. Invitations to the press would be sent but, before this, a chat with Alain in Paris was always useful. Amy, remembering Jean's advice on how to treat Bertrand, tried to see the world through his eyes.

'You still have a great deal to do.'

'Yes.'

'Is there a job tomorrow morning which would take you to Montargis? So that you could take me to the station. I'd rather not take you away from more important things.'

Bertrand looked at her with just slightly raised eyebrows:

'No, you won't be taking us away from more important things.' He turned again to Jean.

'We had fair reviews from *Le Monde* last year. Should we risk it? Is this collection good enough?'

'*Le Monde* was pretty positive last time.'

'Let's see the review.' And Bertrand went to rifle the files in the office.

Madame Estienne cleared the table. After a pause, in which Jean and Amy looked up and past each other, Jean forced himself to go to the open door and watch the search.

'Try that red one on the left.'

'Ah, good.'

Completely redundant, Amy left them to it and went up to pack her small suitcase. When she needed to come down again for her last trip to the outside inconvenience both men were still engrossed in the office. The night air was cool. The sanity of a peaceful countryside always helped put your life in perspective. She did love this place and she did love Jean. However, a second loss could never be as destroying as the first. Coming out of the privy, she hoped he would be there wanting to keep her in his life. But there was no one in the darkness and she climbed the stairs with a weary heart. At the top a feverish figure grasped her.

'My darling – I have your phone number. I'll be in touch. I'll drive you to the station tomorrow.'

A brief kiss and he was gone. Bertrand, hearing him come down, stayed by the doorway.

Next morning Amy found only Madame Estienne in the kitchen. She also found the telephone number of a taxi firm placed by her plate. She looked enquiringly at Jean's mother. That inscrutable lady nodded and replied as though recalling something from long ago.

'The boys have gone to Paris.' Then she too left to tend the aubergines.

9

'You drive too fast, Michel.'

Adèle's fiancé looked hurt.

'I was only keeping up with the one in front,' he said in a plaintive tone. 'And the one behind,' he added in defiance of the slap on his arm, 'we were just the pâté in the sandwich. We had to keep moving not to become real pâté!'

Too young to lose belief in her immortality for long, Adèle laughed, as Michel hoped she would.

It was September 2nd, a Saturday, and they were back from the August migration to the beaches in the south. They glowed sleekly with sun and health and were on their way from Paris to help fill brother René's house with weekend chatter. Adèle was twenty-two, younger than René by ten years – one child born either side of the war. She was petite, blonde and fragile-looking, appearing much younger than her years – kept a child by her parents with whom she lived. When Michel had picked her up from their apartment Monsieur Védrine had accidentally let slip, 'Jacques and Mathilde went some time ago. You'll never catch them' – a dare Michel could not resist. After all, the road was newly built for speed; its thrill was novel, therefore essential. Adèle tried again.

'They'll be calling for Patrice. We've probably passed them already.' He smiled another charming grin, so she lay back and trusted her life to him, adding laconically, 'It would be more sensible for René and Madeleine to come to Paris.'

'Oh they will, they will. We have all winter.'

'If your editor is kind.'

'He's very kind.'

'Not too many trips away?'

'Not if I can help it.'

It certainly would be a turning point in their relationship if Michel put it before the oyster of the world that was beginning to open to him, thanks to the May riots of the previous year. His photographic skills now took him to fascinating places. Sometimes Adèle wondered how they had managed to get engaged at all. She really wanted a man as reliable as her father. But she was a glamorous-looking girl and was herself attracted to glamour even though, unlike her sister-in-law, Adèle did not value her own career. Researcher with a women's magazine, Adèle's interest in family matters was more than professional. It was pinning Michel down which was now the full-time job.

They arrived at the Old Town by the southern route, its double bends inching up through poplars standing like guardsmen. Jacques and Mathilde were already there with Lucien. Patrice had been called away.

The reason for meeting here while the weather still held became apparent after the meal, sitting on the balcony with the sun setting over the plain while they relaxed with coffee and cigarettes. It had been some time since Jacques had seen his godson, René, and he seemed older. The young had to work hard to get on. After the war, of course, Jacques had walked into a top job. There was more competition around now, inevitably.

'How are we to get René and Madeleine to take a break next summer?' he asked.

'Perhaps they slipped away unbeknown to us,' his wife suggested.

'Us – no – we can't stop work for a whole month. It's

a ridiculous habit. We had the occasional weekend, didn't we darling?'

Madeleine threw him a warm smile, recollecting their private time together, which had been rather more substantial than René was letting on. Jacques peristed.

'You're too young to be so ambitious. You should relax more and enjoy life.'

'But that's what we're doing now,' protested Madeleine.

René had just produced an extraordinary coq-au-vin. In its time the bird had been a real cock which had spent a long and active life growing to great size – its neck alone was the thickness and richness of lamb. Simmered in a Burgundy reserve, 1964, the meal had become a commemoration of the bird's life as well as a celebration of their own. René was pleased with his work. The flavour had compared well with the meals produced by the family cook he remembered from before the war. Work in their kitchen divided neatly between them and Madeleine's experiments with shapes and colours of puddings were often trial runs for her work.

'Too much Matisse this evening,' Adèle had said, looking at the bright fruit purées.

'Rembrandt next time,' her sister-in-law had replied, knowing how fond Adèle was of chocolate sauce.

'Do you think we could tempt them with a round the world cruise?' Michel now wondered.

'Boring,' René retorted.

'World cruise, solo style, then,' Jacques fantasised, 'like Louik Fougeron.'

'A romantic idea, and René is a romantic,' said Madeleine.

'But I can't sail!' he cried delighted. 'Obviously a non-starter.'

'Romantic ideas usually are, darling.'

'Did you know,' said Lucien, 'that Monsieur Fougeron

picked up a wild kitten in Morocco and it almost stopped him. It chewed the wireless aerial off, tore open his food bags, and...' – Lucien fell over his words in excitement – '...it wasn't a kitten. It was pregnant!'

'What did he do? Throw it overboard?' asked Michel. Lucien was shocked.

'No,' Mathilde continued. 'He had plastic bags for floating his films to ships. He put her in one and pushed her off. She was picked up.'

'Suffocated?'

'No,' Lucien went on firmly. 'I saw a photo of her. She's called Roulis. She's very pretty.'

'There you are. You go to sea to become famous and it's the cat that everyone remembers.'

They laughed, and settled back to their coffee. Life was very comfortable this evening.

'How is the exhibition of the decade going? Any hold-ups?' René's curiosity could not be suppressed any longer.

'The Henry Moore? It will definitely be coming over in June. I might even have a gallery to put it in.'

René laughed with the understanding of a fellow curator, but for Jacques it had continued to be a difficult summer. The owners of the Gare d'Orsay had resisted his persuasion and he was now having to look elsewhere. It had all begun with the robbery, he felt, though, for heaven's sake, that had not been his fault. The interview had been uncomfortable, of course, though the questions not as pitiless as they could have been. Yet, the interviewer's politeness did not conceal the fact that doubts were being raised about Jacques' skills. In fact, it played off Jacques' own courtesy, leading him to incriminate himself:

'*Is Tonsin on your staff?*'

'*That's right.*'

'*And he tended to follow instructions?*'

'*Usually.*'

74

'*To reduce the number of guards by two during the summer would not seem advisable, of course?*'

'*No. Have you asked Tonsin about this? The reason might well have been that these guards insisted on their own summer holiday.*'

Hired watchmen were notoriously badly paid – how reliable could you expect them to be? It was about time the Ministry put them on the payroll. Jacques could not, of course, say anything so critical of the institution he had worked so long for.

Nevertheless, the fact that Tonsin had felt able to take this course did not reflect well on Jacques' ability to keep the organisation together – a point that Paul was quietly repeating among colleagues. Jacques had just heard from his secretary of a new initiative from the Ministry to reorganise Paris's museums. Were it not that he abhorred committees perhaps he could have prevented it. As it was, semi-private buildings would not be opening any more. This, too, sounded like Paul's style and the public would be the losers. The power that Jacques had always held very lightly, trusting he was trusted with it, was being taken away. All he could do was stick with the principle which had worked for so long: focus on the next project. He now had another theory as to why men took to their yachts. It might be better to pit yourself against the harsh, unpredictable – but unprejudiced – elements.

For others in the party there were still jokes to be enjoyed in the infamous robbery. When Jacques finished his musing he realised the conversation had moved on. Michel was relishing its impudence.

'If the thieves hadn't stopped for champagne and caviare they'd have got away with more.'

Mathilde came to Jacques' defence.

'There had been a guard, but he was at the other

side of the building. By the time he'd worked his way round, they were nearly finished, and since the theft happened at the end of July, all the families living near the building had been away. No one saw anything.'

'Paris does become a ghost city in summer – asking for trouble really,' said Madeleine.

'It sounds from the papers as though the thieves had brought the champagne with them,' Adèle added. 'All rather bizarre.'

'No. It's kept for clients,' said Jacques.

'I hope Herr Braunmüller won't be backing out from the Moore; because of the increased insurance;' Madeleine had the gist from her husband.

'We are still working on it. Things look hopeful.'

'And, at least,' said Adèle, 'Henry Moore's works will be too heavy to steal.'

'They could be eaten,' said Lucien, looking for a way to introduce something more interesting into this talk.

'What do you mean?'

'Monsieur Mangetout could eat them.'

They laughed.

'It would have to be metal sculpture. And he's more interested in consuming objects from the consumer society.'

Mathilde thought this latest Paris entertainment rather repulsive: a man who cut up and ate bicycles in public. He had downed the occasional Renault, vacuum cleaner and television set, but was most at home with the old velo. Repulsive or not, he was interesting to talk about.

'Some people say what he does is a form of art,' Adèle pointed out.

'Yes,' added Michel, 'he changes the way you think about ordinary objects, and that's what art does.'

'Does art have to make you think?' asked Madeleine.

Jacques felt an urge to reply philosophically and

suppressed it. It would be out of place here: too serious and pretentious.

'Well, art makes me...,' he paused, wondering whether to add "a lot of money" and decided against it, '...think that I'll have another cup of coffee.'

'Dad!'

'Yes, a bad joke, Julien. I'm much too pleased to be out of Paris to think at all.' He sank back into the chair, and looked at the view disappearing from dusk to dark.

'Only at the moment though,' Madeleine added. 'Born in Paris, always a Parisian. You wouldn't move if you were offered the chance.'

'I might. I'm just a country lad at heart, hoping Patrice will take up farming, so I can get my feet under his table. As I'm doing here of course.' Lucien took up the idea.

'What you need, Dad, is to run a gallery right in the country — such a good gallery that people would come out of Paris to see *you*.'

'Like the one at Ivrez, you mean?'

'Yes!' he said enthusiastically.

'René's just been there, haven't you darling?'

'Yes,' René continued thoughtfully, 'and they have a really curious exhibit,' he said, recalling the quiet slim beauty swinging her mini-skirted legs on the high stool. 'An unusual addition to their collection.'

'Oh, really? What are they up to now?'

'They have a waif living with them: a girl from England – at Ivrez. Not a painter either. Just a girl, living with them.'

They paused to take this in. Even Jacques and Mathilde thought it rather odd.

'Perhaps it's to help Madame Estienne.'

'Not as far as I could see.'

'Would you send to England for help in the kitchen?' The ten-year-old had a practical turn of mind. 'Au pair?'

'Aux frères.' René added for Michel's benefit. 'It'll be interesting to see what emerges when they come up for their show here.'

'Will you be coming to it?' Madeleine asked Jacques.

'I might.' He was half-hearted. 'I've never found them that exciting. They're too imitative.'

'Bertrand sometimes shows more flair. What of "The Padlocked Penis?"'

'A witty idea, but obviously biographical, don't you think?'

'It makes a statement, yes. I don't think you can write it off as just biographical – I find it original.'

'No. His work has only the one private message. There's nothing universal about it. Not many artists in one generation can have genius. We have to be honest about these things and not let friendship cloud our judgement.'

'I think inspiration can be catching,' Madeleine said. 'Genius is worked at as much as born and it's exciting to see how artists develop.'

René agreed. 'I wouldn't be in the business without that.'

Jacques let them win. René liked to have his own way and Jacques knew he would be there at the opening.

10

When Amy's taxi turned onto Deptford Broadway, she saw a poster against the Vietnam War. It jolted her. Her disappointments were petty in comparison with the brutality, the napalm, the genocide of that campaign. There was to be a demonstration the following Saturday. She would bury her self-pity by going. She had nothing planned for the weekend, nor any weekend for that matter. Jean would now go back to the girl in the Post Office of course. London looked sane to Amy by comparison: sane and sterile. Her refuge of a flat welcomed a refugee. The desert of her head spun. The relationship had ended in such a cruel way. But Doreen, downstairs, greeted her warmly.

'I've brewed a pot of tea. It'll make a change from coffee.'

Amy gladly abandoned the unpacking and joined her in her kitchen, trying to focus her double vision on Doreen tending to pot and kettle, when the picture was constantly blurred by memories of another woman moving about another kitchen. Bringing herself back to the present she thought of the poster.

'I think I'll go to Hyde Park this Saturday, Doreen.'

'What on earth for?'

'The anti-war demonstration.'

'Oh yes, of course.' But it was a strange thought on returning from holiday and Doreen returned to the subject that interested her. 'Were your friends pleased to see you?'

'Well, they were very involved with their work. They

didn't really have much time for me. But it was an interesting break.'

No way could events of the past week be bowdlerised into acceptable conversation. She wished it had been a conventional romance; Mrs Miles would have enjoyed it. Amy continued with the expected noises without giving anything away and succeeded so easily that she was disappointed. A challenge would have relieved her pain by forcing her to talk about it. Doreen, though, was too occupied with present realities to delve below surfaces. She was trying to get a grass stain out of her teenage daughter's blouse. Amy looked at it nostalgically and refrained from asking how it had got there. Her motherly companion broke the silence in her matter-of-fact way.

'Well, it's a relief to get back to work, isn't it? I never find holidays are all they're cracked up to be.'

'No,' agreed Amy, looking into Doreen's unconcerned face.

Putting the key back in the lock of her own door, she could hear the phone ringing. She answered it in her fractured state of mind and the voice at the other end was araldite.

'Amy. I only have a minute. I was forced to leave with Bertrand. He made me choose between you and him. It was so sudden.'

'I know.'

'Will you meet me in Laon?'

'Yes.'

'In about a month. I'm writing. Must go. I miss you.'

'I miss you.'

'I choose you.'

* * *

His first over-wrought letter arrived three days later. It began: 'This is the second time I have written this letter as the first time I don't think I put your full address, but if it did arrive, don't be surprised to be reading the same things over again.' Mental stress came out too in the precise instructions which followed. They could have been written by an underground freedom fighter, thought Amy and, in a way of course he was.

'I had better mention our contact first.' (This was Marcia Chabot, a friend of Madame Estienne's. Her name was not written down, not even for a reader across the Channel.) 'It is absolutely necessary to put your letter in one envelope and write on it "for Jean-Claude" and then put that envelope in a larger one addressed to the person we both know, but without putting my name on it. It's safer this way.'

'Amazing!' thought Amy.

'I'm arranging to go to Laon for the weekend of 25–26 September' – this was three weeks away – 'Write to me to tell me the time when you will arrive. I understand so well how much you detest the situation here but, believe me, I suffer from it at least as much as you do. And it seems to me we do not know each other well enough, despite the passion for each other, for me to suddenly break the friendly relationship I've always had with Bertrand. I think you'll be hurt to read this and you'll say I'm a coward and a hypocrite. You may be right, but if so the wisest thing would be to forget me. Cowards are not worthy of a great love. As for me, I love you as you are; without knowing who that girl was who arrived from the north one Saturday evening in July. I can still taste your skin on my lips and the pleasure of your mouth and body. I feel as though my hands are shaped to your breasts. I hold you and love you a thousand times.'

Now back in an on-going affair Amy became clear-headed. She would still go to the demonstration. She must not lose her sense of perspective again. She had a physical need to see him, but would be as good as he at hedging her bets. So she told no one at work about this third trip to France and booked a flight for the early hours of Saturday morning, returning Sunday evening, so they need never know. The airport was a little one at Beauvais, outside Paris; she could catch up on sleep on the rail connection into the city and on the one from there to Laon. She sent the details of this to Jean, first class and via Madame Chabot as he had described – therefore delayed.

Ten days before leaving, the question of whether he would receive the letter in time took on sudden urgency when Amy discovered she was pregnant. She tried a 'don't-panic-do-it-yourself' test, and the results were horribly positive. She thought of her mother, living in the USA – but no, she was not close enough in several senses of the word, so she steeled herself for the humilating lecture she would receive from her GP. Dr Falconer strongly disapproved of unmarried women 'sleeping around' as he would put it. She was old enough to know what the results would be. He might even try to persuade her to have the baby adopted. During the walk to the surgery, though, the terrible fear of becoming an outcast faded. She was glad she was pregnant. Her life was not ruined at all. She would now find the nerve to make this relationship work against the odds. Once face to face with Dr Falconer, it was easy to persuade him that getting back with the father was the only option. The hedges round her bet had been ruthlessly stripped of their leaves but the view of her life ahead was clearer.

* * *

The excuse for Jean going alone to Laon was to be a fault developing in one of his electronic gadgets. He phoned René Védrine, who was delighted to be brought into the plot: amused too at Jean's meticulous planning.

'It would be best to leave the phone call until Wednesday or Thursday. That makes the weekend the obvious time to come up. If the call is any earlier in the week Bertrand may wonder why I wait so long. You won't forget?' he added with a desperate lurch in his voice.

'No, you can count on me.'

'Right.'

'I thought it would be Jean!' René exulted to Madeleine as he put the phone down. 'I've always thought of him as a closet hetero.'

On the Wednesday evening, two weeks later, he phoned Bertrand with such a convincing tale of problems that anyone would think René was used to lying. Bertrand listened unconcerned. While there, Jean could also gauge the reception they were getting. Jean feigned reluctance, ending his grumble with, 'But, if I start early, I could be back the same day.'

Bertrand responded warmly. Jean wasn't restless after all. They were back together. That woman was forgotten. The warmth was still in his voice as he repeated Jean's message to René.

'Yes, he thinks he can get it done in the day.'

Unbeknown to him, René was laughing.

Jean winced as Bertrand smiled at him trustingly, and helped him to more wine. Jean's guilt in the days that followed became so burdensome that the safest way was to channel it into his work. By the afternoon of the 24th September he could barely face his partner's kindness, and his nervousness was obvious.

'It's not so terrible having work go wrong,' Bertrand said sympathetically, himself feeling vindicated in not venturing into electronic gadgetry. Fortunately, it was Friday; after lunch came the welcome distraction of visitors. Jean volunteered to show them round, enabling Bertrand to stay in his studio, since the following day all the responsibility would fall on him. Again he had to weather the pang of Bertrand's appreciation. However, the social activity kept Jean's mind busy and gave him something trivial to talk about over dinner. That night they made love as usual, and at 4 a.m. Jean put on his better work clothes and crept out of their room.

He did not drive straight to Laon. The early start was to surprise Amy by meeting her at the toy-town Beauvais airport. He would make it up to her for having abandoned her when she had left. Concentrated as an arrow, he ate up the kilometres and, sleeping-walking through Customs, Amy saw him at the other side of a wooden barrier, part of a dawn group but utterly apart from it, entirely out of his element. Not only was he dressed from a different century but even his face appeared changed. For it was the idea of the woman, not the person herself, that he remembered and the fixation showed. Like her, he was remote from lack of sleep. In this alien place neither could put on a superficial display of affection since real affection was not yet part of the relationship.

'This has to be perfect,' was Jean's thought.

'Perhaps it's all over,' was Amy's, as they nodded coldly to each other and walked out of the aerodrome.

The early morning, though, was perfect and a few kilometres of close proximity thawed them. A crisp September mist smoked the fields. It seemed there was nothing on this earth but them and the prairie-like plain sweeping eastwards under an evaporating haze. After a couple of hundred kilometres, Laon appeared on the horizon; rising phallically out of the belly of the plain as dramatically as Amy had remembered. She turned to smile her pleasure at being with Jean and they laughed as the reality of being together struck them. Coming closer to the town, perched on its single high rock, myths of giants throwing stones seemed the most obvious explanation for its existence. It was a million miles from the phoney airport.

They drove through the lower town and up the serpentine road for breakfast in the square in front of the cathedral. The September sun was warm enough to sit outside.

'The first of many,' Amy pledged in coffee.

'Mmm,' was the reply. It seemed there was one hurdle after another. No sooner were they mentally together again, than he had to dislocate himself to phone Bertrand. From his troubled expression Amy judged this was not the right time to add the news of the living egg inside her.

'Where's the studio?' she asked instead. He had mentioned an empty flat where they could stay instead of a hotel. As it happened it was available for a long rent.

'Just down that street,' and he nodded towards what seemed to her a solid wall. 'We'll be able to see it this afternoon.' Then the anxiety came back to his face. 'First, I think I'd better phone Bertrand to tell him the repair will keep me overnight – get it over with.'

'Yes I expect you should.' She paused, wondering where she stood, and added, 'Do you trust me?'

'Yes, but this isn't the time to break it to him.' The strain showed in his voice.

'No,' she said as sympathetically as she could. 'I'll be in the cathedral.'

*　*　*

Monique's blood had boiled when the thick envelope from London arrived, addressed to Marcia Chabot and written in the handwriting that had seared itself into her memory when Amy stood in her shop buying stamps. It must involve Jean who had not been in touch with her since then and, by chance, the postman confirmed it.

'It's a funny thing,' he said. 'This morning I stopped for a word with Marcia as she was getting into her car. I couldn't help but catch a glimpse of that package from London I delivered last Wednesday. You know, the one I showed you?'

'Mmmm?'

'Well, it was sort of in a bag on the back seat. It looked unopened.'

'Yes, that is odd,' Monique said, pretending indifference. 'Perhaps she'd just re-sealed it.'

'Yes, p'raps.'

'Did she say where she was going?'

'To pick up some crochet work Madame Estienne had done for her.'

So the package had gone to the gallery. Her jealousy had a righteous feel, fed as it was by the thought of an intruder breaking the gallery up. The lives of several families had improved because of business brought by the two men. Now this prosperity might all fall to pieces. She too could find a motive to see Madame Estienne and to have a word with Bertrand. Madame Estienne grew asparagus. Monique phoned to buy some for the weekend. What did she care if Jean was there too, she thought recklessly, not knowing of course that Bertrand suspected her with his partner.

So, as Jean and Amy sped north, Monique edged her little car into the gap Jean had left her, relieved it was his car and not Bertrand's that was the one missing. The field was open.

The weather was fine, so she looked for Madame in the allotment. Business begun there ended with payment in the kitchen where she found Bertrand. He stared in amazement as she walked in. This was the second most unwelcome woman he knew and her visit was ominous but he acted as the impassive host and eventually she steered the conversation towards the guest they had had at Ivrez during the summer.

'I met your English friend some weeks ago.' Bertrand's gaze hardened.

'So,' Monique thought, 'I was right.' Her probing increased in vigour. 'She seems to have made a lot of friends in the village. Madame Chabot for one.'

'Marcia Chabot?'

Did she meet Madame Estienne's friend? Bertrand could not remember. He looked narrowly at Jean's mother who replied innocently, 'she never mentioned it to me.' For Marcia had given the letter directly to Jean in his studio, as instructed.

'Well, she wrote to her. I recognised the handwriting. You know how nosey a village is. We're all curious about a stranger.'

Monique did not care how unconvincing her explanation was as long as the warning got through. In fact, the more unconvincing the better. And it worked. Bertrand's mind came out of its paralysis. Monique was transparent. She had no interest in strangers. If this one was an exception, it was because of her interest in Jean. Therefore, what was she trying to tell him about this letter? Could it have been for Jean? Marcia had called during the week. Outwardly he did not react.

'Only Madame Chabot can answer your question.'

'Yes, of course. How's the exhibition going?'

'Well, we think.'

Madame Estienne interposed. 'We'll know more tonight. Jean's up there now, doing a repair.'

Bertrand was irritated. Why give away anything to this woman. Monique immediately picked up on it.

'Oh, Jean's away this weekend, is he?'

Bertrand was even more irritated that she found it her business. But he still replied with a veneer of politeness. 'No, just today. He'll be back tonight.'

She was partly reassured.

'Oh, really? Well, thank you, Madame, for the asparagus. I'd better get back and get on with some work myself.'

Jean-Claude steadied his hand to dial the number. This would be the first direct lie he had ever told his partner. It was the mark of breaking away and at this moment he was not sure he could do it. Swallowing hard, trying to breathe easily, he waited for the receiver at the other end to be picked up. He must talk normally. Bertrand was in conversation with a customer in the courtyard, about to go up and open the gallery for him, when he heard the ring. Though surprised to hear from Jean he found nothing suspicious in the complaint which came down the line.

'I've got to do some soldering to this wretched thing – looks as though it'll take till well into the evening, and then it'll need testing. René's offered to put me up for the night.'

Bertrand replied without thinking:

'Fine, see you tomorrow.'

'Fine. See you then.'

The release of tension in Jean's voice was audible. His lie had worked but, thanks to Monique, not his reaction. He was just too relieved and the tone fell into Bertrand's mind like the last piece of a jigsaw. The letter from Amy last week. The phone call from René last week. Laon in the North of France, near enough for a weekend visit from England. The phone-call now to stay the night. What a lot of planning had gone into this. The ground opened beneath his feet. So many people were involved. The girl, René, Madame Chabot and – it brought tears to his eyes – Jean himself had plotted against him. All this time he had seemed so content, so loving, but all along he had been planning a complicated treachery. Through his whirling thoughts came the voice of his customer who had followed him into the kitchen.

'I'm hoping you still have it, Monsieur Barenton. Now there's the perfect reason for buying it. My daughter will be getting married next month.'

'Married!'

Struggling to keep his balance, Bertrand went up the stair ahead of him and unlocked the gallery, feeling not that he was the king in his castle, opening up its treasures to the lucky few, but that he was at everyone's mercy: a menial, abused – a clerk in an office! With an effort he fought off this despairing memory. He found the man's further questions offensive and struggled to maintain his urbane manner.

Though unaware that he had given himself away, Jean was shaken by the strain. Coming out of the phone booth, he could not remember where to meet Amy. He returned automatically to the square and was taken aback to find her seat at the café empty. He looked in the boutiques and, with increasing anxiety, went down the street towards their intended place of rendezvous. She was not there. He had lost her completely! It was only when he came back and leaned against the Cathedral to collect his wits that he remembered who was inside it. Along with the relief, there came a renewed sense of himself, possibly an independent self. Amy was beginning to wonder whether he had dumped her again but, when he came through the door, she saw that the wait had been worthwhile. This was a much warmer, more confident person than the one who had left her an hour before. For the first time, they both realised, he was whole-heartedly glad to see her.

The exhibition was doing well. When they went in they saw children absorbed around the supposedly faulty electronic man, whose limbs were busy deconstructing themselves into weird shapes. The sequence ended with a return to upright normality and Jean's conscience learned some more robustness from it. Perhaps Bertrand's life too would not only come apart, but would be reassembled. René came towards them. Professionally, he was pleased with the way things were going; he was immensely curious about the couple, and he was very pleased to see Amy. He offered them lunch which they were delighted to accept.

'This would go down well in Paris,' René said. 'But it's selling well here so there may not be enough left to think of putting this same exhibition together next spring.'

He paused, wondering whether the men would be having another joint display. Jean offered no clues so René moved tactfully towards the possibility that interested him.

'Your work has become very interesting Jean. If you work a little faster than I've known you do in the past, we could put on a solo exhibition.'

Amy glowed. René was doing her work for her and with rather more tempting offers than she had.

Jean tried the idea out in his mind. 'Yes, I could do that. Could I find a forge here though?'

'I think that could be arranged,' René said, enjoying the situation, soaking up the clandestine romance, enjoying

90

the power he had over their futures. And he liked his food. He lingered over lunch, not admitting to himself the advantage he was taking of them. On the one hand grateful, yet for the immediate moment, increasingly resentful, Jean and Amy sat powerless as he stole their stolen hours. It was four o'clock when the trio finally broke up.

'We can leave the car.'

They walked across the Old Town's square and into the fissure in the rock Amy had seen before. It was a narrow alley between buildings; narrower than London alleys but no darker since these grey stone buildings were only three small storeys high. The path they were following bent, then opened into a courtyard surrounded on three sides by weathered apartments. René had given them the keys to one. It was on the first floor so light broke into the large room at the back but the front faced another alley. It would be a less privileged place to work than Ivrez, but they would not talk about that yet.

Together they looked in amazement at the bed – such a luxury. Despite the lost afternoon they still had a full twelve hours without being haunted by a third person. They slowed down their love-making with tantalising pleasures, beginning with the slow removal of each other's clothes, then the hungry, slow, insatiable kisses all over and the tactile sensations of skin on skin. The second most noticeable feature of Jean's lithe, wiry body was the scar across his ribs. Amy ran her finger along the red weal.

'How long ago?'

'Nearly fourteen years.'

'Does it give you any problems?'

'No. They're all in the past.'

'Are they?'

'Completely in the past.'

His hands were again shaped to her breasts. He caressed them and her soft belly, and teased the inside of her thighs with his fingers. Though work-worn his hands were sensitive. She sighed with pleasure.

'And we are the future?' she asked, thinking of the three of them.

'Yes,' he replied, unaware they were not alone.

Amy's hands had slipped further down from his scar and stroked his penis. It was hard and seeking. Her insides ached for him. Together, they sank into the well-known, yet timeless, ecstasy.

The main problem was Madame Estienne.

'She won't want to move.'

'Bertrand will hardly want her to stay.'

'She's never lived in a town. My mother intends to be buried in Ivrez. But there is the person you sent your letters to – Madame Chabot. She's a widow, with a large house. They're old friends. Perhaps we could work something out with her. My mother is only sixty-five.'

The object of these plans was clearing up after dinner and puzzling over the change in Bertrand since the morning. Now he could not stay in one place for more than a few seconds and there was a ten second delay between her speaking and his hearing, and then his replies were irritable. Heaven knows what he'd been saying to the visitors. He resented them, but they had been a distraction. When the time came to close the studio, he wanted to delay it, to prevent having to face up to what he had learned. Impulsively he invited an old acquaintance and his wife, who had bought an abstract, to eat with them. But, eventually, Bertrand was alone with Jean's mother.

'When will Jean be back?' she called, on her way out of the room. Bertrand found it impossible to reply, the muscles in his throat were numb. 'Long way, Laon,' Madame Estienne continued prophetically, and closed the door behind her.

Alone, his hand hit the table so hard the glass he forgot was in it broke and cut him. Blood snaked over his fingers. He lurched out of the room in search of air to drown the horrors suppressed all day. The irony! He had loved her! He'd insisted she come back. He'd been so sure she felt something for him, there was some meaning between them. That she could bring meaning to his life. And he had been bitterly deceived. She was out to destroy his life – the only one he had known which had worked; the life he'd put so much work into, which gave his only fulfillment. He would hunt her down and kill her! Tears mingled with his anger and the release cleared his mind. All Jean had had was a stolen weekend. When he came back Bertrand would continue the pretence that the repair had been genuine. But he needed to know more, to know how to react. Could he find the letter? Bertrand contemplated the door to Jean's studio, just visible in the dark. It was never locked. There was a chill as he violated the space inside. A dusty jacket hung on one wall and Bertrand went through its pockets, feeling the physical presence of Jean's body in the rough fabric – feeling a jealousy for them both. Trembling, he brought his torch up to read the slip of paper one of them contained.

Amy still held back from telling Jean about the baby. They had only had a brief time of pleasure together. A baby seemed to be a way of telling him that the fun was over. In this she misjudged him, but it seemed to her it would be easier once she knew he wanted to live with her, of his own free will.

'We can't expect such a gem of a flat to stay empty for long,' she said ruefully. 'But perhaps flats are easy to find in France.'

'Not as good as this one. It would suit us very well.'

She hid her surprise.

'It would. It's almost as though it was all arranged for us.'

'The owners aren't sure whether to sell or to rent.'

'Could we persuade them to rent?'

'That was René's idea. He would ask them to let for a year.'

'What do you think?' She held her breath. A half-hearted 'yes' would be no good. To make this work Jean had to take an initiative and she doubted that he would. His life had not moulded him for decisive action. If he was half-hearted she might mention the baby, but now she had left it so long it would appear like blackmail. While these thoughts went through her head, she realised Jean had spoken.

'I think we should take it.'

He had come to the same conclusion. A blind leap was the only way. A phone call, a cheque in the post – it drew on a joint account – another phone call, and they were promised the keys in four weeks' time.

'Will you be able to work here?' Amy asked. 'It's not what you're used to.'

'As long as you're here. I only need a place to make sketches. And what about you?' he asked, feeling unutterably generous towards her. 'Aren't you giving up your career?'

'I could find a better career in France.'

94

11

In this spirit Jean drove back to Ivrez. It was late afternoon – Sunday. There was no one around. Bertrand's customers had completed their business, and he had gone into Montargis. Madame Estienne was in Ivrez. Jean had the opportunity to search out his belongings. There were not many of them anyway: a few tools – a few clothes; the lack demonstrated a childish dependency. It seemed to him he was leaving his parents', not his lover's house, no longer a child but to be the father of one.

He went to his studio and changed from one old jacket into the older one hanging on the nail. His hand slipped into the pocket and rested on the slip of paper kept there to warm him while he worked: '16 Orchard Hill, Greenwich, SE7; 01-649 0196: I love you and want to spend my life with you, Amy.' He had an idea for an abstract. With the talisman by him the first sketch flew from his fingers. It came effortlessly – the best idea he had had in his life. It would be made in spiralling metal, a hermaphrodite in which the male-female shape flowed like a strip of DNA. Entirely absorbed and happy, he forgot the problem ahead of him until the sound he was waiting for killed his concentration – a car coming along their bumpy track. There would be no putting it off: he would tell Bertrand now. His whole life was at stake.

Bertrand had picked up Madame Estienne on his way back from Montargis.

'Have you ever thought that Jean might marry some day?' he asked.

'Not very likely.'

'But wouldn't you like that? To have grandchildren? Of course it would mean moving away from here,' he added, hoping he had not made the idea too attractive.

'No, that's not going to happen. This is our home.'

Her tone was final. All she wanted after the struggles she had known, was to end her days peacefully where she was rooted. Bertrand was glad to be sure of this. He dreaded the confrontation. If he even acknowledged to Jean that he knew of the new situation he might help it succeed. Speaking of it would bring it into reality. 'I love you and want to spend my life with you' spurred his self-preservation.

Jean was rehearsing his farewell speech as he came out of the studio but instead found his hand warmly shaken by André and Emilie Colvert.

Bertrand had invited them, as innocents, to share this crucial meeting. Their car was now squeezed in behind his.

'Long time since we've seen you, Jean.'

'Pierre has work he wants to show you.'

Emilie, too, dared to encourage her talented son and, Jean's head buzzing with their eagerness to share recent news, he was swept into the conversation. Despite himself he was glad Pierre's talent was proving more than an adolescent whim. He actually became interested, while Madame Estienne, uncomplainingly, ministered to their culinary needs.

It was getting late. If the plane had arrived as scheduled,

Amy would be back in London now, preparing for work next day; preparing for her routine day. Jean moved in his seat and glanced at his watch. Somewhere in the distance André had plans.

'This area has you, but what we need is a central link in the city – Montargis would be fine. An Arts centre – somewhere ordinary visitors can learn about the work of the region. Millionaires may give you your income, but as a region we need to be more inclusive.'

'I've been looking at the mill by the side of Auto 60. Perfect place if it was renovated.'

Emilie's enthusiasm filled the kitchen, and Jean looked at them both, distantly, through ripples of emotions. Bertrand had doubts.

'Ivrez is secure. Artists let us have their most precious work because they know it's safe – you would need security in town. It would become impersonal, just a business.'

Jean looked at his watch again, making the time-adjustments between England and France.

'Expecting someone?' André laughed.

Bertrand answered for him.

'Ignore him. He's just back from Laon – there were problems with the exhibition.' The lie choked him.

'You look worn out, Jean. Perhaps we should be going.'

Bertrand allowed himself an openly antagonistic glance at Jean. It had not been the drive that had worn him out. Jean, in his confusion, could not offer a defence for his preoccupation and stayed silent.

'Long way, Laon,' said Madame Estienne for the second time that weekend, thinking of herself as a baby abandoned there on the steps of the Convent of Saint Margaret.

'Maybe it's better not to confront Bertrand,' Jean began to think; 'maybe it's better to say nothing, just to go.'

His mother continued. 'We're glad to have him back.'

97

Had she read his thoughts? He looked closely at her tough, aging body, the impassive, uncomplaining face. She too was his responsibility.

He recovered his love in the studio next day. Ideas for the sculpture continued to grow. He recovered his certainty. Tonight if he did not phone, Amy would. He would let her phone. He needed something from the outside to force the truth into the open. Bertrand's plan was working; as each hour passed his nerve weakened. But it would be easier to tell his mother.

He could always be sure of finding her alone somewhere outdoors. And his opportunity came when it started to rain. Taking an umbrella with him so as to make his point he went to the vegetable garden where she worked on unheeding, her shawl pulled over her head.

'This is getting too much for you – this outdoor work?'

She shrugged. 'I'm used to it.'

'What if you didn't have to do it?'

'What else would I do. Sit about?'

'There's your crochet and lace-making.'

'I'd get stiff as a corpse.'

She didn't treat the questions seriously enough to stop what she was doing so he changed tactic.

'I'm thinking of leaving Ivrez – setting up my own studio.'

'Ridiculous!'

'But what would you do? Bertrand might not want you to stay.'

The name reminded her of Bertrand's own questions.

'Is there a woman?'

'Yes.'

'That woman this summer?'

He nodded. Thoughtfully, she returned to her hoe. At least she knew. 'That was half the battle,' he thought. She would get used to the idea.

*   *   *

When the phone rang that evening Bertrand was taking a last look in the gallery for any little detail in the lay-out which he might improve on. At this time in the evening he was often struck by changes he could make, especially in the visual relationship between objects. He loved his gallery – it was the nearest thing to perfection that he knew in this life. He heard the phone ring and then stop when Jean answered it. Bertrand would wait to be called. Their friends usually wanted a word with them both and it would be a good moment to normalise relations between them. They had still hardly spoken. In a split second he realised the other possibility. Agonised, he flung himself awkwardly down the stairs where Jean was in intimate huddle with the receiver. Bertrand grabbed it.

'Hello?' he barked. There was a click at the other end and he turned angrily to Jean. But stopped. This was what Jean wanted, so he must control his feelings. He must not say things which could not be taken back. Their eyes met for a moment in mutual goodbyes. Then, to Jean's surprise, Bertrand relaxed.

'There's no one there.'

'Who did you think it was?'

'A difficult customer,' and he smiled.

Jean was forced to begin.

'You know I'm going to start up on my own?'

'Nonsense: how will you get any work done? You'll be back to worrying all the time about making ends meet. And how will your Mother live?'

'You'll see. René is helping.'

'Ah, René. He has his eyes on her.'

Bertrand mentioning Amy first, in this twisted way, ended Jean's attempt. He got up and went through to

99

the kitchen. Now that they both knew, he was free to go ahead. That night he quickly phoned Amy to reassure her.

Bertrand's voice had shot fear into her. But the child calmed her. Procreation was gathering to steamroller any obstacles out of the way. And she knew Bertrand's secret. His weakness gave her confidence. On the phone Jean had been strong on the romance but weak on action and London was so far away. To get him to move, she must go to Laon. Fortunately, she wasn't getting much sickness. Apart from wanting to pee all the time, she felt well. She must move now while she was still mobile. She had to tell someone and it could only be Doreen Miles.

Amy described the complications in an abstract way as though Jean had an ongoing affair with a local woman. Doreen was level headed.

'Are there children?'

'No.'

'Then there's no problem, surely?'

'There's a kind of financial hold, and years of habit. Working there is easy for Jean. But he's paid three months' rent on a flat away from Ivrez – only he'll find it hard to move into it without knowing that I'm already there.'

'You wouldn't sell your flat here, would you?' Doreen was appalled.

'I'll let it for a year. It'll be easy. If things don't work out, I could probably live with Sarah and Stephen till the baby's born. And the father's French. It would be right to stay over there to give things a chance.'

It was all logically thought out – such a sensible form of madness. Weighing things up, Mrs Miles commented,

'Well, the madness has already happened I suppose.'

'It has,' Amy agreed emphatically, 'and the baby gives me something to work for.'

*   *   *

After the phone call, everything began to go on at Ivrez much as before. Daily momentum carried Jean along because his new work was going extraordinarily well. It had a confidence and originality which sharpened his style. He threw himself into it. It would be stupid not to finish it before he left. This was what they both needed to launch themselves financially. It was all inspired by Amy; she would understand. Once this was done he would join her. He wrote to explain.

Amy, too, was driven – by the life inside her. It *was* life! She was caught up in living again, positive about the future. A death would be answered by a birth. She placed her flat with an agent and devoted some time to packing up objects precious enough to figure in some imagined, distant home. These she would leave with Doreen. The phone rang. She grabbed it.

'Jean?'

The reply came in another voice.

'Leave him alone.'

The chill ran down her spine. How did he know her number? Still, it was better for Bertrand to know for sure. No playing games. No need even to say 'sorry' – such a hypocritical thing to say. People did change partners – he would have to accept it.

'This isn't something we can talk about.'

'When I catch up with you I will kill you.' His voice was thick with hurt. Then the line went dead and the chill soon passed. She would not be going to Ivrez. Laon was a beautiful and civilised town, far from him.

By the end of October the flat became theirs. She was ready to cross the channel for the fourth time that year, this time by ferry and followed by a trunk of essentials.

Once on the train from Calais, the promised land disappeared behind carriage windows submerged under an October drenching. It was a lonely arrival, only made possible by the support of René and Madeleine, and Amy could see the doubt in their faces as they met her at the station. She fought to keep an air of control as she struggled with her bags through the puddles towards them. They were so suave and poised: the rain shimmered around their car and dared not touch them:

'You see I'm pregnant,' she burst out as she climbed into the back.

'Ah.' They exchanged a look.

'And I love him. And this is what he wants too. But it is crazy.'

'The best things always are. We'll get him here.' A warmer smile came over from Madeleine.

And, at least, the owner had seen that the flat was clean. Daily existence till Jean arrived began to look possible.

'I'll need to get some work – anything – at first. I could work in a shop.'

'That would be the easiest to find – till something better comes along.'

A word next day from Madeleine to the chemist's where a card asked for an assistant, and the job was Amy's. The shop owner found the romance of her situation irresistible. 'Lucky it's a chemists,' thought Amy.

She summoned her courage and phoned the gallery at Ivrez. Bertrand answered. She put the phone down. A letter would have to do.

Dearest love,
I must be nearer to you. I know there are problems for you changing your life. But you'll see from the

postmark that I have moved into our flat in Laon. René got me the spare keys, and Madeleine has helped me find a job. Everything is working out wonderfully, and your new home is here ready, with your loving Amy longing to be in your arms again.

She sent it care of Madame Chabot. The next day she received Jean's forwarded from London.

Dearest love,
Forgive me for not phoning you back. It hasn't been easy telling Bertrand – each time I try something interrupts. But thoughts of you inspire my every moment. I am doing work that will make me really known, I can feel it, and then our lives will be so much easier. I am not forgetting you – I love you, I love you, I love you, I adore you. Jean.

Clearly he *was* forgetting her, but the note predated hers. It was OK.

Two days later, while Bertrand was sifting their mail, ready to burn anything with a London postmark, Jean was reading Amy's note slipped to him in the village. He was shocked to read where she was. It challenged him. But it also proved she loved him. It was he who had written of a great love and here she was, responding. He wrote a card and posted it before returning to the gallery.
'In three weeks I will come.'

12

Inevitably, the chemist's initial, romantic response had sobered. She began to wonder whether Amy should go home.

'You must think about yourself.'

'But I feel fine. And Jean will soon be here.'

She looked hard at Madame Colbère, defying her to question this assumption.

'It's a difficult situation.'

'Yes, and if I'd stayed in London, there'd be no hope at all,' Amy continued reasonably.

'Well, you have got a little time. Make sure you're eating well. And what about antenatal classes?'

When Amy returned to the apartment the wind was whistling across the rock. The city itself could have been prehistoric, bubbling up through volcanic cobbles, petrified into stone shapes by the wind. She lived on an island suspended from the clouds and, she thought, shaped fantastically like a snail. As the weather was clear, she walked out of the compact shadowy streets and beheld a panoramic vista of the plain stretching westwards into the haze of the horizon. The wind whistled and pulled, pressing her into the ornate railings. Behind her, woodlands curled in the curving tail of her island. Its steep slope led to the plain where the modern town sat, encircling the old like a slipped halo. To get to the chemist's Amy trod the calf breaking, near vertical stairways, and returned by the bus's serpentine route.

The first weekend gave her time to reflect. She had made this move blindly – had had to do it that way, it was a move that had to be done. During the week she had taken instructions, done what was needed and put her identity into the closet. Back at the flat, Saturday afternoon, she felt as empty and alien as the stone walls of her surroundings. It took an hour of going over the reasons for her being here before some courage returned, strengthened by facing the windy outdoors. On the Monday it struck her how alien working at the chemist's was. René had said he would look for a post in Laon's gallery – something she was trained for. At present there was nothing. On her way back, thinking to bring life to the empty flat, she went to buy a few flowers from the shop nearby and saw that they too were advertising for an assistant. The pay was similar and this way, as she explained to a sceptical Madame Colbère, she wouldn't have to travel from the old to the new town. She also felt better in the fresh air, than she did working under strip-lights. Yes, Madame Colbère was convinced; she did not appear to think that this showed even more instability than Amy's having arrived here in the first place.

She was right about one thing – it was important to get to grips with the French medical system and, as a chemist, Madame Colbère was happy to help establish Amy's claim on it. With this, her identity received more support. She was treated as a valued individual not a cipher, not a statistic, despite unanswerable questions, such as:

'And what of your husband's family's medical history?'

Only when, or if, Jean arrived would anyone really believe her.

* * *

105

Three weeks! – Amy put the letter away and flew into an orgy of home making. The room to be Jean's studio looked subdued in the autumn light but, yes, she felt, dusting off a layer of neglect, it had atmosphere. To welcome him she would fill the place with flowers, a rural and erotic smell. Jean's letter meant he would arrive the weekend after next. There was no phone in the flat so, via Madame Chabot, she sent another note, giving him the phone number of the flower shop.

After sending the card Jean's ability to keep the promise ran into trouble. The DNA piece would be fragile until finished and it was excellent work. They needed this to start their lives. He found himself unable to phone Amy: there was nothing to tell her that she wanted to hear until the piece could be moved. He was, however, no longer sharing the bedroom and he avoided seeing Bertrand except when his mother was present. Bertrand no longer heard surreptitious phone calls, no obvious clues to Jean's plans, but the widening gulf told him of a break. One afternoon he came in and watched as Jean worked.

'We've been friends many years,' Bertrand said eventually.

Jean was silent.

'I couldn't have achieved anything without you.' Bertrand had had time to think over this truth. Their roles were reversing and Jean searched for neutral words of defence.

'I didn't plan this.'

The evasion produced a bitter response:

'I hate the whole business of love. Except for you.' Yet, the one thing the three had in common was that their search for love consumed them more than anything else.

Jean struggled to keep Bertrand's feelings at a distance.

'There's nothing to say. Everything's changed.'

'What's so special? You've had others.'

Jean looked at his partner with surprise. Bertrand had known of his double life all along. The moment of honesty brought them close again. He looked away. This was not something he could explain.

'It's unfinished,' he ended lamely, hating himself. Opposing Bertrand was dispiriting and he had given him the answer he was looking for – one implying that the relationship with Amy would eventually be over. If only Bertrand could be brought round to look other truths in the face. Seeing the worn expression on his face, Jean hugged him in a brotherly way and that night slept in their old room. Bertrand held him to him as a brother.

The next evening, before their meal, Jean leant on the gate looking into the wood. He'd been stupid the night before. There'd been no physical love, but the friendship mattered. Still, it made him stupid. It was easy enough to choose in your head but not so easy to carry out the hard decisions involved. And he'd had a letter from Alain – 'This woman is playing with you. Don't let her destroy your lives.' Alain could not see the situation from Jean's point of view of course. The pressure was on. Absorbed in his thoughts, he did not react immediately when he saw a Citroen rather like his own backing down the lane. But his attention sharpened at once when Amy's friend, Stephen, climbed out.

'Bonjour.'

'Bonjour.'

Since Stephen's fluency was completely exhausted by this exchange he drew from his pocket the letter with Sarah's explanation. The light was gone from the sky and Jean waved Stephen eagerly towards the kitchen. Was this letter for him? Was it to do with Amy? Something that would tilt the scales – give him his conviction back. Animated, he strode across the yard.

'Nous téléphoné,' Stephen tried to explain as they walked, baffling Jean still further. What Stephen was failing to communicate was that Sarah had phoned, Bertrand had answered and put the phone down. They did not know, nor even want to know, why because this journey could not be put off and Stephen had come anyway. None of this could be made clear until, inside the kitchen, Jean read the letter. During the pause Stephen nodded towards Madame Estienne, who was producing tantalising culinary aromas. She returned his look approvingly, noting that, physically, the two men were very alike: lean and muscular, used to physical labour and able to endure tough times.

'Vos peintures,' Jean said at last, showing his disappointment that Stephen was here on his own business.

'Oui,' affirmed Stephen. Not all had been sold last year. Obviously, he needed them now for income over the winter. Jean nodded reluctantly and Stephen followed him up the stairs to Bertrand's studio where they were being stored. They passed Bertrand in the gallery. Stephen's innocence regarding the affair between Jean and Amy, even of the fact that she had returned alone to stay at Ivrez, stood him in good stead. He felt no awkwardness, nor did he find Bertrand's coldness anything new. But, over three journeys, as he and Jean manouevred his paintings down the stairs, he did begin to wonder at an extra strangeness that was coming at him from them both. Was this going to be the briefest of visits, with himself immediately booted out into the hotel? He did not have the language skills to forestall it by keeping them talking into the evening, and he was thankful when he saw that Madame Estienne had done what was necessary. Four places were prepared at the table.

He did his best to keep the conversation going during the meal and, since he was the only one in a good humour, there was plenty of silence to fill. With drawings, and more key phrases from his notebook, Stephen tried to give an impression of how lucky the family had been; how they had found a really great house – thanks to the people of Veuillans – a house in the countryside but near the little town – and between Lyon and Grenoble – big cities, just what he needed for selling work. What he now needed were contacts in these cities. Geneva too, would be good, and he continued to struggle to convey this. At times, in enthusiasm and linguistic frustration, a paragraph of fluent English shot from him, followed by his hearty laugh at its futility. Madame Estienne nodded, and looked seriously sympathetic.

Bertrand understood most of what he was saying, especially the lapses into English but, even in better times, his philosophy was never to attempt anything he was not good at. He could never make a fool of himself with pidgin-English – certainly not with pidgin-French. If only this family had never arrived. And now, here they were again just when he might have built on the minor success with Jean last night. These intruders were colonialist English trampling on his future. He could see that Stephen kept reminding Jean of who was waiting, probably in Laon where 'René was helping them'. But, realising from Stephen's behaviour that their guest knew nothing of any of this, Jean too found he had little to say. It was Madame Estienne who was left to respond harmlessly to the pictures, phrases and smiles. Then Bertrand suddenly turned to Stephen with immense affability.

'Did you say your house was in Drôme? Very fine country around there. I remember it well – spent some time there as a boy. Have you been through the Bourne

Gorge? Quite spectacular, and Puy has the most beautiful cathedral in France.'

This was said in fast French, which Stephen could not understand. He stared aghast and Bertrand concluded with an answer to his own questions.

'Oh, I see, in Isère. How splendid.'

With a malicious smile he returned to his supper. The rudeness was utterly different from Bertrand's style of haughtiness and Stephen's transfixed stare showed he understood the insult. Jean, embarrassed, tried to explain. At last Stephen found one of them listening to him! He interrupted, fastening on the opportunity to repeat the only question that mattered: where could he sell his work? For the second time he brought out Sarah's key phrase that he'd learned by heart:

'Ou vendre les peintures en Grenoble et en Lyon? Les contacts?' Now that Jean was concentrating he caught the meaning.

'Ah, oui.' As it happened there was one man he knew well. 'Grenoble – Marino Verchese.'

Stephen could not make out the second name and quickly presented Jean with his notebook and a pen, heaving a sigh of relief as the words took shape in more durable form. An Italian might be more communicative than these two.

As the clock struck ten, Madame Estienne got up from her chair and left. 'Now I'll be chucked out,' was Stephen's resigned thought, preparing to get up too. He could sleep a bit in the car, and at least be home sooner. But she came back through the staircase door with sheets, and hung them over the back of the chair she'd vacated, pointing to Stephen and to them before leaving the room. The whereabouts of the bed, though, was a mystery. Bertrand had left the table and was standing, sullenly, in the doorway. Stephen was tired. These men had gone

110

mad but he had what he came for so, glancing at Jean who was watching Bertrand warily out of the corner of his eye, Stephen rose and lifted the precious paintings to a safer place, some face to the wall on a chest in the corner, some propped up against it. Then, feeling equally mad, he picked up the sheets, pointed at them and did an elaborate Italian-style 'I don't know where to go' gesture. Jean smiled ruefully, went over to the door at the foot of the stairs and led the way. It had been brave of Stephen to attempt this visit alone, and he was pleased with himself. He had succeeded and he said goodnight to Jean in unapologetic English. Jean descended to face Bertrand once again.

Towards the end of the three weeks Amy gave up hope: still no phone call. Bertrand must have locked him in the tower. Past habits must have taken over. She wanted Jean so much. The future was a blank. The devastating realisation struck her that she had no future without him. Miserably, she read again a letter from Sarah, forwarded from London: a considerate letter, telling of difficulties overcome and a home found. Amy had so much to say which could not be said. What had happened between her and Jean would cause a rift in their friendship. Yet she couldn't stay in Laon much longer without him and she might simply have to throw her pregnant self on Sarah's mercy, since her own flat in London was now let. What a catastrophic mess everything was. On the Friday she forced herself not to prepare for his arrival, working late and not bringing back any flowers. She was right. He did not arrive. Nor on the Saturday. On the Sunday evening she wrote some sort of letter to Sarah, went out to post it in the early hours of Monday morning and from exhaustion, eventually slept.

About 6 a.m. she had an extraordinary dream. It seemed to her that a warm body had slipped between the sheets and enclosed her protectively. She rolled over and slid her free arm around the neck.

'Was it hard getting away?'

'Impossible – but a moment came.'

A few hours earlier Jean had told Bertrand his plan was unchanged and left. There had been no more scenes. His almost-finished work, wrapped in layers of sacking, fitted tightly in the back of the car. It was still not quite finished because Bertrand had surprised him in the last few days with another task. A buyer in Auxerre phoned with a fiddling job either of them could have done.

'He asked for you and you can't offend him,' Bertrand had said, knowing Jean was superstitious about not discarding those who had bought his work in the past. Fuming he had lost time, but he redoubled his efforts and was ready enough and more determined to go. A few mementos, a photograph of his father, the receipt from his first big sale, a case of clothes, and all trace of his existence was removed from Ivrez. The fire of the forge had been left to die down but the lingering warmth was enough for him to doze by for a couple of hours, while Bertrand, through the wall, lay stonily awake.

The damp smell of autumn grew fainter as Jean turned from the narrow, green lanes and onto a deserted autoroute. He was pulling up his roots but he felt the profit, not the loss. He and she belonged together – of that he was sure. They were part of an ordinary world of marriage, children and success. It seemed to him that he had grown up.

'Are you asleep?' he asked her.

'Half awake, half wanting you, half thinking, half

dreaming.' Words could not express the wonder she felt at this miraculous reversal of events. 'Four halves,' she added wryly.

'It makes two of us.'

13

Jacques turned out of the narrow rue de Varenne on the left bank, near the military district, and into the drive of the house which had been Auguste Rodin's home for much of his life – heading for demolition until saved by the sculptor's reputation and bought as his museum. At the entrance an attendant was sweeping up leaves.

'Good afternoon, Monsieur Duclos.'

'Good afternoon.'

The iron gate swung open with ceremony, recalling the house's eighteenth-century origins. It was Monday and the museum closed to visitors. Between October and March they did not swarm in quite the numbers that they did the rest of the year and only one small, disappointed group watched him drive in. The front garden was windswept and deserted, apart from three men in overalls digging a channel in one of the side paths. Jacques parked the car and approached the imposing entrance optimistically. One of the advantages of housing such a beloved artist, a national hero, was that numerous bequests had made the museum self-financing. It was owned by the National galleries but rested very lightly on their purse strings. Jacques was pleased to think that he would be less bound by red tape if he could show the Henry Moore exhibition here. A tall woman, her face weather-beaten, appeared at the top of the steps.

'Good afternoon, Marianne.'

'Hello, Jacques.' She came down to meet him. 'Forgive

the work going on here. We have to seize every moment when the gates are closed to get repairs done. The water is back on.'

Jacques nodded, followed her up the steps and in through the massive French windows. The office was upstairs but, since they had the museum to themselves, she led the way across the worn parquet flooring to the glass doors at the back and the comfortable seating which had been arranged there.

'Aperitif? Coffee?'

Jacques declined. 'In some ways,' he said, 'this building is better than the Louvre.' He looked up at the larger than life-size bronze "Walking Man" in the middle of the entrance hall striding its way towards them with muscular determination. 'The building has a human scale but it doesn't cramp these monumental figures.' He could envisage a Moore "Mother and Child" replacing the "Walking Man".

'It is the best place in Paris for large works.'

'Yes. We need another gallery like it.'

'We do. Well, let me show you round.'

Jacques stopped to admire a work by Camille Claudel, Rodin's pupil, model and lover: "The Unrelenting". It commemorated his eventual discarding of her. It was a strong, wild piece of work and hinted at the mental breakdown that was to follow. As he admired it, Jacques' eyes checked for its removeability. Again, Madame Nicolet saw his eyeline descending floorwards. As he looked up he noticed the quizzical look.

'We need all these rooms. You know it's crucial.'

'During his life Rodin shared the house with several artists,' she replied carefully, knowing that Jacques' request was impossible under the terms of Rodin's will. 'Matisse and Cocteau, as well as Claudel.'

'A curious quartet.'

'Whereas, Moore has something in common I think.'

'Yes, as much as two artists ever can have.'

He was glad to have his doubts talked away, until they walked into another room totally dominated by the five larger-than-life "Burghers of Calais", in chains.

'Can nothing be moved?'

'This can, as it happens. It's being shown next spring in Berlin.'

'We haven't been able to get the Gare d'Orsay, you know. Its owners have plans of their own. I was depending on it. I thought we had it. So, although the Moore exhibition is on its way, in fact we have nowhere to put it.'

They were now in the garden, passing Eve clutching her nakedness away from their gaze. Not far away was her spouse, similarly shy, contorting himself into the position of discus thrower. By contrast, further down the garden, a muscular John the Baptist strode out to preach with glorious self-confidence despite his own very blatant naked organs. How would Moore's non-sexual figures compete cheek-by-jowl with this physicality? His colleague began to sympathise with the dilemma.

'Two rooms downstairs can be cleared, but not the "Walking Man" I'm afraid. Some smaller pieces can be stored upstairs, but others have nowhere else to go. Most of the work in the garden, though, could be put in less prominent positions. Apart from the few that are permanent fixtures.'

'But the gardens are large,' Jacques conceded. 'We can expand out here.'

The autumn air was turning cool and he saw Madame Nicolet shiver. He offered his hand.

'I won't come in again.'

'Very well. If you decide on us send a list of the works and we'll discuss what's practical. We'll be as helpful as we can.'

116

'Fine. I'll contact you directly then.'

'Yes, we're a free agent.'

'Splendid.'

As Jacques walked back to the car he passed the cast of Rodin's most famous work, on its grassy plot to the left of the driveway. He rested his elbow on the plinth of "The Thinker", leaned over the bones of Rodin and his wife, and thought about it. Could Rodin move over sufficiently to allow in a visiting giant? Visitors might enjoy getting two shows for one. They might think them twin romantics, a view that neither sculptor would agree with. Jacques considered the muscular forearm of the statue, its very physical, bent posture: the most sensual depiction of intellect he could imagine. A stunning gravestone. How clever of Rodin to keep one of his best works with him. The statue sat above his remains like a question rising from the sculptor's brain that would hover there for all time. Its robust physique was not unlike Rodin's when alive, so he was immortalised in two ways. The plinth had no plaque, no other commemoration at all. It was the three-dimensional image that Rodin intended we should never forget. And how could we? Except for a few weeks when the near virginal asceticism of Moore would sit alongside. If Rodin made the spiritual physical then Moore made the physical spiritual. 'We could state the contrast,' Jacques thought, 'make some sense out of the combination.' If there were problems it would strengthen his hand for acquiring a better site for the future.

14

'Eiyee!'

Jean lifted his head from Amy's belly.

'Your ear is worse than the stethoscope.'

'No heartbeat yet. Only your tummy rumbling.'

'The rumbling of lust, more like,' she added running her fingers through his newly washed hair.

'Fine with me,' he said, coiling his naked limbs around her. 'It's because it's your first pregnancy, but lust is infinitely better than being sick all the time.'

His knowledge made her smile. In the evenings he pored over books, describing diagrams and timetables to her. He responded to the provocation of the smile.

'Well, you know I'm as much a mother as a father.' She punched him. He kissed her fist.

A little light fed through the recessed window in their cave-like apartment – less now it was November – but Jean liked to imagine he could see a delicate embryonic curve under the skin. He traced an outline on her tummy with a gentle finger, sending her into a passionate tremor. For some reason these days she lusted after him all the time, and tried not to think of him at work in case anyone asked about the rush of blood to her face.

'At this rate you'll be more worn out than me,' she said once the plunging and rolling were over.

'I'm making the most of it. Of everything – counting the days to the birth. I'll be there every moment. You won't need a midwife.'

'No regrets?'

'None at all. And you?'

'No. My life had ended in England. You have given me a second one.'

The low window looked straight onto the alley but three-foot thick walls muffled the sounds. Their privacy was womb-like, as Jean put it, reaching up with his left hand to touch the skin of the ceiling. As he did so, light glinted on the gold band round his fourth finger.

The idea of marriage had come to him on the drive up from Ivrez. It would show the world he and Amy were not to be separated. A wall had been put up between himself and what was behind. With a mischievous smile Amy clasped her ringed hand round his.

'It was a good wedding.'

'One of the best. Even if we'd had to sleep on the floor.'

A private joke, repeated for the pleasure of seeing her laugh. Days before the ceremony, the owners of the flat had taken a fancy to their abandoned antique and the journey to the Registry Office had included a visit to a furniture shop.

'Can you deliver today?' Amy asked the assistant cheerfully, 'we can't start the honeymoon without a bed, can we?' The assistant looked out of the window at her partner, he assumed, skulking outside and returned her a humorous look. But then an Aston Martin pulled up and from it stepped Laon's most glamorous woman. She began an animated conversation with the 'tramp' – not even Jean's best suit quite brought him into the modern world. The addition of Madeleine, though, changed the assistant's expression to one of genuine interest:

'We'll see what we can do.'

Jean was slightly better equipped for life in the studios.

There were six working down in Semilly: Yvonne Talabot, a dynamic and innovative sculptor, the most famous of the group; Tomas van Leirsberghe, another sculptor, a Fleming with strong political views he wanted Paris to hear more of; the painter, Hébert Chapu, by contrast, a quiet, introverted man, a troubled person who tended to disappear for weeks at a time; another painter, a local man, Philbert Marin, easy-going and gregarious; the sculptor, Jean Legrand, also aimiable and, finally, one more woman, by chance a friend of Madeleine's, Génevieve Lacotte, who worked with stained glass. They all got on well because no one could afford to waste time.

Jean found his way there following René – noticing that Semilly had once been a separate village and was now a suburb divided from Laon by allotments. The studios were in a conversion of the church and of the priest's house next door, from which congregation and pastor had fled to less drafty quarters. The late nineteenth-century buildings stood at a bend in the main street, part of a continuous row of houses looking across to another row of houses. The place was functional and Jean was pleased to find he had a choice, either to share the open interior of the church or take an individual studio in the house next door. In the back of the van that he'd borrowed was the DNA sculpture – still nearly finished but now with a buyer waiting. After brief introductions, he followed René up the stairs to a room recently cleared of junk. A bench, a chair, a table and an area reinforced for heavy work made up the interior.

'The welding equipment is kept over there.' René pointed out of the window. 'Otherwise, this is it!'

'It's just fine,' said Jean, planning to alternate according to his needs and, as René left, he dashed down the stairs after him, pulling a slightly dog-eared piece of paper from his jacket pocket. It was a cheque for the sum of the rent on the Laon flat, drawn on a joint account – his and Amy's.

'It's made out to you but it's for Bertrand. I can't send it directly. It would hurt him terribly. But he's used to receiving money from you.'

'I'll have to say it is you settling up accounts.'

'Yes, that's fine. It still won't seem quite so ... personal. And he won't see Amy's name.'

Quite an eloquent speech for Jean. René patted him on the shoulder and left. His second protégée needed him and he turned to her needs with equal enthusiasm. He was an indispensable part of both their lives and now, with Jean here, René's reputation would not be damaged by finding Amy a position on the Art Gallery payroll. She was qualified, she was partnered, and the work was much the same as that in Greenwich: negotiating loans, organising exhibitions, writing publicity. The more indebted they were to him the easier it would be to turn events to his own account if things went that way. The game itself would be interesting.

Two naked figures padded into the kitchen.

'Ah, quick – the floor's cold!' They hopped, giggled like children, hugged each other for warmth, and took back coffee and rolls to their inner sanctum. Lying in the pleasure of each other's company, the pleasure of the warmth and of the food, Amy spoke carefully of the near miracle of their lives.

'The way things have fallen out ... it's as though this life has always been here, waiting for us to come and take it.' It was a less clichéd way of saying: 'This was meant to be.'

For, once they had made their decision, everything had gone without a hitch. Now, some of Jean's new work, naturalistic bronzes he called 'Couples', sat on the table along with the lay-out Amy was working on for an exhibition of Watteau's drawings. The banker who had bought Jean's DNA sculpture had offered him a commission for a much more ambitious work. A truly large sum was agreed. Their success was startling and they could afford a weekend reviving its inspiration.

Some at the wedding, though, thought they were too much like children. When the couple had hesitated in the large doorway of the Registry at the Town hall, they seemed to Alain Degré like Lilliputian discoverers of a Colossus. The ceiling was decorated with dynamic classical figures which Amy, for a moment, felt dwarfed by. Seeing her wandering gaze, Madeleine appreciated her own life – just how ordered and secure it was. Never had she had to snatch at happiness in such a precarious way. She shepherded them forward. The registrar was polite and efficient, concealing the fact that time was short, and she sat them in front of the desk in the two chairs dedicated to official coupling. They obeyed as though caught out in a prank which now had to be remedied. The bump in Amy's belly was not noticeable, but the wonder of Jean's arrival still intoxicated her, making her a touch giggly and curiously irresponsible. She looked at the impressive leather chair which had propelled thousands who sat in it into a new element. 'It's a kind of ducking stool,' she thought, and a smile escaped her. Jean looked enquiringly, but...

'Marriage is a serious undertaking,' the face opposite interrupted, 'even though this is not a Church ceremony.'

They nodded, Jean thinking of the break it represented in his life, and wishing that his mother could be with them. For Amy, this life had no connection at all with any previous existence and it was impossible to think of her parents as she passed Jean one of the rings. Sure that she had their full attention, the registrar then continued with the legal question of whether either of them knew of any impediment to the marriage.

'No,' Jean said a trifle thoughtfully, 'there's no legal objection,' and no one else in the room said anything to the contrary. They put on the rings, signed as instructed, and it was done. The registrar had a minute in hand and wished them well.

Amy was plaiting patterns in Jean's hair. Usually his habit of wiping his hands through it made it brown but, after washing, it revealed an ambition to be yellow. The doctor's questions made her wonder about his origins.

'Was your mother blonde when she was young?'

'Yes, she was.'

To his relief, Amy did not pursue this.

'Were you brought up in Yonne?'

'No.'

He offered nothing more, and hoped to sound more sleepy than resentful.

'Perhaps it isn't fair. You've had a tough life. Perhaps that's why you aren't at all curious about mine?'

The question at the end was in hopes that he would engage. But Jean could not.

'It's the present that counts. The past is like a dead skin. It will trip you up if you don't leave it behind.'

'But your childhood is so far away. Isn't there something you can tell me?'

In so many ways they did not know each other at all.

'Well, my parents were brought up on a farm near here.'

'Both of them?'

'Farms... Lived on.'

'And near Laon. How strange for you, coming back here.'

'I suppose so.'

'But it would explain the fair hair.'

He waited in silence.

'Like blonde Italians in Milan. A north-south crossover point.'

'Yes.' He felt safe enough to fill in some gaps. 'Before the war my parents didn't like what they heard coming from Germany. Picardie was already a graveyard and they didn't want to see anything like that again. We hadn't much money but we moved to Anjou...'

Amy waited.

'We did find agricultural work and there was enough to eat – most of the time. We didn't do badly. Anjou was occupied by the Nazis, of course. Most of France was.'

'Of course.'

He thought of Érec Jacquin, a boy his own age, who stole back a salmon the soldiers had taken from his mother. The boy had been killed by one accurate shot. Nothing could be said about that. As Amy contemplated his silence he found an optimistic point to pick up at.

'After the war the change was wonderful. Like being reborn. That's why I know we must leave the past behind.'

'Yes, I see.'

As I've left Bertrand too, Jean meant, of course. In the silence she had felt a touch of his dangers. Now it was her turn, even though Jean did not ask and she had nothing profound to offer.

'My first memory was of the war. Soldiers camped in our drive. It was about 1946 and they'd just been demobbed. Apart from that everything was quite ordinary. A decent education. Perhaps I'd have liked more interest from my parents. They were divorced when I was twelve.

124

Both remarried. My mother's in America now but my father occasionally gets in touch.'

No mention of John. Parents, though, brought something else to Jean's mind.

'I've been trying to work out how to persuade my mother to come back up here.'

'When we have a house and a child, she'll be curious.'

'Sometimes I have no idea how she thinks. She is a very reserved lady. Very North European. But, we're doing all right. Thanks to René, we'll be able to rent a house soon. Maybe we can tempt her then.'

'Thanks to your excellent work.'

They snuggled up together again.

Amy had been none too pleased with René during the wedding. He had been showing off – showing them off as his protégées at the lunch he had treated them all to.

'Tomas, Géneviève, Philbert, Hébert, Alain. Here are our runaways. Be kind to them.'

Alain Degré was the last-minute surprise, driving up from Paris as an old friend of Jean's. More likely Bertrand's spy, René guessed. That would be no bad thing.

'You're better off in France, Amy,' René went on. More than happy to agree, she was, however, less compliant over his reason.

'England's just a troublesome little island off Brittany.'

'How can you say that?' she replied as charmingly as she could.

'Believe me, it's true. Been a thorn in the side of Europe for centuries. I don't mean you, of course – you're one of us now.'

He was not joking, nor was he even aware that he had said anything out of the ordinary, but Hébert laughed uproariously. Alain, too was amused, and blamed General de Gaulle. This venerable figure had done much for French pride in the last ten years, sometimes to the point of absurdity. Amy was not amused. René might be their godfather but she could not accept these assumptions, particularly his confidence that she would not dare challenge them.

Quite casually she countered, 'Oh I don't know. The two countries aren't all that different.'

Insult to France registered instantly on René's face and she sweetened the barb with a playful smile. It reassured him. Sexual fencing was the one alternative he could be happy with. Unaware of this conclusion, Amy moved to easier subjects.

'We've bought our bed and, thanks to Madeleine, they actually delivered it this afternoon.'

'The shop's contribution to a happy marriage,' Madeleine replied.

'Yes: food and love,' said René, 'the French never sell you short on those.'

'How trite,' thought Alain. And Jean's vacillating over sexual orientation was tedious. But even Bertrand was prone to it. One day men like themselves would be completely at home in society just as they were. They would stop trying to fit in. The work they left was far more enduring than any children might be and, in male love, there was greater freedom. He pitied Jean's domesticity, remembering him twenty years ago and wondering how long this aberration would last. If it did, it would definitely be the ruin of Ivrez.

'How is your work going?' he asked.

'Very well. You must see it before you leave.'

The next question was something Bertrand wanted an answer to:

'Won't you need an income ... to rely on?'

126

The rent of the London flat kept their income steady but that was none of Alain's business, especially as Amy knew he disliked her. Instead, she showed a more active card.

'René has got me a job – a proper job,' and she smiled at Madeleine to show that her gratitude had nothing intimate in it. 'In the gallery. I shall pick up my old trade of administration.'

She would, of course, have to leave this in about four months, but that too was none of Alain's business and, as though taking her up on the unspoken thought, Jean added confidently, 'I have the winter to build up a new collection.'

'I have more ideas too,' he quietly enthused across the table. He was sure of himself now, equal to any criticism from his one-time friend. 'In a year or two,' he thought, 'I will be as famous.'

As the two of them cuddled in their nest Jean thought of the two months absence from Ivrez. Alain, he guessed would be in regular touch. Several times at the wedding it had been on the tip of his tongue to ask about his mother, but it was the tip of a dangerous iceberg and he veered away. He had written asking her to join them but she had not replied. He could not help but wonder what was going on there. Perhaps Bertrand had found a new partner. 'Surely he would have done,' Jean said to himself and, with that conviction, decided to let Ivrez sink from his thoughts.

15

'Ask me first!'

Pierre Colvert stood, humiliated for the first time in his life and regretting the arrangement for him to work at the château. Bertrand's attempt to be sensible was breaking down. Pierre needed space and it was no hardship for Bertrand to let him drive over during the day to use the furnace room next to Jean's studio which Bertrand himself now used. The rooms were too close and disagreements erupted.

'Why didn't you say you were going to disconnect the furnace?'

'But I did,' Pierre replied through gritted teeth.

He needed to hang mobiles. Preventing fire was an obvious precaution and all Bertrand used was the welding torch and the arc. Nor would it be difficult to reconnect the furnace later. Bertrand was so sensitive to anything which undermined his position. It was tiresome.

'Don't try to run the place,' Bertrand fired at him before going into the kitchen to let Madame Estienne comfort him with another cup of coffee. He had not thrown her out. How could he? He needed her. She kept alive the belief that Jean might still walk through the door. Memory re-ran shots of the past with a clarity which startled him. They imposed on reality many mornings when he glanced towards the gate thinking he'd seen his friend there. He'd been too sure Jean would not leave. Failure left him punctured and it seemed he was closer to Jean and understood him now better than when contact had been taken for granted. Since the end of October the gallery had been closed. Anyway, winter was the time to build a new collection, he did not expect to sell much. For a month he had floated unthinkingly and was re-surfacing encrusted with an extra layer of bitterness. But at least he was back at work, attacking the metal with venom enough to corrode it. Two new pieces were half done and, over the coffee which he really needed, having worked half the night, he mused on more grotesques.

'Bertrand?'

'Mmm.'

'Will you open the gallery next weekend?'

'There's no reason not to,' was his inconclusive riposte before lapsing into silence again, during which Madame Estienne put the two empty wine bottles from dinner of the night before as quietly as possible into a sack.

'You could put the advertisement in *Le Monde* then, as usual. December has been a good time for us.'

Bertrand continued to look at her morosely under the excuse of the alcohol. Instead of taking offence, Madame Estienne pitied him. Bertrand could rely on his bulk to disperse each night's wallowing and she knew his mood went deeper than two bottles of wine. Lack of sleep had much to do with it and there were good reasons for that. Without replying he went out to his work, glad to find that Pierre had gone.

'Jean couldn't really have married that minx,' Madame Estienne muttered to herself, and it went without saying that she would not be replying to his letter. Let the force of her disapproval bring him back. 'He couldn't have done it,' she muttered again, as she thwacked the dirt off her brush on the outside wall, relieved to hear the noise of Bertrand's soldering starting up again across the yard.

Alain had reported to him after the wedding, giving as true a picture as he could. Financially, disaster did not loom over the couple in the way that Bertrand wished. Alain compensated for this by playing up the impression he had that work arrangements were not very good. Jean had grumbled that he had to fit in with other sculptors, younger men; he did miss the independence of Ivrez. Alain did not add that, despite this, Jean's work continued with its fresh lease of life. Bertrand had pressed him for personal details. How happy were the two together? He forced the truth out, as far as Alain knew it. Bertrand must stomach it all. He had to be on the inside of their life to tear it apart. With enough information he would know what to do when his moment arrived. Alain winced at the masochistic questioning. Pierre's father, too, was concerned. If Bertrand went on pretending he could get Jean back he would end up a real mess. He'd ruin himself and the gallery. He needed someone to get him to face up to reality. Genially, André advised him.

'Sell while the gallery still has a reputation and move into Montargis where there are more people around – take over the mill Emilie is having restored.'

Bertrand had watched the face speak these words. He watched as though a slug crawled over it – as if any gallery could replace the one he had created. He watched in wrathful silence. His whole identity depended on Ivrez. And, he thought blackly, there were too many songs about fat, lonely old millers. He would not let them turn him into a pathetic joke.

For the rest of the day he was hard at work. He now found Jean's studio a better space than his own, upstairs. The outdoor noises, the bucolic sounds, which had once been a distraction, fired the revulsion against life which kept him and his work going – as did the pain of Jean's absence, sharpened in Jean's workshop. A half-finished piece of Bertrand's now lay inside the door – an animal hanging by its entrails. It would be an apocalypse, he thought with satisfaction – probably his own. He set up the welding equipment to torture it some more. 'This will be rather more than Alain expects,' he thought. Bittersweet anticipation made him remember Madame Estienne's advice and he went back in to phone. Surprised he'd responded, she voiced another thought.

'Jean's never been very bold. He'll be back.'

Bertrand smashed the receiver onto the phone. Hearing his unspoken wish out loud sounded like mockery.

The evening was as dismal as any that autumn. The fire and the wine failed to dispel the misery. Ten o'clock came. With the chimes Madame Estienne put aside her crochet and left the room. The solitude was unbearable. Not even Oedipus could help. Madame Estienne had fed the dog which now lay by the hearth, eyes closed, one ear pricked in case his master remembered him.

The door opened and Pierre came in. He placed a couple more bottles on the table and started to open one without waiting for comment.

'At least I needn't join you in drinking your cellar dry.' His tone was jovially truculent. He'd already had a couple of glasses. Bertrand squinted up at him. Solitude was unbearable but so too was intrusion.

'What makes you think you're welcome?' he snarled.

'Of course I'm not welcome. Does it matter?'

'Nothing matters.'

'Nothing in the damn world,' he said, determined to keep up with Bertrand's mood. He poured drinks for them both.

'Your young life is blighted is it?' Bertrand sneered.

'Not at all.'

'Out with it. Give me the sob story, then I can kick

131

you out,' Bertrand's anger was real. When would this family leave him alone?

'No sob story.'

'Then why've you come back? Did you drop a pretty mobile?'

Pierre took a thoughtful sip at his glass, and a good look at Bertrand over its rim. He looked wild: hair uncut, more grey showing than a few weeks back, beard grown, a shapeless old smock on and heaven knows when he'd last washed. Obvious pain in his face. Into his glass, Pierre said casually:

'I had a corny idea that I could console you.'

Bertrand snorted. 'You go for fat old men do you?'

'You don't really think badly of yourself. You couldn't do such brilliant work if you did.'

'I'm defying fate,' he muttered, angry at having to put this into words. Pierre was undeterred.

'Then you've succeeded.'

Bertrand was forced into considering his irritating guest. He was about the age Jean was when they'd first met. But Pierre was Mediterranean: dark, tall, self-confident, and with beautiful brown eyes – sharper, less mournful than Bertrand's own, and the sparkle in them showed that everything was still possible for him. Nor had he finished what he had to say.

'There's a new cinema opened in Montargis. It gets the best films. Jean Renoir's *La Bête Humaine* is coming round again. You'll have seen it.'

Indeed Bertrand had, with Jean of course. Pierre sat down.

'Cinema reshapes the inside of your mind, don't you think?'

'You think it'll be therapeutic for me.' Bertrand's contempt was acid enough to strip paint. Pierre seemed not to notice.

132

'I find film therapeutic. No effort is involved and yet you have to let go all thoughts to watch it. Very often, after going to a film, I find the answer to other things that were on my mind.'

For a moment this dinner-table psychology seemed attractive to Bertrand. But how could he bow to the superior wisdom of a callow youth. Instead he parodied it.

'Do you never watch critically?'

'I'd rather not. I prefer the purging.'

All rubbish, but it was better than being alone so he suspended his antagonism and let the boy's chatter fill the air. Feeling more secure, Pierre let down his guard.

'Coming here was a test of my nerve,' and he smiled. He had a beautiful smile.

'You thought I might set the dog on you? I might yet.'

'Oh Édipe's all right.'

'Then what did you fear?'

'Your anger ... whether I could withstand it,' he said looking steadily at him as though the anger were a balloon that could be pricked by a look. At the mention of his name Oedipus had opened his eyes then, realising his mistake, closed them again.

'I might test your nerve, though,' Bertrand went on and paused for effect. Pierre looked at him closely to judge whether this was a response to his own earlier pass. Bertrand looked steadily back, playing with the same possibility before continuing.

'When...' he forced himself to say the name '...when Jean and I rebuilt this place we often risked our lives – up on the roof. There's a narrow parapet up there. I bet you couldn't walk along it with a bottle of wine inside you.'

But even if Pierre sometimes talked like a fool, he wasn't one.

133

'You're absolutely right. Nor could you.'

There was the glimmer of a smile.

'Still, would you like to see it? There's a trap door at the top of the stairs.'

'If you go first.'

Bertrand inclined his head and got up, a little unsteadily. He had had more than the usual two bottles and he led the way carefully up the tower staircase. There, in the ceiling outside the guest room, was the square trap. There was just space enough on the landing to allow Pierre to join him as Bertrand took down a pole and opened the door-catch with its hooked end. Then he pulled down the folding ladder.

'That just leads to the roof space,' Pierre challenged.

'And from there to the roof.' They looked at each other again – nose to nose.

'Another time.' Pierre's eyes sparkled.

'Another time,' Bertrand echoed and put his arm round him. Pierre firmly removed it.

'Not till you're sober. And stink less,' he added, returning down the stairs. In the kitchen, going out through the door, he called back good-humouredly:

'Let's do something civilised, like go to the flicks.'

Montargis is the Amsterdam of Burgundy, with roads crossing two small rivers and two canals. It wears its location elegantly, the quiet waterways lined with graceful eighteenth-century buildings sitting behind avenues of trees. The place oozes culture, its history linked to Rome before Paris, and the town is rich in museums. Pierre's parents would have a money-spinner once they got their own art centre opened here. Bertrand insisted on driving. He looked quite sober, bordering on tidy, if not dressed with quite the careful eye of a year ago. Still Pierre wondered whether two months of alcohol would have damaged his reactions.

'An old drunkard is a safer driver than a callow youth,' Bertrand declared on seeing the doubt in the boy's face and, to prove his point, reversed the car onto the lane. Bertrand had had time to wonder about the young man's motives, bearing in mind Pierre's father and his paternalistic advice.

'Why did you come back the other evening?'

'I admire you ... despite your moods.' Bertrand pulled a face. Pierre went on emphatically.

'I've grown up knowing Ivrez. I hate to see you like this.'

'You're likely to see plenty more then.'

'Yes, I know.' Determinedly, he changed the subject. 'You must have been here about sixteen years. Almost the whole of my life. Can't imagine the place without the gallery.'

'Then don't.'

'Were you from Paris originally?'

'Everyone's from Paris originally.' Bertrand was back to snarling.

Well, if private life was a 'no go', films were just as interesting. It mattered to get Bertrand to engage in something – anything. The new cinema in Montargis had two screens and, as well as *La Bête Humaine*, Chabrol's new film *Le Boucher* would be showing. Which did Bertrand prefer? Pierre was a fan of Chabrol's.

'He's as sophisticated as Hitchcock but a countryman like us – makes him even better. Did you see *The Road to Corinth*? Spy thriller.'

Bertrand had not, but gave up trying to block him. The boy would chatter on anyway. And he did.

'I also like the way he shows women.'

'You're interested in women?'

135

'Very few are interesting, but if I found one who was I could be.'

He looked squarely at Bertrand who did not respond.

'On the whole I prefer men. But in Chabrol's films the women are specimens – they behave as though they are under a spotlight all the time. Action is very concentrated, deliberately self-conscious. The men too in a way. All the characters are drawn as cold fish, specimens for analysis. From the start you know what is going to happen, and the result is chilling. Chabrol's just as good as Hitchcock.'

The cinema was a kilometre beyond the town, a recent and seriously comfortable viewing space. There was also a good restaurant, so Bertrand treated his young companion, aware that he himself needed to be put into a better humour – but for what he wasn't altogether sure. However, the seats were roomy and well upholstered: something else to help put him at ease.

The film began with shots of the iron-age paintings in the Lascaux caves, then moved to a wedding feast in a Dordogne village. Bertrand prepared for the usual alienation but a touch of reality was there. The line 'weddings turn sour soon afterwards' attracted his interest. Perhaps there would be a point of view nearer his own. After some twenty minutes, though, he had decided this was a trivial film, and a slight subject. The actors were too elegant, clean, clinical. In the scene of the funeral cortège the rain was pouring yet you were conscious of how pleasing, how elegant, the effect of the umbrellas was, not the fact that someone had been murdered. Popaul's taking the lighter he'd dropped at the scene of his second murder from Hélène's drawer was stupid. It incriminated him. He only needed to see it there to know she suspected and for the audience to feel her danger. Clearly, this was not going to be a therapeutic experience for him. The film was too deliberately staged. Life is full of accidents, he thought, and thrillers needed the same dangerous quality. The only thing of any interest to him at all was the butcher's compulsion to murder women. Curious that it was so similar to the plot of *La Bête Humaine*. There, if he remembered rightly, it was a compulsion only to murder the woman Jacques Lantier loved.

Pierre was relaxed against him. From time to time one or the other found themselves responding to the proximity. Each time, Bertrand's mind reminded him of the reality. It was such a clichéd response to feel he had to follow romantic expectations. He was not a young thing exploring life, wanting to change partners. The situation was as phoney as the film, as artificial as the plush upholstery. When Pierre looked at him a touch expectantly at the end, he shook his head, and Pierre registered the message. They returned to the car. Bertrand would drive him home.

The road they took ran beside the Canal de Briare which still served as a waterway and, just behind, parallel to it, was the small Aveyron river. Pierre suddenly asked Bertrand to leave the road and turn left at the bridge ahead. Was this for a more determined move, Bertrand found himself wondering. This would be more original than the back row of a cinema. Why not? Perhaps Pierre's optimism could give him something he needed. He turned left over the long, low bridge and stopped, as instructed, on the bank between the waterways.

'Leave the headlights on, we'll need them.'

Then Pierre jumped out, ran round to Bertrand's door, opened it and took his hand with an eager smile.

'Come with me.'

Charmed by the gesture, Bertrand laughed as he was pulled from his seat, and he followed Pierre obediently to whatever this tryst was to reveal. Pierre had keys in his hand. To an apartment? He was impressed by such confidence. They crossed the weir and, as Bertrand looked forward, he saw Pierre's mother's beloved mill. Pierre was unlocking the door. He glanced back, still eager.

'Your experience would be invaluable.'

As the truth sank in rage blinded him.

'You whore!' he cried.

Pierre turned round, mouth open in surprise. Bertrand took hold of him and threw that silly face into the river. If you are dumped by your partner the whole world thinks it can manipulate you. Black anger enveloped him and he went back automatically to the car. Opening the door he realised what he had done and looked back. It was all right – the headlights showed a figure dragging itself out of the water. He drove off. Let Emilie come and pick up her son. She was probably lurking round a corner.

16

It was a preview and they were in the clients' room behind the gallery at the Atelier St Germaine. René was familiar with most of the artists, but not with those from the southern part of France and it was a point of honour for him to keep up with anything new. After a walk round the first room, he retired with Paul for the obligatory glass, and to prophesy on who would still be known in twenty years' time. René had just sat one more of the interminable Louvre examinations and, with the Higher Diploma out of the way, it was useful to his future to be drinking wine with a valued member of the grapevine. He put out a few tendril thoughts.

'Are you pleased that the extension to the Carnavalet is going ahead?'

'Very pleased. The Paris archive is vast. We've no chance of keeping it properly without more space. Just because Malraux's gone, it doesn't mean his plans have to be dropped.'

Paul often talked as though he were the man giving the new Minister his ideas, but they had all seen that Chevalier Aubert was not a spoiler.

'From what I've heard, Aubert is a lot easier to get along with.'

'Definitely more of a committee man.'

'Won't the focus on the Carnavalet take the spotlight off other things nearer your heart?'

'Oh, I don't know, money isn't tight. For example...' he could not resist, '...a new collection is being donated to the Louvre – modern works.' René looked slightly surprised. Jacques had not mentioned this at their regular dinners but it was true that his godfather was increasingly less of one, professionally speaking.

'Can the Jeu de Paume cope?'

'Maybe not, as things are at the moment, but that opens up opportunities.'

René looked enquiringly and Paul buttered the carrot.

'It's time we had a fresh look at our organisation – twenty-five years since the last shake up. There are going to be quite a few changes. Some old heads rolled last year. Now it's time to bring younger men on. The Conference next January will be a lot more lively than usual. Will you be there?'

His inflection in the question revealed more than a passing interest. To René the meeting would be a piece of tedium, another exam, but one he would certainly endure to get a transfer to Paris. The enthusiasm in his voice, as he replied, was almost genuine.

'Yes, I should think so.'

'There'll be some votes at the end. Crucial to have support if we're to get change.'

Paul was making assumptions:

'Hang on, I haven't heard the arguments yet.'

'No, of course not. I'm not trying to buy your vote. But I thought you might see things my way.'

This was always possible but René also had other needs on his mind.

'I'll be working on the Watteau exhibition, for Laon, of course – it will take up a lot of time. It's hard to get hold of his works. Most are in New York or Berlin. But we think we can manage a small collection of theatre drawings: musicians, dancers. actors. And of course...'

Paul picked up his drift.

'In the Louvre we do still have his Pierrot – Gilles.'

'I realise it isn't lent lightly, but it would be a perfect centre piece.'

'I'm not the top man,' Paul said invitingly.

'But aren't you the wheels within wheels these days?' The question suddenly sounded satirical. 'It's what I hear anyway.'

Paul was reassured to hear his reputation keeping pace with his aspirations. More significant was the fact that René had come to him rather than to Jacques. It demonstrated Jacques' lack of influence these days. Jacques was not a political man – more of a mixer with the artists and a bruiser of the bureaucrats. However, the request put Paul on the spot because he disapproved of informal loans.

'We've become very sloppy over how we care for these works. That's one of the things I'll be talking about. I want us to draw up a set of regulations – absolute regulations, not just guidelines that everyone ignores.'

René tried to look impressed, but could not see what the fuss was about.

'For example, this gallery we are in now is a private gallery – fine in its way. But, at the moment, they could pull strings to make use of national works.'

'Well, obviously, Laon's *is* a public gallery.'

'And it's all to the good that works are seen. That goes without saying. But, in future, we are going to have to be more disciplined in the way museums are run. Casual arrangements lead to trouble.'

René thought he could detect criticism of Jacques; of himself too, of course, and defended them both:

'Casual, Paul? Curator to curator?'

'Informal.'

'Send me the forms.'

But there were no forms.

'We can't draw up a system until it's agreed at the Conference.'

141

'Or until everyone has agreed – after the Conference. Do we halt everything until then?'

'No. You know the normal arrangements still stand. It's these ad hoc chats I'm uncomfortable with.'

'I'll put it in writing.'

Paul had to see the sense of this and their conversation had added weight to his own concerns.

'Your views on this would be valuable.'

'I'll definitely be there.' Still, friendship was not entirely dead and René added, 'There are some good men running things at the moment.'

'Yes, and they've had a good innings. Done excellent things post-war. They just don't have their finger on the pulse any more. They're losing control. We have a new Minister, and it's time to act.'

'Do you have much support?'

'I think so.'

The message was clear. Jacques and the other old hands would be encouraged to retire. Knowing René's family connections Paul added, 'Think about it. It's the only way to go.'

They continued their tour of the rest of the exhibition.

'A constant stream of talent.'

Here, René agreed whole-heartedly.

'The French do know how to produce genius.'

'You also have to work in Paris to be in on it.'

As they walked through an archway they found an example of Alain Degré's work.

'Are you his agent now?'

'Just recently,' Paul said modestly. 'You also have to work in Paris to make money.'

And a cut on sales of work of that calibre would be good money. But inherited wealth put René above commerce. It was promotion that he deserved. He turned away politely and found himself looking at a painting of

142

a naked Amy Estienne. Looking closer, he was amazed to find that this was not his imagination. The painting was not by Jean-Claude of course – he was strictly a metal man these days – but by the Laon painter, Philbert Marin, and not even Marin's abstract style could disguise her blooming health. The nude study was disproportionate, contorted. Nevertheless, it showed an Amy self-contained and glowing: eyes curiously proud, hair up, revealing such a neck, such breasts and then carrying that fertile belly. There could not be a better advertisement for pregnancy. René gasped as though Amy had stripped just for him.

'Yes,' Paul commented, 'someone's found a beauty there.'

René collected himself, made a mental note of its number and went on with the tour, taking in more of the advice Paul continued to give. Action was essential now, with a new Minister of Culture.

'We need to shape events before they drop into a pattern beyond our control.'

Paul was sure that by this time next year he would either have Jacques' job, or would have climbed the ladder to another equal to it. He was not so rash as to say so, outright, but neither so self-controlled as to avoid dropping hints. René really should come to that Conference: he'd gain a lot from it.

'Right, I will, and, maybe you could see fit to loan some of the Watteau drawings too? They'd all go in one crate.'

It didn't seem that René had heard the argument on his objection to this; yet René needed to be won over, and Paul agreed.

A couple of weeks later and René's sister, Adèle, was hidden in an empty anteroom in an expensive clinic.

She waited until two smartly dressed women had started their sauntering walk down the hall before venturing into the corridor herself, close behind them, and aiming for the same imposing door. Her caution was unnecessary. Clinical routine was never questioned. Had she walked down the hall on her hands stark naked the receptionist would have assumed it was a medical experiment. Not being aware of this, Adèle gave a nod of acknowledgement towards the waiting room as she passed. Since no one had seen her come in, she preferred to forestall questions by acting as though everyone should remember her. Then she was through the doors and onto the Champs Élysées which lay, as usual, as wide and dangerous as the Seine. Cars were moving at extraordinary speeds, slotting in and out across lanes, rear lights streaking the darkness like threads of red silk. The Arc de Triomphe was a fountain of light and, high above, Christmas lights added their colour to the spectacle. Adèle reached the pavement ready for whatever disappointments the rest of Christmas would bring. For Philippe was still in Beirut, having a good time no doubt.

Walking down the street, she glanced at the fashionable boutique windows, noting anything worth a return visit. An overblown fur stole for aunt Clothilde, she thought unkindly; an English deerstalker for her father, and a rather smarter hat for her mother. Fit to wear at a wedding. She moved on. In another window a handsome male mannequin stared vacantly at her in the likeness of Philippe. She paused, looking into its painted eyes. The dummy was an empty likeness, a parody of the image that Philippe had been reduced to during the last three hours. Why had he stayed in Beirut? Since they were both from a generation who made their own choices in life, his staying away could only be wilful. Perhaps it was all over. He'd made her unfaithful.

She hurried on. Her parents' flat was not far away and, turning into Rue George V, she saw a figure ahead who looked familiar.

'Bonsoir, Madame Gilbert.'

The concierge was laden with packages and, to quieten her guilt, Adèle helped her with them. Then she took the lift to her parents' large flat on the top floor.

'My poor little one,' her mother greeted her. 'What did the doctor say?'

'Everything's fine.' Adèle sounded as though she were dying and Madame Védrine put her arm round her.

'You went to the best clinic in Paris. I'm sure they knew what they were doing.'

Adèle could not respond so her mother moved to the only other possible reason for her low spirits:

'And, here you are all alone at Christmas, it's too bad. Go through and phone him.'

Her mother could always be relied on to sympathise – a little too much perhaps and Adèle went obediently into the study. The series of eye tests had ended the previous week but Adèle had called in again to pick up a report that could have been posted. It *was* the best clinic in Paris, and a private practice, so how Adèle and the doctor decided to spend their Christmas Eve afternoon in his rather splendid rooms behind the office was no one's business but their own. Her mother's sympathy obviously distanced Adèle from her since it was her own revenge, not Philippe's absence, that was troubling her now. She came back out of the study.

'He isn't there.'

'Oh, it's more than a Christian should bear.'

'But, if I'm not a Christian...'

'I understand, my pet.'

But she didn't understand. She couldn't. And her mother never responded to goading. It was infuriating.

Her mother went back to the kitchen followed by a rather stout Pekinese that had good reason to love her. Adèle went over to the window and threw it open.

'I'm suffocating.'

Her father gasped as the cold air hit him.

'Have a heart, Adèle. Have you phoned?'

'He wasn't there.'

Madeleine's thoughts at that moment were also with her sister-in-law. Philippe had rather leapt at the chance to work in Beirut when his senior had turned the job down simply because the assignment started four weeks before Christmas. No wonder Adèle felt abandoned, unconsidered and Madeleine wished her sister-in-law's wedding might be the reason for the piece of work she was engaged on at present. This commission had her working behind a securely locked door – as hidden from the world as in any convent chapel, she thought, fitting the last of the emeralds into their filigree platinum frame. In her well-organised world she would both finish this and arrive with René in Paris in time for mass and Christmas Eve dinner with his family.

Adèle's mother put her head round the sitting room door.

'I could do with René's help.'

'Mmmm?' Monsieur Védrine looked up from his paper.

'I could roast the partridges with tarragon and onions or do them as a casserôle in this sauvignon I have here.' She held the wine up, as though it might inspire him. 'What do you think?'

'Either way. I really don't mind,' he said genially.

Claudine shook her head.

146

'Doesn't help?'

'No.'

'Mmm. "Pigeon and partridge clustered round."' He hummed a line from university days as he cogitated the difficulties of choosing between two equally delicious menus. 'Let's say the roast then.'

Claudine retired, satisfied. These small debates restored some sense of adventure to their thirty years of culinary routines. When the phone rang, no one was expecting it. Adèle came out of her melancholy and went into the study.

'Philippe, where were you?'

'Travelling a lot. Can't say over the phone.'

'It's so long since I saw you. I never thought four weeks could be so long.'

'I thought I'd be back by now. But you could come to Beirut. The Hilton here is fabulous. All kinds of famous people passing through.

'Yves Montand? Yul Brynner?'

'Well, more your Greek shipping tycoons. And one or two spies I expect.'

Rather less enticing, but if it were possible... With a now animated face she interrupted her mother preparing the canapés for the poultry's last resting place.

'I know what I shall do for New Year.'

'What, pet?'

'Spend it in Beirut with Philippe!'

As the cloud came down over her mother's face Adèle tried to make the idea sound very much more ordinary.

'Obviously he won't be working or he wouldn't have suggested it.'

'Is it safe for a western woman?

'Of course.'

But if Philippe is called away you'll have to stay in the hotel, all alone.'

'Beirut isn't like that. It's a civilised city.'

'Is it, love?' her Mother replied, doubtfully. 'You're so young.'

She was twenty-two, Adèle silently protested. The conversation, though, was left unfinished for she was not entirely sure that her mother was wrong.

'Come back soon,' was her plea to Philippe when she phoned him back. Good form then demanded that she put aside her turbulence to help with the festivities.

The skies over Laon were dark but the clouds had cleared. At the apartment door Amy could make this out in the chink of sky above the alleyway. Then she looked down along the street again and, restlessly, went back in. Jean was late. She was edgy. Work at the Maison des Arts was fine but, as time moved towards the end of the year, there were moments when she had to fight irrational anxieties. This relationship which together seemed so complete and so simple, sometimes lost its reality when they were apart. Were they tempting the gods on their idyllic mountain? Was their life all a figment of her imagination? One day, would an extra-strong wind blow everything away? Perhaps it was just the tiredness that had struck her recently which caused this alarm. But the ending of the year was a time for endings. It would be different if there were relatives, if contact with Madame Estienne were possible. Christmas was a family occasion and their absence of one had hit her more strongly that lunchtime when colleagues from the Maison des Arts had left, laden with family gifts. She and Jean were still known as the runaways.

Jean was driving home through the slush, warmed by alcohol and holiday antics – Hébert chained to a roof support, leg-cuffed into bondage sculpture by a fellow artist. Hébert argued cynically that all art was trickery, but his outrage had rather punctured the pose. Also finished off that afternoon was Jean's present to Amy. It was more realistic than usual, a nymph crouched ready for flight or attack. The face was lovely – sensitive, vulnerable – and the poise of the body was masterly, Jean thought. He found Amy at the door with her coat on, also ready for flight.

'We're going to eat out,' she said.

'Oh, fine.'

'Christmas has to be different.' And she smiled at his bafflement. 'The season demands that we are extra-happy.'

'Right.'

Had she put a bowl of potatoes before him that evening, he would have sculpted them for her as usual.

'And it's more sociable to go out tonight.'

Jean realised what she meant and put his arm round her. He too had felt the absence of his mother.

'Next Christmas we will be a family.'

'Yes.'

She hugged his arm as they walked into town, glad the time away from work was only a day.

The choir finished singing the introit and Mathilde knelt for the next part of the ritual. The mass was a quiet time in which to recover her priorities, to disentangle the knots which built up in her thoughts during the week. Jacques was looking tired. It was a turbulent time and he seemed to be taking on more than he need. Even today she'd had to go to l'Orangerie to drag him away in time to eat with the older children he'd not seen for several months. Thankfully, they could at least escape to Laon at New Year. A few rows behind her and Claudine Védrine rose after the prayer. She loved Christmas. Any season when the church bells rang out along the Champs Élysées reminded her of that glorious moment in 1945 when the people cowering in Paris knew that their ordeal had ended. Whenever the bells rang out now an upsurge of happiness took her over and her prayers beamed out with good will to everyone. To have both her children with her and she and Adrien in good health filled her cup of happiness. René and Adèle were a little self-centred she had realised in recent years, amiably spoilt. Well, there was nothing they could do about that now. Both were basically good-natured and Madeleine had saved René from the worst his nature might have led him into.

The priest intoning the Mass was a visitor and not as good as Father Eustache, yet the ritual was so familiar that everyone would hear the litany even if he mimed it, as he sometimes appeared to be doing. Quietly intoning 'Kyrie Eleison, Christ Eleison,' the ends of his words vanished into the cavernous church, leaving a silence hanging until the responses started up, untidily, unsteadily then swelling with mid-sentence confidence... 'Like an old gramophone constantly in need of the winding handle,' thought Madeleine, whose mind was also veering off on tangents. Her main plan was to devote this holiday to making Adèle's face light up. She had met them in a curious, abstracted way and, glancing across at her, it still appeared to Madeleine that Adèle's mind was vacant – she was just not present with them – obviously thrown by Michel's absence. Madeleine glanced at René on her other side, but he was completely absorbed and she let his devotion revive her own. They were instructed to pray, so knelt again. René had never lost his boyhood fascination for these ceremonies – happy to accept the Church's rules since they were not at all difficult for him to follow. The inevitability of sinning followed by repentance suited him well – his easy sensuality was not made for greater challenges. But what Madeleine appreciated in the Mass was the nostalgia. She could not deny that it made her feel safe, that it was enjoyable to let go all energy, ambition and anxiety, to float for a while in the collective consciousness. For a short time, until it began to feel like collective unconsciousness. Her eyes strayed forward to the backs of three heads she had recognised when they came in: two adults and one a ten-year old boy. The younger adults sitting alongside them were less familiar, but Madeleine could work them out – Patrice and Marie, with one toddler, and the mysterious Cleo, back from Cannes.

The choir was singing the final stirring anthem, from one of Vivaldi's unmistakable Glorias; helping to propel them through the doors. Despite it, the crowded church emptied slowly. It was several minutes before the two families could filter into the procession that was edging past the pews.

'Is there anything we can bring up for New Year?' Mathilde asked Madeleine when they reached polite speaking distance.

'Some of that excellent caviare – René adores it.'

Mathilde nodded and they divided off again into their respective units.

'You can't move to that square, my friend. The dice said eight.'

Adèle took her brother's hat off the Champs Élysées, and back onto the Gare de Lyon.

'Did I do that?'

'You know very well you did. And it's not the first time this game.'

'Well I know where I belong, you see.'

'In jail?'

'I only did it to see you look so prim,' he laughed.

'Well, now you've seen it.' She turned to Mathilde. 'He hasn't changed since the age of eight.'

'I can imagine.'

'That's what I like about him,' Madeleine defended. 'René doesn't take anything too seriously, do you darling?'

The question was rhetorical and ended with an affectionate smile at Adèle. During the week she had settled a little. Another long conversation on the phone had helped. She looked more relaxed.

Jacques was dozing on the sofa. For a few hours he needn't think of how to get those huge chunks of bronze and granite across the channel without any of them plunging to their natural habitat at the bottom of the sea. For a few hours their weight was off his shoulders. The location in the Rodin Museum was finalised but at the moment he wasn't even dreaming of it. His mind had rocketed clean into the ether.

'Are you coming with us, René? There's time for a walk in the park.'

'Yes, perhaps I will.'

He had dropped leading questions to Jacques about life in the Louvre since Malraux had gone but Jacques had simply looked back quizzically. Was he blind or was he untouchable? No one was untouchable; even Malraux had been fired. Surely Jacques realised that René had to look out for his own interests. Feeling uncomfortable now at the prospect of being left alone with him, René roused himself to join the others.

'How are the runaways doing?' Mathilde asked him, as they walked down the hillside.

'Very well. A mad idea seems to have paid off.'

'Who would have thought it? It never seemed possible

that Jean would change his way of life so completely. Does he ever talk about Ivrez?'

'No, not something he could really.'

'Jacques is thinking of arranging an exhibition for Bertrand later this year,' Mathilde added.

'For Bertrand?' René queried, remembering Jacques' words not so long ago.

'His new work is quite different.'

'So it's paid off for them both.'

'But Bertrand's a wreck. Drinking of course. Doesn't seem to sleep. He quarrels with everyone. We're wondering how long he can go on. André's trying to head off something suicidal.'

'Ought we to tell Jean?'

'Hardly fair – nothing he can do, short of leaving Amy.'

For some reason this news upset Madeleine. At her New Year dinner her welcome to the pair was cooler than usual. Jean and Amy had arrived glowing with health and happiness bought at others' expense. Madeleine looked at Amy's bulge and the easy rapport between her and Jean – no longer did they seem so vulnerable – and her mind set against her. A waif was one thing, but with her approaching motherhood earning her thoughtful gestures from all the men in the room, Amy now seemed more at home than Adèle, without Michel. And what had she done to Bertrand? Trying to be positive about this season, which Amy was finding so trying, she enthused about everything; the French custom of having a crib as well as a tree at Christmas, and putting the infant Jesus in it on Christmas day. It was such a family detail. Little did Amy suspect any insecurities in the circle of faces around her, but Adèle looked extra bright and went to make the coffee.

153

17

These days, the mill race on the Aveyron ran slowly.
Pierre had not been in danger. He was fit. He had
weathered running home in soaked clothes through winter
temperatures without getting so much as a cold. No
harm had actually been done to anything apart from
Pierre's pride. Shocked friends thought he should tell
the police but this would have been vindictive and might
have led to embarrassing questions, so Pierre shrugged
the whole thing off and was now in Paris. No one was
harmed and Bertrand clearly needed to be saved from
himself, so Pierre's father decided not to quarrel with
him either.

Instead, André arrived at Ivrez one December evening
with a bottle of Haut-Brion Blanc and two dozen oysters.
Dark as it was he did not need his torch as he left the
car. The lights for Bertrand's welding were more than
enough. They revealed an unkempt figure, like a
Hephaestus, bent over his work in the yard, sending out
showers of sparks and putting such concentration into
his creation that André was able to walk into the kitchen
without being noticed.

'How long will he keep working?'

Madame Estienne was preparing a simple meal.

'Six hours he's been out there. Last night too. He'll
be glad of someone to talk to.'

So Bertrand needed to be interrupted. Like Madame
Estienne, André fell into humouring the sculptor as
though he were sick. He went back outside and stood

where Bertrand could not fail to notice him. 'Heavens!' André thought, 'he is filthy.'

Bertrand switched off the equipment and took off his goggles, not pleased with whom he saw before him.

'I have a cutting you might like to see,' André said levelly.

'About flour mills?' Bertrand asked with heavy sarcasm.

'About you.'

André was piqued enough to show he was aware of Bertrand's misdeeds.

'There's no need to injure your friends.'

Bertrand pulled a face.

'I'll be in in a few minutes,' he muttered.

Once the lights were switched off he could see that the night sky was clear. It would be cold, but he would come back later and the large construction at his feet could be left where it was. He did André the favour of putting his face under the outside tap and climbing out of his overalls before coming into the kitchen. André was quietly chatting with Jean's mother.

'Where's this cutting then?' Bertrand asked, noting their sneaky conversation and the bribery laid out on the table. Patiently, André took from his wallet a page from an Art sale catalogue. One of Bertrand's early works had been resold for six times its original price – not something even Bertrand could be cynical about. He took the paper indifferently; then a broad grin spread across his tired face.

'They must think I'm dying.'

'Your work is being revalued, Bertrand.'

It was extraordinary news and Bertrand could not deny a deep sense of gratification as he read and reread the cutting. This justified his Herculean efforts going on outside.

'And you deserve a break,' said André. 'Madame

Estienne too. Did you know Marcia's invited her for Christmas...?'

'Oh, forget that,' Bertrand broke in. Madame Estienne looked down humbly.

'Not good enough, pal,' André went on firmly. 'Pierre is away. Come and stay with us.'

Bertrand put up more resistance but Madame Estienne gathered the courage to say that she liked the idea. The expression on her face told him that she had no reason to punish herself.

'And Marcia will run me back every day to feed the hens.'

'All right.'

Bertrand caved in. After all, it made no difference where he spent the time. He might even learn something useful.

So, a couple of weeks later, for the first time for fifteen years, since that wing of the château had been brought back to life, the gallery was left locked and empty, and a resigned dog followed his master to the car.

Emilie and André's rambling old house was full of grandchildren who had been told not to ask about Jean. It was Jean they would miss. They were not comfortable with Bertrand and to hide it they welcomed him exuberantly, turning their instructions into a game, competing to see who could wait on him the most devotedly. They took his coat and suitcase, found him the most comfortable of the well-worn chairs, argued among themselves as to who was to show him all over the house. The novelty both touched and unnerved him. It took him back to that hopeful, fearful time when he had been a tutor. He flinched from their small eager hands, fearing a hidden mockery, and prepared himself

156

to endure the week. André and Emilie were business-like. No longer did they talk about his moving but, instead, of finding ways to prevent his total isolation by bringing him into town from time to time. The thought of acting as advisor to several local projects interested him. But during their discussions he remembered why this was necessary. He went on talking but his eyes became glazed and increasingly averted. This was not reality. This was a pretence. Reality was much darker and his attention could not long be weaned from it. Surfacing into a positive alternative did not last long. Over the week his melancholy increased and by New Year he was desperate to have his solitude back.

The New Year's Eve party was to be a small one – family friends only. To Bertrand's relief the visitors only knew him professionally and for a few hours he was prepared to put on the act he had once so much enjoyed – to be the public persona again. It would put him in a position to encourage useful gossip. For obvious reasons, though, the information Bertrand wanted to hear did not emerge:

'I wonder how long the good times will last,' mused a curator from Troyes. 'With the changes in Paris?'

'As long as they don't cut the funds we can work with anyone's ideas.'

'The last eight years have been good for the country as a whole. No one will want to take risks with that.'

The curator from Troyes was close to court gossip.

'There's a rumour that Jacques Duclos is retiring and René Védrine taking over his job.'

Bertrand looked up in disbelief:

'René Védrine is a shrimp. No way could he take over as Head of Modern Art!'

'Yes, rather a wild rumour. In fact, Paul Carlier is a more likely man: very capable, with masses of energy.'

Bertrand had met Paul.

'Not very likeable though.'

'Aggressive. These types tend to settle down once they get where they want.'

'Why are you so sure that Jacques is going to retire?' Bertrand went on. 'Last time I spoke to him he had plans.'

'Retire from conflicts. Not from life.'

Bertrand hoped so. He had a simple faith in Jacques. But by 2 a.m. his attention in such matters was exhausted. A piece of Jean's electronic gadgetry stood on the table – one of the ingenious designs he used to do before the changes of the summer. As Bertrand looked at it the past returned. He recalled the loving time Jean had spent on it and how they had discussed ways to fix the lighting so that the effect would be more shadow than light. The strength of these memories brought to the surface again the sure knowledge that he had no future. No amount of effort could create the same strength of purpose. Now he was living through imitation time. The conversation in the room came dimly to his ears. Hyde took over as another bitter thought came to him. Jean could have married any other woman but not the one Bertrand himself had put such trust in. It was that which destroyed him. He got up abruptly and left this society where no amount of goodwill could create a place for him for the freedom of the balcony. Smoke from the candles at the back of the room bent in the draft as he opened the door and, similarly, the conversation turned towards him.

'Poor chap.'

'He won't be able to stay much longer at Ivrez, will he?'

Bertrand moved further from the closed door but still he could hear them. He looked over the balcony into the night. A cat was elongated along the rail and, absentmindedly, he took comfort in stroking it.

'He still expects Jean to come back.'

'That's not likely from what I hear. Jean's doing very well. Better than he ever did at Ivrez. He's come out of Bertrand's shadow. And they're expecting a baby. Due sometime in spring.'

A baby! Bertrand nearly cried out. So, that really was the end. He had been right to endure this week. At least he knew. The end of everything. End of Jean. Even the cat was squealing like a baby. The sound merged with his despair. It took Bertrand some moments to realise that the cat was squealing because his hand had tightened round her neck. The noise subsided, and he looked at the animal, uncomprehendingly, then dropped it over the balcony onto the path, where it lay dead. Blood trickled over his hand where she had failed to defend herself. He would have to go in. Moving along the balcony he entered through André's bedroom to avoid unanswerable questions before he reached the bathroom.

'Do you get many foxes so close to the house?' the curator from Troyes was asking André in the drawing room.

'Often, in winter.'

A little later they came out to look for Bertrand. The balcony was empty, and they noticed the open drawing-room window.

'Do you think he heard?'

Wherever Bertrand had got to, they decided to leave him in peace.

A fox that night did come up to the house, leaving its prints in the muddy drive. It dined off the cat.

* * *

159

Bertrand appeared late to breakfast next morning, his mind still floundering. His hand was bandaged and drew comment.

'I can't remember,' he said, morosely. It was hardly a lie. 'I think I put my hand on a nail.'

The children came in full of distress.

'Mimi's been killed,' Anélie burst out, rushing to André.

'How do you know?'

'She didn't come into my room this morning, so I went to look for her, and there are bits of her on the path,' she sobbed.

'We heard a fox last night, just before we all went to bed. Did you see it, Bertrand, from the balcony?' André asked, uncomfortable now over Bertrand's injury. When Bertrand grasped what was being said he decided that he had.

'Yes, I did hear a fox.'

'A fox couldn't get a cat – unless it was already injured,' their cousin pointed out.

Anélie was becoming uncontrollable.

'There,' her mother put her arms round her. The conundrum would have to be forgotten. 'We'll bury her, and you can think she's helped keep another starving animal alive. So in a way, she's still alive really.' Anélie's sobs quietened.

How petty and irrelevant it was. If only he could go. Anyway, what did anything matter? He was one of the world's abortions.

Further South, in Veuillons, there was a rather more successful family Christmas. So much was going on at James's school and in the hotel where Sarah now worked. Rushing here and there in an effort to meet everyone's needs, she toyed with her employer's invitation to take a room for a few nights. Stephen, too, liked the idea. It would get the family out of his hair while he dug himself into finishing a couple of abstracts – rock shapes, earth and sky colours, capturing a sense of wind. It all took his absolute concentration and he cleaned the windows of the spare room, where he was working, every day to squeeze every ounce of light through the pane. Pity he hadn't time to convert the stable into a studio. It was hard enough grabbing what time he could on the abstracts while finishing the portrait in town.

Sarah put the idea of staying in the hotel to James in a half joking way. His response was a very solemn shake of the head. Security and status depended on going back to their own place every night, even if late in the evening and Sarah tired out with serving office parties from across the river all day, and James asleep on his feet after making Christmas bric-a-brac and rehearsing the school Shepherds' Play.

This would be part of the community's Christmas – to be put on in church during midnight mass. Ali-ba was found a crib of his own in the hotel and Stephen was dragged into town. But the thrill of such an impressive theatre, the church, kept James wide-awake in his role of non-speaking shepherd. It was an important event, played before a packed church, for there was here a dedication to festivity that the family had never encountered before. At the appointed time James, with a group of youngsters, walked solemnly down the aisle in his shepherd's robes leading two bemused sheep.

When mass was over, food was served and, at 1.30 a.m., they drove home with two sleeping youngsters, one draped over a Yule Log, and the car laden with food – cooked, thank heaven. For the next five days Sarah would not lift a finger, she lied to herself.

* * *

Hearing from Amy was now a cause of wonder. It no longer produced the anger of two months before when they had received her first, depressing revelations.

'What does she think she's playing at? Aping us in a move to France; breaking up two of your best friends, risking your future and hers. Getting pregnant, for heavens sake! I never thought she'd be so infantile.'

Stephen defended her. 'Must have taken courage to go and stay with them – complete strangers. Either that or she didn't realise what she was doing.'

'Reality will hit her in no half measure once the baby arrives.'

'Perhaps that's what she wanted,' he replied in a moment of clear-sightedness.

'It will hit us too,' Sarah added bitterly.

Then they heard of Jean's arrival. No abandoned pregnant woman was thrust upon them and the Christmas card brought yet more surprising news. The couple were married and very happy. A new perspective moved into the frame.

'We hoped the trip might help her get a fresh approach to life,' Stephen pondered. 'And it really, really has.'

Sarah laughed: 'We brought her here, and had no idea what was going on.'

'Thank heaven I got to Ivrez before he left.'

'I wonder what could have moved him to do such a decisive thing, leaving so much behind.'

'The baby? Love?' Stephen looked unromantically at his spouse.

'There must have been some need there.'

'And it wasn't Jean who sent the invitation, was it?'

Stephen left the implications hanging in the air. The possibilities were beyond their experience.

* * *

162

On New Year's Eve an anti-cyclone produced a hint of winter, interrupted by a warm front. Under its cloud a slight ground frost changed to tiny droplets, a coating over the vegetation too thin to run off. The cloud quickly broke up, shafts of light squeezed through once more and, as the family set out on foot, the sky had again turned solid blue. The sun's rays skated horizontally along the earth, catching on tussocks of the varnished grass and making them glow a rich green velvet. Walking up through the valley the air was breathless – branches of trees still, as though pinned to the sky – so calm Stephen could feel the earth thinking. He paused and Sarah and James gained some space.

'What are you doing?' Sarah called back.

'Nothing. Just listening.'

'What's he saying?' Sarah asked, smiling. The first words that children form have unrepeated significance.

'No, not that.' Though, now that he had stopped, Ali-ba in a harness on his back added sociable half-words.

In that quiet moment Stephen had decided to stop trying to paint at all until he had converted the stable into a studio. The commission in town was nearly finished; next he would put his back into the conversion and finish that in a couple of months. It would be easy. Winter here was almost spring-like and Sarah had a job that took daily pressure off them. What was more, they had sold the Alvis. It had produced a good sum so it was only right to plough part of it back into his work. The potential of the stable was superb. If he replaced most of the riverside wall with glass it would provide a view looking right down the valley. 'Wonderful! What wouldn't he be able to do with that inspiring view!' He smiled round at Ali-ba and began to canter towards the others, bouncing the toddler in his seat.

'Gee up, gee up.'

Their neighbour's farmhouse came into view.

'It's Étrée-Wamin all over again.'

'What?'

'Drinks with the farmer's family.'

'We've come on since then.'

'I wonder how Marie-Louise is. We'll have to invite her down in the summer. We've plenty of room.'

As they arrived at the farmhouse door a young woman they had not met before came out with a bucket. She encouraged them to go in before disappearing through a door across the yard. A sweet smell wafted across before they closed the kitchen door behind them.

Josephe and his wife, another Marie, were in their fifties. Their son was also out, doing most of the heavy work now. The two younger girls, one of whom they had just passed, had migrated to teaching professions. The other, Marianne, and her husband, Georges, were busy in the kitchen. The arrival of the foreign family refocused their conversation.

'We've heard a lot about you. Are you settling in?'

'The commission has been a good start. The Mayor asked Stephen to paint a portrait of his wife.'

'You don't want to hear about that,' Josephe barracked without bitterness. 'Marcel's losing his socialist ideals.'

'From what Stephen says, they are treating the idea as a bit of a joke,' Sarah went on. 'Doing it for us I suppose.'

Stephen wished he could translate Geneviève Valèry's comments, put to him in English: 'When it's done, we'll hang it over Sylvie's pool-table. Put them all off their form.' It was not his work that was the joke, but rather the idea that they should be so bourgeois as to find themselves suitable models. Portrait painting was not his strongest card though, unless in a surreal style and, despite the jokes, it was important not to produce a cartoon. The work was good practice, bringing him back into a discipline. None of this could Stephen add to the present conversation and he slotted patiently back into trying to follow what other people were saying. Sarah had not exhausted the theme of painting.

'Once Stephen has built up a collection this winter, he'll be taking them to a gallery in Grenoble.'

He looked at her sharply. That was only one of the ideas they had talked about. She knew he had thoughts of building a studio first. Last night, no decisions had been made either way. And, in fact he was now totally decided on the other plan. Sarah saw his expression and dropped the subject. But Marianne, the youngest daughter, and her husband loved Grenoble.

'So much goes on – night-life, restaurants. Skiing at weekends.'

'And,' her husband added, 'the University is behind some of the most advanced technology: hydro-electricity, nuclear power – you name it.'

'How about selling paintings?' Sarah asked cautiously.

'Everywhere in France has its galleries.'

'Not much encouragement there,' Sarah thought.

'Grenoble is good at international contacts. I could imagine it would be an advantage not to be French. Stephen, you must stay with us when you come.'

Josephe turned back to Stephen, thoughtfully.

'Are you getting to love your new French car?'

Stephen could follow this question and its humour. The Alvis had gone to a good home but, naturally, he felt the difference getting behind the wheel of the Citroen. Josephe understood what a wrench it had been and a theatrical grumble would not be misunderstood:

'Well, we have a supply of rubber bands, so repairs

165

aren't a problem.' After the laugh – after the translation – he added, 'and the problems with the Alvis were usually rubber bands that snapped.'

Josephe went on in his thoughtful style, 'We have an old van – it'll need some work on it. But if you can do this, you could use it. When you go to Grenoble, Sarah will need the Citroen.'

The elder daughter came back in.

'It's all ready. You can come across now.'

Without learning what "it" was the visitors allowed themselves to be shepherded towards where the sweet smell still hung in the air. Inside the byre stood the small herd of cattle: twelve Friesians, now graced with red and green ribbons, and the byre was generously hung with greenery. On the ground was a pile of sweet-smelling, oily, grainy slabs.

'Cattle cake?' asked Stephen.

'Yes. Sarah, would you like to feed your namesake? They're all female of course James. And we're giving them a New Year feast.'

Acting out biblical stories had taught James a few basic facts. He looked from the farmer and his wife to the decorated beasts and suddenly said, slightly puzzled,

'Josephe et Marie.'

'Yes!!' they cried among guffaws, 'not to worry – there's no baby in the straw. Just the cows' winter feed. Any excuse for a party!'

That evening Stephen stuck by his original plan and Sarah did not conceal her irritation. He was still such an impossible dreamer!

'What of earning money? The whole point of being here is to become better known.'

'It would only take a couple of months and the sale

166

of the car brought in a lot of money,' he protested. Sarah had become so hard – she did not value his self-sacrifice in selling the car at all. 'It's only fair that I use some of it on my work. I need somewhere *to* work.'

'You've been using the spare room.'

'The light isn't good enough.'

The question, like many, recently, was left unresolved.

18

Bertrand put the phone down on another concerned friend – this time Alain, who felt more sorrow than anger. It would, indeed, be a sad loss if the gallery folded. But Bertrand had no use for anyone's exhibitions – no time left. His mind was quite elsewhere. He had discovered something beyond the understanding of these mercenary people and he would follow its logic. He called to Madame Estienne as he left, 'I'll be in Nevers today.'

She looked up in astonishment.

'Again?'

He'd be away all day like last time. Bertrand was already crossing the yard and did not hear.

The road was good down to the Nièvre. It followed the Loire along its broad, sweeping valley, hidden at the moment behind the winter murk. Snow and rain fell intermittently, as though the sky was unsure which was appropriate for this low-lying region. Eventually he reached the faceless suburbs of Nevers. The bland, repetitive houses conveyed a denial of existence which suited his mood. He turned off the main road at the same place as last time and, a little further on, arrived at the equally expressionless high eighteenth-century walls of St Pierre prison.

He had his ID and waited in Reception for an attendant to escort him. The room was quiet; there were no arrivals nor discharges. Bertrand looked through the glass towards where he would be going, looking forward to checking the reality against the dream. Why should he have dreamed of a prison? Black bars from floor to ceiling – ominous enclosure. It expressed what his life had become; this was a bitter fact he lived with, yet the dream had given him feelings of happiness. It was home and he had been reluctant to wake up. The memory came back, vividly, and gave energy to his work. At night he had brought the image into his mind so as to fall into the same cell as he slept, but there was nothing. Night after night, there was no repeat. The Governor of Nevers prison, though, had been intrigued by his enquiry. A well-known artist was looking to develop a creative sense of confinement. The Governor was a liberal man and had replied.

The corridor Bertrand was in was impersonal, efficient, as in a hospital – white tiles, easy to clean, and the new sodium lighting which spread brightly into all corners, creating a different kind of oppressiveness from the one Bertrand was looking for. Then an official greeted him.

'A group of men are being moved just now, sir. We can go down in a few minutes.'

Through the window, Bertrand saw, through a further window, a small group in their pyjama-like outfits being escorted to, or from, one of their daily routines. This group, or one like it, would be in the education wing, where he would join them.

'We can go now sir.'

Bertrand nodded and took a step forwards, with just a little nervousness. But it wore off in the ordinariness of the passages through which they marched.

The workshop was large and kitted out with tools which, for obvious reasons, were kept in a strong room. Several guards were on hand to watch and to frisk. As

169

Bertrand arrived, a couple of prisoners at the back were completing some skilled joinery in the form of veneered cabinets. Others were grappling with more basic work, cutting sections out of planks of wood and, from a separate room, Bertrand could hear the hiss and crackle of electrical tools. All the men were dressed in striped pink and white tunics: a gentle colour to instill gentle behaviour. The men did not talk much; in this place nods and gestures conveyed as much as questions and answers. What Bertrand had not anticipated, though, was the effect of identical dress. Individual personality was removed; even facial differences were obscured as the men worked on, thoughts buried inside restraints. They were long-term convicts, men who had dared to do what he planned to do. Not all of course, but some had killed. Across the space Bertrand's eyes assessed them keenly in brief, discreet glances. He sensed a brotherhood. How many of these could give him confidence for his own plan? They could probably even give him ways to carry it out. What would they say if that were what he started to discuss with them now? How many, he found himself wondering, in such close confinement, were also lovers? Their movements and postures, like their faces, gave nothing away. Many would be, Bertrand thought, it was part of the degradation of the place. Degradation? Why that?

In front of him, on the bench, was the supply of metal he had asked for and the welding equipment. Pretending indifference, he passed sketches to three men sitting in front waiting for him to start, glad to avoid work. Bertrand tested the equipment. Then the other men were instructed to leave their jobs and take up the rest of the seats. They did so, resentfully it seemed, or perhaps they simply carried resentment with them, automatically, whatever they were told to do. When all

170

the captive audience was assembled, Bertrand turned to face them. Introductions would have been crass so he went straight to the point.

'For reasons of speed, I'm using metal thinner than you'd need for a permanent sculpture. Otherwise, those curves' – he indicated the sketches – 'would take several hours to beat into shape. However, this' – and he cut a metre length – 'is quite pliable. Curved in towards the hammer, at the point where a bend is wanted, it stretches quite quickly.' Bertrand worked for a few moments with the flame and the hammer until the point was demonstrated. 'Thinner material is better to practice on because corrections are comparatively easy.' Some lags with years of safe-breaking behind them found this infantile but, as usual, did not show their thoughts.

Now Bertrand was moving into the more creative aspects.

'You'll see this design is minimalist. To make the human figure, what is mainly needed are the right proportions between size of head, length of spine, and length of arms and legs. It needs a good eye and practice. So it's best to start with sketches until your eye is trained.'

As he talked, he continued working, bending out a skeletal shape and neatly welding the joints, until a crawling figure appeared, one arm stretched out forwards and one leg backwards, giving it balance.

'Head first down an escape tunnel,' a wag in front laughed, and others joined in.

'Ah, yes.'

Bertrand was pleased to get a reaction and not sure whether to reply. He decided he would.

'There *are* practical uses to this work once you are outside. Decorative metal work, fencing, or even making security grilles...,' and he looked directly at the man who had shown a sense of humour. The man, though,

171

found it more difficult to take, rather than to offer, a joke and his lips contracted into a sneer, not a smile. The two hours were over. The guards came forward and the men slowly prepared to obey, body language always making clear their preference for independent action. One stocky man, who had only been half watching, came forward.

'Monsieur, what good do you think your display is to us?'

The man was weather-beaten, or life-beaten, and looked at him through narrow slits of eyes, resulting from years of mistrust and cruel calculation. The strength of his contempt in the word 'Monsieur' interested Bertrand.

'That's none of my business.'

He swept pieces of broken metal into a pile giving himself the briefest of moments to dart a look at the questioner. Bertrand was already picking up prisoners' ways.

'We give you your kicks,' the man dropped out of the corner of his mouth as he sloped off into line.

Bertrand did not mind. What the man had said was absolutely true. It gave Bertrand a new kind of thrill – a touch masochistic – and he held back on his smile until the prisoner turned away. The remark was an invitation. The man had understood him well enough to know he could get away with the provocation. Little did he know just how far his invitation might be accepted and Bertrand's imagination leapt to the possibility of their meeting as equals. The man could kill him if he liked. He would have no further use for himself, by then. The attendant came in to escort Bertrand back.

'Are there photographs of the prison before it was modernised?'

'There are a couple of cells in the basement, unconverted – used for storage, sir.'

'Have you time to show me?'

'If you like sir.'

They went down steep stone steps, into the old well of the prison. This was a different world – dank, and feebly lit by a few naked bulbs. The cells could have been from an old police station; rows of bars and a barred door offered nowhere for a prisoner to hide. One of the cells was almost empty.

'Would you mind...?' Bertrand gestured and backed up the question with a sane explanation. 'Seeing the inside will give me a stronger sense of incarceration.'

Nodding with polite gravity, the guard pulled out a large key from its place in a desk drawer and turned it in the lock.

'The dimensions, too, are valuable,' said Bertrand, maintaining his professional poise.

'What a prisoner's life used to be was little more than incarceration. Lock them up and forget about them: that was society's attitude. Not like today. Now we're more optimistic. Ten minutes and I'm off duty, sir,' he added as Bertrand pulled the gate to behind him.

An iron seat projected from the wall. He tested it gingerly but it held him. The stone interior had been recently painted a dull brown, scratched in places by crates and boxes and the paint had obliterated signs of earlier scratchings. He could only imagine the pain and privation that had been endured in here – unheated, always damp. There was, high up against the ceiling, a tiny grille barely above the level of the ground outside. It allowed in just a little light, a little air. He himself wouldn't last two months in here. Yet the place cheered him. All options were closed once you entered here, all hope could finally be abandoned. Remembering the ten minutes, he came out again.

'Thank you for letting me try it for size,' he quipped.

'Oh, we'd need two for you sir,' the attendant responded jocularly as he locked the door. Then he straightened up and prepared to apologise. But Bertrand was not offended. How extraordinary. This insolence, which outside would produce fury in him, seemed kindly meant here. He had surrendered his problems. Even unhappiness is a fragile emotion, he discovered. He could be happy within it. Perhaps that was the meaning of his dream.

'We have someone here who would interest you,' the attendant went on as they climbed the steps and Bertrand's mind immediately flicked to the insolent prisoner. 'One of the Neuilly robbers made the mistake of coming back from Morocco. He'll be off for trial in Paris in a few days.'

Bertrand smiled again. Life was full of ironies.

It was nine thirty and Bertrand still not back.

'This can't go on much longer,' Madame Estienne thought sadly. 'We're nearly finished.'

No exhibitions, no visitors, no attention to the outside world ... and now Bertrand's manic working had been interrupted by these trips away. The neglect couldn't go on much longer. Their resources were coming to an end, she thought, unaware of just how much Bertrand and Jean had saved over the years. She would have to write to Jean after all, make it clear he had to rescue them. She went into Bertrand's room to sit at the desk and wrote in a not quite steady hand. It was desperate work for an old woman to be forced to take the initiative like this. She wrote, insisting that Jean come home, fighting the tiredness that seeped into her. Bertrand's leaving her with no explanation wasn't right either. This lack of purpose in the house was wearing her down. The address of the Laon gallery was in the office book. She'd thrown away Jean's address so René would have to take this to him. At last her effort was finished and she laid the letter by the phone. In the kitchen she put the blanket of ashes on the fire and then went to bed. She was soon asleep. Oedipus came in and lay on the mat in her room with his head on his paws.

After a while, he got to his feet again and padded back along the passageway into the kitchen, greeting Bertrand with a wrinkled forehead. He did not understand what he had done to lose his master's love. Bertrand was looking at the name and address on the envelope. He would post it tomorrow. Maybe it would help. Patting Oedipus absent-mindedly, Bertrand helped himself to food. The basement cells had been exactly like the imprisonment of the dream. Not that that was surprising, all pre-twentieth century prisons would be much the same. The picture he had had was like something out of *The Count of Monte Cristo*. He sat down with a plate of soup and Oedipus rested his soft muzzle on his knee. What would be the next move? He could not really believe that Madame Estienne's appeal to René – whatever it said – would be the answer. Bertrand lifted his head and looked across the room. He had no idea what to do. He was quite, quite lost. But today's discoveries reassured him. Now, he trusted fate. The moment would come for his revenge against life, and he would be put in a cell like the men he'd met. He could forget then. He imagined the judge's face if he asked for an eighteenth-century dungeon. They'd find him a loony bin! He laughed out loud and Oedipus wagged his tail, eyes fixed humbly upwards, seeking attention. Finding this wasn't enough he licked Bertrand's hand. Bertrand glanced down and noticed it was still pocked with claw marks.

19

Amy was buying flowers at the shop where, a few months before, she had worked.

'I was sorry to lose you,' cheery Madame Tremand was saying, 'but very glad everything's turned out so well.'

'Yes, hasn't it.'

Amy smiled warmly back. Since New Year her doubts had gone. Jean was deep at work on his mammoth commission and his happiness with it cemented their own. She had also begun to appreciate how friendly the people in Laon were. Madame Calbère had phoned at New Year with her good wishes. Now Madame Tremand's little girl was weaving around her. Amy gave her some chocolate. The little girl immediately insisted on sharing it. Very glad that she had had this idea of buying flowers, Amy went back for a few moments to the flat to arrange them and to visit the loo yet again. As the town was small, the extra few metres did not tire her. Besides, this last week her old energy had returned; there was energy even for ideas. It was as though her body had finally got over the shock of dividing its attention between two people. She had put on weight in the expected places and it no longer slowed her down. Ideas had come to her of how to move into an independent career within the art world: exciting, but too embryonic to broadcast. Leaving the flat, she anticipated with pleasure the welcome Jean would find when he arrived home first that evening to prepare his honest country cuisine. Warm, despite the wind, she returned to the gallery.

Jean had ducked outside for a few moments at midday to get the benefit of the cool snow that was falling. Working in metal meant you were always too near an oven. This morning he was finishing a model for the Banque Régionale. The studios were busy and he needed to work fast – so much rested on the income he would get for this. To express 'the Bank' he was searching for an economic ideal, if it wasn't a contradiction in terms. Not that he objected to the commercial nature of the work. It brought him fully into ordinary society after living on its fringes all of his life. He was taking ideas from early Soviet art, which provided a strong design into which he could incorporate symbols of trade and finance. This display, welcoming customers into the new head office, would stand the full height of the foyer. Jean went back in and threw himself furiously into finishing the model. After all, his mother was never ill. Should the wheel and the shield, he wondered, be clearly recognisable, or merge into a single shape? Surely he had been right to ignore her letter. He broke off and went upstairs to make further sketches. Either design would work. He would speak to Mr Perrachan and see which he preferred. He phoned, arranging to see him the next day. Then, still disconcerted, he phoned Amy at the gallery.

'I just wanted to know what you were doing – right at this moment.'

'Pen in air, debating with myself whether to support the white argument or the colour argument for the walls. Don't you think a very pale colour would be less dead than white? Unless it's whitewash?' she added roguishly.

Jean understood the allusion but did not laugh as spontaneously as he might have done and, after a short conversation, rang off. It had not worked. The rumour he had heard that morning that his mother was in hospital still dominated his thoughts. Talking to Amy had not miraculously answered his question as to whether this might be a trick on Bertrand's part. Obviously, when her letter came soon after New Year, he had had to ignore her pleas, but could she have written because she was feeling ill? So he phoned Alain, even though it was still the middle of the afternoon. Alain, not pleased to be interrupted, responded as though Jean were to blame for not knowing.

'Well, yes, it was pleurisy. It was a month ago she went into hospital. Didn't you know?'

'Which hospital?'

'She's home now.' And Alain rang off.

So Jean phoned Marcia Chabot. But this conversation did not put his mind at ease at all. His mother was not recovering. She seemed to have lost interest in life. It was another call, more urgent than her letter, and one he could not ignore. So it was a very subdued Jean waiting at home for Amy with one of his mother's recipes – though this was a useful way into what was on his mind. Amy looked at him in disbelief.

'But you can't go.'

'I can't not go. She nearly died.'

'Think what will happen.'

'Nothing will happen.'

'Bertrand will crucify you.'

'I don't think so.'

'He's been alone for three months. What if he's not the man you remember?'

'Well, I've changed too. I'm not so easy to push around now. And he could have let me know of Maman's illness. He didn't. That looks as though he's managing.'

Amy could not believe how naive Jean was being. It was he who had said the past must be left behind, that it would trip them up otherwise. The bond between them could be lost if he went now.

' Your mother's getting better. Wait till the baby's born. Then we'll all go.'

'According to Marcia she's not getting better,' he said, wretchedly. 'If she died I'd never forgive myself.'

It was still dark when Jean rose, a few mornings later. Amy stirred too. It took time for her to heave herself into a sitting position. Her physical awkwardness produced a pang. She was vulnerable now she was losing him.

'Don't forget us.'

'I won't desert you.'

A few moments and she took her arms from round his neck.

20

February had the countryside fully in its grip and Jean
was dragged south through squalls of snow. For all his
words to Amy, once on the road they felt like bravado.
He would stay just long enough to decide what to do
for his mother – that was all. The rest of the arrangements
could always be done back in Laon. Before starting out
he had wondered whether to phone or write. But arriving
unannounced would give him the strength of surprise
so he had torn up the letter to his mother, then regretted
it, but did not write another. She was sitting up now,
Alain had told him, able to take an interest in events.
How soon would she be able to travel? She'd need to
be coaxed from her bed. Ivrez was a chilly place in
winter; no wonder she was reluctant to leave it. This
line of thinking reminded him of Ivrez's sleeping
arrangements. But there was the guest room, and he
paused on the outskirts of Paris to buy himself a sleeping
bag.

He had stopped in a suburb where there was yet
another small gallery, run by Vernon, another of their
group from twenty years ago. Jean hadn't seen Vernon
Caillart for at least ten and, out of curiosity, he paused
at the gallery window. Slickly painted greetings cards
and prints were on display. So, Vernon had given up
being an artist altogether. He had always been more
interested in gossiping. On the other hand, perhaps the
cards were just to bring in customers. Jean opened the
door gently, hoping not to attract attention, and slipped

into the empty shop. Inside, there were prints by a number of different hands, and all were imitations of styles that had become fashionable – geometric abstracts, Miroesque designs and leanings towards Andy Warhol. Jean's curiosity was satisfied but, turning to leave, he was intercepted by a beaming Vernon who remembered him rather better than reason expected.

'Jean-Claude!' He embraced him warmly. 'How's the new life?'

'Oh, fine,' Jean fell automatically into his old wariness.

'Great about your work. I read a piece about you in the paper. Always thought you'd make it. I said to Alain, all those years ago, that you'd catch up with them one of these days.'

This was not just nostalgia. Vernon had added him to his list of people worth knowing and Jean could not deny that this first piece of public recognition brought a pleasant glow. His ebullient friend was in no danger of running out of hyperbole and Jean sifted Vernon's words carefully, discovering in himself new social skills. He was pleasant, unpretentious, not letting Vernon see his true thoughts, but without catching Vernon's falsity, and they parted on good terms. The short five minutes had been proof of how right Jean had been to change his life. And, on returning to his car a little later with the bag, the difficulties that lay ahead shrank with *Alice-in-Wonderland* speed. Of course he would not stay long at Ivrez. Arrangements for his mother's travel could always be made from Laon.

Would Bertrand have forgiven him? It seemed now there had been too much friendship underpinning their time together for this to count for nothing. After all, Jean had been moving in this direction for some years, and Bertrand had known it all along. Pictures of Bertrand in the better times, years ago, came to him. There was

181

no reason they couldn't both do well. In happy anticipation, he phoned impulsively from Montargis.

'How's mother?'

'I've had to nurse her.' Bertrand made no attempt to hide his resentment.

'But she's better now,' Jean stated firmly.

Bertrand's finger traced a pattern in the dust on the bureau: 'Recovering, I should say.'

'Soon she'll be living with me.' He couldn't say 'us.'

'She won't be a burden on you.'

There was silence from the other end.

'I'll be there soon.'

'Mmmm.' The web of lines under Bertrand's fingers interested him. He put the phone down. Pleased to be talking to him again, Jean had not let him know he was actually close by. But Bertrand had guessed. He put the phone down and went to prepare a light lunch for his patient.

He had not made a good nurse, resenting the burden and the fact that he could no longer go to Nevers. But he was doing what was asked of him. At the hospital they had shown him how to turn her and support her once she was able to try her weight again. It was all part of the trial he must endure before justice could be done: penal servitude before the crime. He seemed to be drifting further and further from his goal but he would suffer it. He would be patient until Jean was brought back. At least Madame Estienne gave him the perfect reason not to plan for the summer. Both of Alain's letters had gone straight into the fire. She was the perfect ally, disliking the fact that Bertrand was the one to care for her.

'You must tell Jean to come back. This is his job,' she protested as Bertrand washed her.

'Yes, he'll come,' Bertrand had replied. But Jean would

182

not believe in her illness if he received the news directly from himself. So he told everyone except Jean. Once the message was passed to him Jean would come of his own accord and with his mind open, as this morning's phone call showed. Fate was revealing its hand.

Madame Estienne co-operated all the way. The nurse who called clucked again disapprovingly as she showed no real will to get on her feet.

'Think of the burden you are to Monsieur Barenton.'

'It's not Bertrand who should be looking after me.'

'No, exactly.' The nurse was encouraging.

'No, exactly.' Madame Estienne had replied this morning, mockingly, but low enough not to be heard. Reluctantly she allowed herself to be guided around the fire-heated room. Jean had phoned; that was Bertrand's news this morning. She must not look too well when he arrived. Still denying the reality of the marriage, she thought he would settle down for the sake of the woman who had devoted her life to him, and then she would recover her health. Bertrand, though, spruced himself up. His beard almost met his eyebrows, the embers of his eyes kindling between them, rather like Fidel Castro's, he thought with distaste, as he sought to restore a more civilised exterior – one calculated not to startle Jean back north.

But it was a new and positive man who appeared in the kitchen doorway while Bertrand, humbled, was washing up the lunch pots. Jean embraced him warmly and Bertrand responded with a deliberate kiss.

'How are you?' Jean asked and went on before Bertrand could reply, 'You look well.'

The soup Bertrand had just laboured over unsettled Madame Estienne's stomach. The sight, the smell, the carrying away of rejected deposits demanded all Jean's attention and he devoted himself sympathetically to his mother's needs. By the end of the afternoon he was

183

able to contemplate her as she slept. She had become frail. Her features had lost their outdoor sculpture – smoothed with fever, she looked almost young. But there was nothing wrong with her heart; there was no reason for her not to travel back with him in a few days. Bertrand came in.

'I've made you something to eat.' Jean looked up and weighed up the trim beard against the dark circles round Bertrand's eyes. On the whole he *did* look well, Jean thought with relief, maybe even tougher than before. Perhaps he *had* found a new partner. In the kitchen his optimistic thoughts tumbled out.

'You know, Bertrand, when my mother comes up to Laon you'll have her room and a spare studio.'

'Half of Ivrez is technically yours,' Bertrand responded drily. He'd never discussed ownership before, but then Jean had never implied that Ivrez belonged only to Bertrand before. Jean drove on.

'What I mean is, you mustn't be alone here – and there's no need. Pierre Colvert is looking for somewhere.'

Bertrand smiled. Jean was behind the times.

'A replacement for you?'

'Of course not. But you know him, and I've found working with younger men stimulating. You do think his work's promising.'

'Do I?' Bertrand appeared to consider the idea. 'He's a trifler – a designer.' It gave him pleasure to adopt Jacques' phrases. Ignoring this, Jean phoned Amy before she left for home.

'It's going to be all right. Mother will soon be up, and I'll be back to find us all a decent house.'

'How long?'

'Two or three weeks.'

'I miss you all the time.'

'Me too.'

184

Jean took his things up to the guest room and by the time he returned to the kitchen his adrenaline had subsided. He was thinking better.

'What's this brilliant work you've been doing?'

Bertrand's eyes glinted. 'I'll show you.'

Jean made to go back upstairs.

'No, not there – I need more space.'

He moved to the outside door, beyond which the February sky was black.

'Now?'

'There's a better effect in the dark.' So Jean followed to the once familiar studio. 'I've fixed up some lighting.'

Bertrand flicked the switch and Jean gasped. His room had been invaded by corpses. Low lighting threw shadows over cavernous skulls and impaled limbs. Broken contortions, which could just be made out to be based on the human form, lay twisted and gouged on the floor and on the shelves. Some were elongated, forms pulled on a rack. Another, very small, which Jean could hardly bear to look at, was a baby. After the shock, Jean recovered his critical faculties. He looked narrowly at Bertrand.

'They are good,' he conceded. 'Fearful of course.'

Bertrand's cold humour shot like nails.

'You like them?'

'You haven't been wasting your time.'

'No. I intend to show these in Paris. Alain thinks well of them.'

'And Jacques?'

'Yes.' 'I'm very pleased at that,' he said in his still bitter tone.

At least Bertrand's life was taking shape. Jean nodded in pleasure at the thought. Bertrand, seeing the comfortable expression decided to undermine it.

'But I like them best here. This place expresses my meaning.'

185

A private exhibition for me? Jean's candid blue eyes looked enquiringly, and he added out loud. 'You'll soon tire of a show with no audience.'

'The best work is always done on a precipice, don't you think?' Bertrand retorted. 'I hear you've produced some impressive things too.'

He smiled. 'Our lives have always run in tandem, haven't they? Perhaps we're on the same precipice.'

'I'm here because of my mother,' Jean replied firmly. 'I'll be sleeping upstairs,'

A couple of days later Jean tried to talk seriously to his mother. It was not easy.

'A house in Laon!' she said in horror. Of all places. Surely Jean would realise what she had against the place.

'A new home, where we can look after you.'

'Not at my time of life. Bertrand needs someone here.'

'Bertrand's doing very well. Looking after you. What if the cold in winter's too much for you now?'

'Nonsense. The anxiety made me ill.'

Jean ignored the blame.

'Won't you want to see the baby?'

This raised her interest. The flicker in her eyes produced another in his. She fought down the curiosity and replaced it with facts.

'You're breaking up Ivrez. It'll be the end of the gallery. It'll be the end of Bertrand.'

Jean phoned Amy.

'She won't listen. I'm coming back.'

Almost as though she had heard, Jean's mother was rushed back to hospital that night after an asphyxiating coughing fit. The doctors pronounced a further lung infection. No further plotting would be needed for a while yet. Departure was postponed.

186

'Madame Estienne.'

The name took Amy by surprise but she was glad to hear it broadcast so publicly. It reminded her she had rights.

'Madame Estienne, the paintings have arrived.'

'Right, Ricard, tell René I'm coming.'

She took her time getting up from the chair. The baby was her only companion and moments taking him into account were like a conversation. It was six months now. The doctor had let her listen to the heart-beat through the stethoscope and had introduced her to his hiccups. She was sure it was a 'he', in compensation for Jean's absence. But her energy levels were still strong. She was no longer plagued with aches and weariness. Now, especially, it was essential for her to keep active and forward-looking.

When she reached the main office several staff were gathered round as René lifted the masterpieces out one by one, carefully unwrapping each of the Watteau drawings to examine and record them. Amy was struck by how modern they looked – fresh.

'Fresh?' René queried with a smile. Everyone knew it was Watteau's stylishness that made him great. But Amy's naiveté was always charming. What Amy saw was the casual poses and a surprise in the sitters' eyes as they glanced up as though they'd heard the click of a camera. Then the figure of Pierrot emerged – an innocent, too naive to pose, clumsy, waiting for the order to go. All the staff stood round in delight.

'It reminds me of Philbert Marin's work, don't you agree?' Amy suggested to Estelle, a cousin of his.

'Some of it – his circuses.'

'Yes,' Amy agreed eagerly and, a couple of days later, she took René to a restaurant, not to eat – it had

187

gastronomic prices which would have identified them as lovers – but to see a couple of Philbert's works on the wall, both of clowns. These figures, too, had vitality. She took with her the rather fine camera Jean had bought her at Christmas.

'Jean and I think he's the best painter in Laon,' she said as she focused the lens. 'Do you think we could bring his work into the Watteau exhibition in some way?'

Amy was working hard at giving herself control over her life but there was effrontery in this suggestion; she was but a secretary. René did not respond to that, glad instead that she was bringing them closer.

'Perhaps we could do something,' he said amiably vague. 'A small exhibition in the foyer maybe.' Her pleasure made him a touch jealous at her concern for yet another man not himself.

'Philbert's done paintings of Jean and me,' Amy was saying as she took further notes. 'Not that they would fit in here,' she added, hurriedly.

'Yes, I know. I've seen one – of you.'

'Where?'

'In a Paris exhibition,' he said with deliberate keenness.

She flushed. It was a personal painting. The pose had been for Jean, while Philbert painted, and done during that first intoxicating month. Things were rather different now. The watching René was very pleased to have provoked a response. He'd pierced her defences and brought them closer still. He tried to imagine her face if he told her he had bought the painting. He would tell her soon. Amy was obviously contriving to see more of him – her loneliness was moving her in his direction. Soon, he would give her much more than the painting. Had Amy not been busy putting away the camera she might have noticed his expression. As it was she only became aware of the silence and looked up enquiringly.

'Come on,' he said in his usual affable tone and headed for the door.

A couple of days later came the weekly visit to the clinic. As ever, she was told that all was well.

'You're lucky. Naturally slim. You'll stay active till it pops out.'

A group breathing session further raised her sense of well-being. Then she went to phone for the return taxi.

'Amy! I should have realised I'd find you here.' Madeleine had materialised in the corridor. As her doctor was away she had to call at this public place to pick up her contraceptives. She was as impeccable as ever, an image off the front page of a magazine, out of place in the real world, though far from embarrassed at finding herself in it. Impulsively, Amy invited them both to dinner, then instantly regretted it. She was making herself ridiculous. Anyway, Madeleine would probably find an excuse not to accept. But, too well bred to deliver an open snub, Madeleine decided to defer this until later.

That evening, still keeping to a proactive agenda, Amy phoned Madame Chabot.

'You know how vague Jean can be. I'm concerned about how his mother really is.'

'Oh, much better – Jean brought her round here a few days ago.'

'Then she'll be coming up to Laon with him soon?'

'Going where?'

'Here, Laon.'

'Heavens no! She's adamant about that. She'll not leave Ivrez.'

Was this the wiles of Madame Estienne or the wiles of Jean? Amy controlled the blow.

'Surely Jean wants to come back.'

'Oh, of course he does. This can't be easy for you my dear.'

'No.'

'When is the baby due?'

'June' – Juin and Don Juan's baby – she flicked the bitterness from her mind.

'If nothing's worked out by then, we can arrange for you to have it in Montargis. You can stay with me.'

When René reached home that evening he appeared tired. 'The February blues', he called it. He was troubled by his secretary and the painting of her, wrapped in brown paper in a gallery store room, inflamed the trouble. Recently he had been allowing himself the pleasure of undressing it, done just before coming home that evening. 'This is crazy,' he thought as he peeled back the paper tantalising himself in a juvenile way as the naked body was gradually revealed. At home with his beautiful Madeleine, it all seemed absurd. 'I ought to sell it,' he realised. Emotional disturbance was tiring, Laon was boring, and that tiresome girl was becoming an embarrassment to him unless he could contrive an opportunity with her. Madeleine brought them both a drink, and put her arms round him from the back of the chair.

'Have you heard about Adèle?' she asked.

'No. What's happened?'

'Nothing alarming. She has a new boyfriend.'

'Can't say that surprises me. Never thought Michel her type. There's a hard streak in him.'

'This one's a doctor. The eye specialist she went to see last year, no less.'

'Well, well.'

'It happened after the tests were over of course.'

'Of course.' He paused. 'I hope it goes well.'

'So do I,' Madeleine said with warmth.

The affection Madeleine had for his rather wilful young sister always surprised him and he turned round to give her his first real smile of the day.

'I have to go back to the studio,' she said after their kiss. 'I won't be long.'

'Do you have to? We *do* work too hard, you know. How would you like a weekend somewhere warm. Rome, say, or Athens?'

'Yes, I would like that. I would really like that. We'll talk it over when I get back.'

In the car Madeleine also thought this the perfect excuse for not eating with Amy. They could not confirm a date as they would be leaving soon. Once they came back she could forget about it.

Yet, here they were, sitting at Amy's table, with René enthusiastic, and Madeleine annoyed for having let him know the purpose of her call. He had found reasons to change her mind. After all, they had helped get the pair together. They had some responsibility towards her now she was abandoned by her husband. His disappointment in his wife worked. Madeleine had studied his face but, as far as she could see, René's attitude was purely paternal.

'I'm afraid this is going to be a boring evening for you,' Amy said when they arrived.

'Not at all,' said Madeleine. 'We're concerned about you. Do you know when Jean is coming back?'

'Well, of course I have to wait for him to phone – and he does. His mother is recovering very slowly. And

191

he won't be able to move the Bank sculpture until it's finished. It'll need special transportation. But I have told him I can't stay here alone much longer.'

'Where will you go?'

Of that, she was not sure. She'd be lynched if she went to the village at Ivrez. She had wondered whether a third letter to Sarah was possible; such a humiliation though – a confession that the marriage was over.

'There's Madame Chabot in Ivrez and I do have friends in the south of France.' The doubt in her voice told René that she needed him and there sprang to his mind the perfect place for her stay. He would find a time to suggest this. For the moment he pulled out a harmless compliment.

'Well, despite your worries, you still do an excellent job at the Maison des Arts.'

She had to smile at the encouragement.

'Do you have any news from Ivrez? she asked him.

'Nothing worth giving. I've only spoken to Bertrand. He's putting together a one-man exhibition.'

'Coming here?' Her tone was sharp.

'No, no,' René went on reassuringly. 'Paris.'

That night René lay with his hand on Madeleine's flat belly.

'What about us?' he asked.

'Not here. I want to go home first. Or we'll never go back.'

René sighed. The only hope of working in Paris was through Paul and since the Conference he had been silent. If Paul's plan had misfired René saw no way of appeasing his restlessness. Madeleine could move back any time. Her business was doing very well: most of her clients came from Paris and Brussels. It was him holding her back so he had no right to complain. Now Madeleine pursued the idea in her own way.

'We must talk to Jacques again. I'm sure a post could be made.'

René did not argue but, since the robbery, Jacques did not seem to be in a position to help any more.

Life at Ivrez was settling into a routine, for Jean had to keep working. His car passing through the village from time to time caused interested speculation, discussed daily in the Post Office. Repeated exposure cauterized Monique's feelings and it was mischievousness which took her over late one afternoon to see shy Jean transformed into the married man. She timed it well. Both men were finished for the day and Jean welcomed her with open arms. Flirting with her would demonstrate to Bertrand that he was indeed 'straight'. Her response was a little more barbed.

'No one expected to see you again so soon. Tired of marriage?'

'Not at all,' he replied, with his arm still round her. 'You ought to try it.'

'All the interesting men have left Ivrez,' was her pointed reply as she disengaged herself but, seeing no guilt disturb him, went on, 'Perhaps I can persuade father to move.'

It was the trap she was in which caused the bitterness. For Jean she was no threat. After a long talk that morning his mother had promised that after Easter, with winter over, she would at least visit his new home. The battle was won and Jean took a pleasurable revenge against Bertrand, treating Monique in a way which made clear the old liaison. Bertrand, in fact, looked on with great interest. She might be useful to him. As she returned to her car she found him there.

'Should I congratulate you?'

'On what?'

'Last September – you were right.'

She shrugged: 'Well, it's too late now.'

'If only she would go back to London,' Bertrand continued. 'If we could get her down here and frighten her.'

The flicker in his eyes was alarming. People were right, there was something dangerous about Bertrand these days. And was the 'we' a bargain that, in return for her help, she would get a little bit of Jean? She climbed into the car without answering and Bertrand returned to the house. No, Monique would not be any help. But, at least, the look on her face told him she would not be back. He did not want interlopers getting in the way.

In the days that followed Jean nearly matched Bertrand in the hours he put in. The sooner the wheel construction was finished, the sooner he could go. His style could not have been more different from Bertrand's, but there was one thing they had in common. There was no denying that Jean's work now had equal fluidity and confidence of line.

'We've never worked better,' Jean was happy to say one morning over coffee. Bertrand pretended not to notice the cosiness of the 'we' and bent it into a more detached statement.

'We should both be grateful – look forward not back.'

Jean shot him a delighted look.

'Should we talk about selling Ivrez perhaps?' Bertrand went on.

'Eventually, I suppose, but I'll leave that to you.'

'No. This place is yours too. I'm thinking of moving back to Paris. We should celebrate and move on.'

194

Jean was overjoyed. They had reached the turning point he had so hoped for. They could part but stay friends.

'A farewell supper - a stag night!' he laughed.

Madame Estienne looked on in quiet horror that evening as she heard them discuss various improbable alternatives.

'André Colvert would buy it. Emilie would prefer it to her mill.'

'Or Guillaume might buy it back from us. Turn the whole château into a hotel.'

'Or let it out to his friends. With suits of armour for one of their weird parties.'

As their fantasies over dinner grew more inventive, selling the place at all looked less and less likely to the watchful Madame who approved of the amount they were drinking. The men's laughter made them increasingly conscious of each other again. Mutual admiration mingled with affection and a sense that Bertrand was right, even apart their lives did move in tandem. Reminiscences blossomed, they returned to letters written fifteen years ago. Some of them love letters. Laughing over a photograph of themselves taken in 1960 Bertrand pushed Jean sprawling onto the bed. Still laughing, he soon had Jean's trousers open and Jean felt his penis harden as Bertrand took it in his mouth. The night was spent in drunken oblivion. In the morning Jean was distraught.

There had been a late fall of snow and Laon's poplars had paused in their springtime surge. Amy could not live alone in this flat any longer and Jean had not phoned her for a week. He had appeared out of the night and had now disappeared back into it. She would have to take up Madame Chabot's offer to stay with her to find out what was going on. Going to claim her man was such an unhappy cliché that she resisted making the move. It would only confirm the end. As she washed the pots from that morning there was a knock at the door and René appeared.

'Jean asked me to call. I phoned him.'

'Lucky René,' she thought. He continued.

'While he's away, we mustn't let him be forgotten. We can hang those last sketches he made in the Library.'

'That is a good idea.'

His loyalty to friends touched her and she welcomed him as the one stable point of a world that kept tilting sickeningly.

'I can't understand why Jean hasn't been in touch. I do wish I could phone him.'

'Artists are no good at everyday realities,' he replied. 'They just get moved along by events. You'll have to get used to that.'

Amy flinched. 'Did he say anything to you about when he'll be back?'

'He was vague, the way he usually is...' And he smiled as though Jean had simply forgotten to pick up the shopping.

'Would you say he was very close to his mother before he met me?'

'Can't say. Don't know him personally. But Jean is her only relative.'

'Then why won't she come up here?'

'Has he said that?' This interested him.

'No, the opposite. In ten days he'll bring her,' she asserted, wanting to knock the truth out of him, whatever it might be.

'Then ten days it is.' He smiled reassuringly. Wanting to be reassured, she smiled back.

'The troubles of love,' he added with a theatrical sigh, and wondering how to make his own offer.

But, instead of engaging with him, as he had hoped, Amy ignored the platitude and went to make him some tea which René always liked. Slightly annoyed at being made to feel redundant yet again, he called out.

'It's the one good habit to have come out of England.'

Again she laughed his comment away as he followed her into the kitchen and inspected the packet over her shoulder. It was his favourite brand. This reassured him. He put the packet down and his freed hand came round her waist to caress the bulge of her belly. She dropped the pot, but before she could pull away his other arm pinned her. He leant against her from behind, trapping her against the sink. His free hand swiftly raised her skirt and found its way into her crotch.

'Jean won't mind,' he whispered into her neck as she struggled to get free.

'Artists don't mind.' His fingers insidiously found, through her clothing, the tender gap and toyed with her clitoris, wanting the sexual response he had thought about a little too often.

'I know you like me.' He kissed her on the neck.

He had thought of her so long in a certain kind of way that it seemed obvious she was similarly lusting after him. Her avoidance of him was just the suppression of desire so his free hand continued its exploration of the inside of her thigh, caressing insistently. Pressed to him she felt his penis moving against her.

'You're unbearably desirable, especially pregnant,' he whispered. Revulsion gave her strength. She moved her feet enough to kick him in the shin and grab a fork. She had underestimated his thirty-two carat arrogance. For a moment they stood, her face blazing. He was not at all abashed.

'Well, Jean's back with Bertrand. Why not accept it? I

197

always knew he would.' His smile suggested, 'and leave you to me.'

'He's only there because of his mother.'

'Oh, she's better now. Sowing the veg. as usual. Bertrand told me himself on the phone. He and Jean are back together.' Bertrand had decided to use René. After all, Jean had used René.

'Think about it,' he said as he left her still leaning in shock against the sink.

When René emerged from the courtyard into the alley he saw a familiar red sports car. Madeleine had heard he had left the office and just wondered if he might be here. It was better to show that she was not entirely blind. René turned smiling towards her as she stepped out of the car.

'She's not in,' he said. 'The news from Jean will have to wait,' and he hugged her devotedly. There was no phone in the flat and Madeleine dismissed her suspicions – after all, the girl was so pregnant.

It was terrible going back to work to make sure press invitations were done – avoiding René and knowing that, because she wasn't screwed, her job was. If she did not walk away then, obviously, her maternity would be the cover for the humiliation of dismissal. The fact that she'd been planning to go anyway did not reduce the humiliation. But she had grown up overnight and could no longer even dream of depositing herself on Sarah. Now she could see the world from Sarah's point of view. There were no such things as easy dependencies. In expecting easy friendship from René she had put herself in a position where he could abuse her without it ever crossing his mind that that was what he was doing. In the autumn she would return to London. That wouldn't be so bad – the baby would be four months. But until then it was Jean who had the responsibility. She would, after all, have to live in the village with Madame Chabot. An embarrassing arrangement for them all but what was life without its embarrassments? The next morning she overcame her dread of driving, hired a car and headed south.

21

Jean was labouring at his work and wondering whether Bertrand would keep his promise to bring the new battery for his car. In a way, Jean hoped not. He would prefer to pay the garage to bring it over.

'Stay here and you can have a new car,' had been Bertrand's invitation. A car! He missed his embryonic family. Bertrand's seduction had at least purged the confusion he had felt on returning. Bertrand had not acted out of love but out of malice. And his mother was as well as she was ever going to be. She'd sat up with them through that dinner three evenings ago without ill effects. It was obvious she too was playing with him. The problem was what to say to Amy. Jean carefully laid the network of radiating threads on the table and took some measurements. Working upstairs in Bertrand's old studio made him conscious of the silence. The thick walls swallowed up all noise. He preferred the studio among the chickens. Even more he missed the buzz and banter of Semilly. Restless, he wondered whether to help himself to yet another coffee, and decided against it.

It was the first time Amy had driven to the château and keeping a sense of direction was not easy once you left the autoroute for the spider-web of minor roads. She had, though, memorised the position of villages; accurately, she realised when the sign for Seurans appeared. On following the road into this village she came to another junction where directions to Ivrez leaped out at her alarmingly. The sign also displayed a silhouette of the château. The cheery cartoon sent a chill down her spine and she wished she could slow the world down. But, inevitably, the distance between Seurans and Ivrez shrank.

As she came to the familiar green lanes Bertrand's threat came to her mind: 'When I catch up with you I'll kill you.' And this was a very isolated place. She could, instead, go to Marcia Chabot's. But it was still daylight and she had to talk to Jean. Young leaves on the trees left gaps and soon the view ahead revealed a glimpse of grey stone. It would be better not to drive too close – better to leave the car here and approach quietly. It was 4 p.m. Would the men be working? Jean should be in his studio in the yard and, even in her condition, she could get that far without attracting Bertrand's attention. She paused, hidden by trees at the corner of the drive, and tried to pierce the château's impassive walls with her eyes. All she perceived was their tranquility – like Bertrand's face with its mask of politeness. If his car were there she would go back to the village. She walked cautiously down the side path and saw that Jean's car sat alone. Wonderful! Her fear evaporated. She almost kissed the familiar metal before opening the gate and walking confidently towards his workroom. It was locked. Perhaps he was in the kitchen. She crossed the yard and found this empty. There was no Oedipus around though – confirmation that Bertrand was away, probably on business and not back till supper. Good. She looked for further signs. Three plates were drying on the side of the sink but the coffee pot was warm. All three had been there for lunch and someone had been in for a later brew. Two cups sat upturned. Dare she assume that it was Jean who had been back to the kitchen recently? There was a basket of vegetables on the floor – a normal evening reunion was planned. But Madame Estienne had not been in the garden when Amy walked past. She could be resting in her room off the passage behind the kitchen. Someone else to avoid.

Amy turned and gasped. Jean's coat was dumped over the trestle at the back of the kitchen. She gasped at the sudden normality, even security that sprang from the sight of it. She must find him. She climbed the steps to the guest room at the top of the tower. The winding stair reminded her how trapped she had been here before; she would be even more now, with her grown stomach. It would be ironic if Bertrand returned behind her again to see the results of that first time. She was sweating by the time she reached the door. Inside was more evidence of Jean, but not the man himself. She sat on the bed for a moment to recover her breath. Only a moment – she dared not wait. She would have to write a note and slip it under his studio door, telling him to contact her at the little hotel she'd stayed in with Sarah and Stephen. On the way downstairs she wondered about the gallery. No sound came from there but she pushed at the door which swung quietly open. The room was empty and showed signs of renovation: small repairs done to the walls, some repainting. Was this Jean's work? 'Back together' René had said, for the coming season. She felt another cold sweat and glanced at the door to Bertrand's studio at the far end. It was the only other place Jean could be. She walked across and put her ear to the wood. A chair scraped on the floor inside. She leapt back. Jean? Madame Estienne? Or might it be Bertrand? The sound of the chair being moved came again. She'd been heard. The escape door at the far end gaped in the distance. She could not move fast enough to reach it. Then the door to her right opened.

'Maman?'

'Jean!' she gasped, and almost fainted into his arms. He was amazed, not only at her sudden arrival but also by her size. He'd been remembering her as the sylph of last autumn. The shock made him abrupt.

'What are you doing here?'

'You didn't phone!'

'I was out of sorts.' He kept his face averted.

'You must come now or it'll all fall apart.' She too did not want to go into details.

'Yes. We'll go now. Do you have a car?'

'Yes. Hired.'

'Fine, mine needs a new battery.' He paused. 'Perhaps we could tow it to the village.'

How could such a trivial thought come into his mind when their future hung in the balance. Seeing her surprise he went on, 'Bertrand's not going to chase us – there's nothing he can actually do. We don't have to run like rabbits.'

'I think he could be quite violent – to me.'

'No. He's his old self again.'

'Because he's got you back?'

This time they were looking directly at each other and Jean's eyes told her more than she wanted to know.

'He thinks he's got you back,' she said more gently.

'He's wrong.' He looked at her tenderly at last. 'We'll go now. You must be tired. We'll find a hotel.'

They went up to the guest room to pack his things.

'And your mother?'

'I give up. We'll make our own family.'

'She'll be curious eventually.'

'Yes. I'll tell her I'm leaving.'

Madame Estienne was lace-making in her room and

thinking how easy life would be once all Jean's interests were back in Ivrez again. He *was* settling down so she would tell him that she would not visit him in Laon after all. She was too set in her ways. If he left, they would never see each other again. Then Jean's voice reached her from down the passageway. Bertrand must be back. But she could not hear the reply. If she could hear Jean, she'd certainly hear Bertrand. These walls were so thick. She got up and came to the open door where the second voice reached her.

'I could go and get the car; it's a few yards up the road. But I'd rather we went together.'

'I'll find you in the kitchen. I won't be long. But I must say good-bye.'

Madame Estienne was unable to make out the words, but the fact that Jean was talking to a woman was undeniable and her eyes filled with tears as she went back to her room. That woman had come to get him. If he left now they really would never see each other again.

It took a few minutes for Amy to find the few shirts and other clothes scattered about the room and put them into Jean's bag. Then she did as he had asked, returning through the gallery to the studio with his precious work inside. She locked the door, put the key in Jean's bag and went downstairs. Thankfully, all was quiet. In the kitchen she picked up Jean's jacket from the bench and waited. Then she heard footsteps outside. Bertrand was back. It changed everything and she moved into the passageway to be closer to Jean. But nothing followed. There were no more sounds. No dog either. She must have been mistaken, but still Jean did not come out of the far room. The door there was closed.

It was a long time for him to be with his mother. Perhaps he'd already said his goodbyes and gone out to his studio. He might have things there to pick up. Yes, he must have left before she came down. Amy went to the kitchen door. Dusk was falling. Perhaps that was why the quietness of the château had settled into something watchful. She was uneasy about emerging into the yard, yet waiting there only increased her fears. She *was* being watched – all her senses told her she was being watched. She pulled herself together. She would go straight for the car. Jean knew that was where she might be and once inside it she would be safe. She looked out at the courtyard – no dog so no master. As she crossed the yard, she saw a light on in Jean's studio. Yes, of course, that was where he was. She'd tell him to meet her outside the gate.

Bertrand's business in Auxerre had run into difficulties – always the way dealing with people he did not know. He anticipated all kinds of stupidity from them and his expectations showed. Well then, he'd leave it to André to arrange the transport. He had already been away from Ivrez too long and was anxious to know what Jean was up to. There was little traffic on the road on the way back, but even that irritated him. Needless to say, he had not brought Jean the new battery. Jean was the bait to bring Amy. Coming down the lane to the gallery, Bertrand saw a strange car – parked. He climbed out of his own to look more closely and could hardly believe it when he saw a sticker for a Laon garage in the rear window – only a few days since he'd given his story to René. 'It had all gone wrong for her,' he thought with satisfaction. 'Now, she'd picked up her skirts and come running for help.' It was the chance he'd planned so long for and he must be careful not to lose it.

There would be problems if she'd found Jean. Not likely though – he was tucked out of sight in Bertrand's studio and usually stayed engrossed until interrupted. The hiss of the tyres on the hired car, as Bertrand released the valves, was a pleasing sound. No car could move now except his own. Bertrand manoeuvred this closer to the turning and left it there with the dog in it, becoming impatient at the time it took his leaden feet to close the last few metres down the drive. At the gate he looked across the yard. The light was on in the kitchen. He went into Jean's old studio, turned on the light there and came out again. It gleamed invitingly through the window. Pressing himself against the wall as much as he could he approached the kitchen, but no – this wouldn't work. If she were there, she would see him. She would have time to get away. With an agility he didn't know he possessed he moved away to the other side of the studio door and concealed himself behind a buttress.

The moment Amy took a step inside she knew that this was a trick. The studio was no longer Jean's. Ground level lighting revealed sickening shapes. She must escape quickly, but the form she'd imagined watching her now appeared in the doorway.

Bertrand took his time shutting and locking the door. He turned and the light shining upwards produced a death mask of his face. It approached the weird mask that was her own face. One of his works stood jaggedly between them. This meeting was a twisted piece of theatre. But Bertrand seemed quite at home with the grotesque. His voice was hoarse.

'Do you remember what I said?'

She resisted him by saying nothing.

'You will never see Jean again. Do you hear. He doesn't want to see you. After tonight you'll never want to see him again either. I will change you.'

'Jean is waiting for me,' she said levelly.

'I could kill you,' he went on 'No one would know. No one has seen you arrive.'

'Jean has seen me!' she said emphatically, hoping to bring him to his senses. His response was the opposite of what she expected. He took hold of her.

'It was all a mistake,' he said intensely. He meant the invitation last summer. The sculpture fell over.

'You'll damage your work.'

'Not at all – it's about this.'

She held his gaze and, as he held her, her physical warmth provoked conflicting emotions. Surprised, his hold relaxed and she pushed past him to the door, searching for the key.

'Jean!' Her voice sank into the massive stones.

Bertrand's hand was on her mouth, stuffing in a rag – it tasted of oil. He tied her hands and left, turning out the light.

Jean's mother was making it difficult for him to walk out of the room. Her tears were genuine. He kept delaying, quietly cajoling her, persuading her, but she was not going to let him part on the terms he wished. Well, if she intended him to feel bad, he would respond by not caring. Feeling bad all the same, he eventually went into the kitchen, where he saw Bertrand splashing cold water on his face. Amy was not there, but the bag he had given her was. Jean was immediately alarmed.

'What's happened?'

Hoping his trembling had stopped, Bertrand straightened up and said, dismissively, 'A horsefly bite.'

'Where's Amy?' Jean barked, impatient with this ridiculous answer.

Bertrand regained control of himself and turned round. His incredulous look was convincing:

'Is she here?'

'Yes. I'm going of course.'

Bertrand shrugged his shoulders. Jean had come down too soon. He was in the way. Bertrand wasn't sure, now, how he could make this work out. He should have bundled Amy into the car ten minutes ago instead of stopping to recover from his own shock. With nothing more purposeful to do he put the kettle on the range in a show of normality.

'So there's bad feeling all round,' thought Jean. 'Too bad!'

Where was Amy? She'd said something about going for the car. That's where she'd be. He would go and find her. Out in the yard, he passed his old studio. Amy recognized his footsteps on the cobbles – they were too light to be Bertrand's. She struggled but could not spit out the gag and soon the footsteps faded. Jean put his things down by the gate, and paused. Something was wrong in the building behind him. He looked back, but could see nothing wrong. His jangled feelings were getting the better of him – he'd go to the car. But still he paused.

Bertrand in the kitchen waited in suspense, watching the figure by the gate. It was only a matter of time. How long would it be before Jean searched for her? And what would Bertrand do then? The moment he refused to hand the key over Jean would know. Bertrand felt sick. He'd be found out, he'd have gained nothing – no revenge – no satisfaction, only Jean's hatred. Now he could kill her. Hiding pitifully behind the door-frame, he watched the dim outline by the gate. It moved again.

It was coming over the yard, purposefully towards the studio. Bertrand watched, fascinated by the disaster about to unfold. Then Jean went into the lavatory. And there was the outside bolt that they'd never bothered to remove. Could he get across the yard before Jean came out? He forced himself to race across. In an instant he had driven the bolt home, overcoming its rust in a single effort. There was a cry from inside and the door rattled. There was no light inside – good. Bertrand stood panting, and brushed sweat from his eyes. He went back to the studio and hauled Amy out. She struggled. Jean could hear muffled cries. The gag came loose and she called his name. Horrified, he called back, his voice echoing. She heard and stopped struggling. He called again.

'Amy. Open this door.'

'I can't.'

She couldn't break free. If she didn't have a miscarriage it would be a miracle. She must wait for an opportunity. It was a battered old door; Jean must break his way out.

'Help me Jean,' she called as Bertrand pulled her away.

Going as slowly as she could, she allowed him to walk her through the gate, up the drive and to his car. Oedipus, baffled by being abandoned so close to home, freed her in the energy of his welcome. But she could not run. She was so tired she could barely stand. There was strong cord in the car. Bertrand bound her arms and tied her into the front seat. Then he turned his attentions to the dog, tying him to the back seat.

There would be nothing too messy – he would tip her into the quarry.

22

Jean gasped. Amy's cry struck like a punch to the solar plexus. His partner was dragging away his wife. Killing her in the woods. He hurled himself at the door but the bolt held. He threw himself at it again – still nothing broke. He stopped and listened. There was no sound at all now, no car starting up. He'd noticed the Renault wasn't there so they couldn't be far away. He must get out. Attacking the door within the small space was not easy, but after some minutes the frame pulled away from the wall, and night air filtered through. Bits of stone from the roof hit him as they fell. He would not be much use under a heap of rubble. But the wood was splitting. He placed one foot on the side of the lavatory and with an almighty thrust burst through. The doorframe collapsed, and the front walls gave way, crumbling behind him in a neat cartoon action. But Jean was uninjured. He made for the gate. There was no sign of Bertrand, only a slight whiff of petrol. Five minutes earlier and he would have collided with the car as it made its way down the track. Now it was too dark to make out anything. The stony path showed no tyre marks; crickets were chirping and the bushes looked undisturbed. Should he follow the path to the quarry on a hunch that could be wrong? If it were right, he would be one man against man and dog. And Amy might need medical help. The Police Station was an impossible eight kilometres away. One of the officers, though, lived close by. Damn his useless car. Jean ran up the lane into the bewildering dark.

Bertrand was forcing the Renault along the footpath to the quarry. The jolting, the dark, the slash of leaves against the chassis, Bertrand's fixed expression – the ride was something out of time. Tied to her seat Amy experienced again what it was to be abused. It was always unexpected, crashing into normality. That was its horror; the injustice of it. And now there might be no way out. She must make Bertrand see where his own interests lay.

'Why ruin your life?' She implored.

His grim expression told her it was already ruined.

'Your work's never been better,' she insisted. 'They're talking about you in Paris.'

He was silent. Would the truth get through? 'You can't expect happiness as well.'

His deafness continued.

'And what about Ivrez? It'll be remembered for the worst...' This was not a thought she could complete.

'It will be remembered,' he replied, his voice low and forced. It was a start.

The car lurched over a stone and Amy was thankful for the baby that she was strapped in. Reasoning was getting nowhere; she would have to barter.

'Once the baby's born I can go. I get my flat back in October. Can't you wait till then? If I go Jean will settle down. He could forget me.'

'If only she would go,' he had said to Monique. But when Jean was a father would he slip back into the life he'd had before? It wasn't likely. Anyway, now Jean knew the worst about him there was no going back. If she weren't so stupid she would realise this. He'd been tipped out of his life. All he could do was end on his own terms. His anger would blast them all to smithereens. Then let the police come.

Despair blinded him, but not enough for him to make

the mistake of driving them both into the quarry. On the grassy plateau he got out, taking the torch to cut open a crack in the dark, and edged carefully forward until he could see the crumbling outline near his feet. A clump of thorn clung to the edge. He leaned the torch against the bush. It shone through the twigs, turning them into flame – a sign. Then he stumbled back to the car. Amy had found the knot in the rope and was twisting it in her pinioned fingers. Bertrand's hands brushed hers aside, but his clumsy fumbling made no progress either – he'd tied it too tight. Swearing, he leaned across the dashboard for his knife. As he attacked the knot the blade slipped and jabbed her through her clothing. She felt the warm blood on her skin and wondered why she felt no pain. Bertrand had cut the knot and pulled on the lasso which held her round the shoulders. She was no longer a person, but a bundle of rags to be thrown as far from him as possible. Desperately, Amy clung to her seat, conscious now of blood seeping into her coat. As her grip gave way she grabbed the cut end of the rope and managed to hook it over the steering wheel, hanging on with both hands. Bertrand pulled until the wheel broke off. Oedipus was barking frantically, frustrated by his leash.

Finally dragged out of the car, Amy dropped into a foetal position and Bertrand discovered he couldn't lift her. His bulk worked against him. Even bending was difficult but he managed to get his hands under her armpits and drag her. He reached the bush, and paused to balance himself. In the car, the dog's frenzy broke him free and he leapt out to help. His jaws went for Amy and his body caught his master straightening up. Bertrand tried to regain his balance but he was too near the edge. He fought desperately to step back onto firmer ground but the earth kept crumbling under his feet, throwing him forwards, and his flailing arms grasped nothing but air. As he went over into the quarry it was not his life but the ironies in it that flashed before him. It was his heavy body, not hers, that thumped and bounced against the rocks, and broke as it tumbled down the side. He was always the scapegoat, the outcast – his hopes were always mocked. She had perverted his life. The dog was shocked. He had never heard Bertrand cry out like that. He forgot Amy and ran whining along the edge looking for a way into the gully. She lay where she was, semi-conscious.

When the car headlamps lit up the scene the police saw her on the ground, her arms still round her knees. Conscious of rescue she began to shake convulsively. Jean knelt beside her, fearing that whatever he did would only hurt her more. He put the blanket round her and helped some hot liquid into her mouth. Her teeth chattered too violently for her to speak. The whining of the dog below had led the police towards a slope where they could scramble down. There they found Bertrand's unmistakable body. He was lying on his back, his arms spread-eagled. His head was cracked open and his eyes still expressed outrage. An attendant bent to smooth the lids carefully down. Jean's silent self-recrimination over Amy was interrupted when the stretcher with the giant figure of his partner on it was carried towards them, silhouetted in the headlights. The group negotiated the cars and the inert body was slowly transferred into a white vehicle. How could he have let this happen? Then another stretcher was brought and Amy was carefully lifted onto it. Jean followed dumbly to the second ambulance, holding his breath as the precious bundle was lowered and passed inside.

As Jean went to climb in with her, a medic he passed said quietly:

'Monsieur Estienne, Monsieur Barenton is alive.'

Relief turned to horror as he climbed in. He could only forgive a corpse. Inside, Amy had fallen asleep. The medic checked her pulse and was satisfied. Through the partition, Jean could see over the driver's shoulder that they were following Bertrand's ambulance in a grizzly procession, slowly negotiating the potholes in the track leading to the village. When the familiar houses appeared, he imagined everyone drawn to their windows, watching them. It was unbearable. He spoke to the medic.

'Will she be all right?'

'She's not in any danger.'

'I'll come to the hospital very soon, but can you let me out here? My mother's all alone...' and his voice trailed off helplessly.

23

He watched as the ambulances disappeared down the lane. The driver of the one in front had picked up what speed he could and bursts of the klaxon reached Jean as the vehicle negotiated bends. Then it faded into the distance. He was standing beside the same policeman's house that he had come to for help a few hours before. Now it was the village taxi he needed to take him home.

The second ambulance reached the autoroute. Amy woke, eyes wide. There were sensations in her abdomen, which she had been taught to expect in another few weeks: an urgent tightening and relaxing of the muscles.

'The baby's coming,' she said.

'How early?'

'Six weeks.'

'No need to worry then. It should be all right,' the medic assured her. 'Breathe steadily, keep calm.'

'Where's Jean?' she asked suddenly.

'He went to see his mother.'

'His mother!' she wailed. Nothing had changed. He had gone again.

'He didn't know the baby was coming. His mother's all alone. He'll come to the hospital as soon as we phone him.'

'Of course.' She thought, too, of another. 'And Bertrand?'

The medic paused.

'Not well,' he admitted, 'but your job is to relax. Try not to worry. Keep breathing deeply.'

Instead of going directly home, Jean asked the driver

to return to the quarry. The dog was there of course, sitting faithfully by the car that Bertrand had trashed. With difficulty Oedipus was cajoled into the new vehicle and the hired driver took them back to the gallery. Such a short time away, and such changes; the building that loomed into view was no longer the same. Once inside, he busied himself numbly – food for Oedipus – a bite for himself. Then he steeled himself for a painful talk with his mother. But she was asleep, oblivious. An innocent world still existed. He left her undisturbed and went to phone the hospital. A night nurse who had just come on duty answered. She knew nothing of what lay behind Amy's arrival.

'Everything's fine,' was all she knew.

'I'll be in first thing tomorrow.'

The final task was to phone Marcia Chabot, then wait for morning. Sleep was impossible, he said to himself as he lay down on the guestroom bed and slept.

Next morning his mother was dumbfounded that it was he, not Bertrand, in the kitchen. Details were out of the question.

'Bertrand's had an accident,' he said. 'I'm going to the hospital.'

'I thought you'd run back to that minx,' she said cuttingly.

'Mother. Not now. Bertrand's had an accident.'

She looked keenly at him and realised he was serious.

'I'll be at the hospital a lot and can't leave you here on your own. Marcia would like you to stay. And she'll find a home in the village for the dog.'

While her bag was being packed Madame Estienne began to get some sense of the size of the catastrophe.

'Where *is* Bertrand?'

'Auxerre hospital.'

For one more time Jean was dependent on the hired car. The driver was a good-natured fellow and allowed him to fix his own to the back with the tow rope. They edged out from the track, Jean steering the Citroen through the window-flap and turning the car onto the lane. There, fifty metres up, was Amy's hired car, lopsided on its deflated tyres. He groaned and called to the driver:

'Can you stop there?'

The driver looked at him sceptically.

'Can't tow two.'

But from the sticker in the window Jean gleaned a telephone number before they continued on their way. This was the second strange cortège in twenty-four hours to wind past the eyes of village windows. One by one, Jean dealt with the problems: his mother would be looked after, the dog was handed over, arrangements were made to pick up the other car while a new battery was put in his own. Jean could, at last, confront the disasters.

The limited facilities in Montargis meant that both casualties had been taken to Auxerre, entailing a longer drive. Inevitably, tales about the two admissions had begun to circulate and the nurse at reception raised her eyebrows thoughtfully as the clock ticked on to 11 a.m. The man cited as next of kin to both patients had still not arrived. Could he not face this? It was not long after, though, that Jean found a space in the car park and, for the first time in his life, entered a hospital. He gave his name and the receptionist left him there, before returning with a senior nurse.

'This is a difficult time for you,' the Sister began sympathetically.'

Jean looked up sharply.

'No, your wife is well. She may even carry the baby to term.'

217

'Which ward?'

Why was this woman holding him up? But her eyes continued to hold him as she went on: 'Mr Barenton is in Intensive Care, in a coma, on machine support.' Without saying, 'He may die at any moment,' the nurse attempted to convey this message.

'But I must see my wife!'

'Obstetrics. Ward 6.'

Jean charged off.

Soon after arrival Amy's contractions had stopped and she was sleeping when Jean was ushered to the bedside. Her arm where the knife had struck her was lightly bandaged. In sleep her face was calm and a better colour. He sat down and let her presence restore sense and calm to his mind. Everything might be well after all. In a day or so, they would be able to run away, back to the honest world of Laon. Then he heard a baby cry beyond the curtain. Looking out he saw a nurse carry an infant from its cot and towards the next bed. Jean looked at her as alarm bells started to ring in his head.

'Is that expected ... for my wife?'

'Maybe, maybe not.'

'But it's too soon,' he protested.

'Contractions began last night, but no serious labour. The waters haven't broken.' The nurse disappeared behind the neighbouring curtain but Jean knew what she was talking about. He sat and willed their baby to hold on until they were away from this mess. Amy continued sleeping and the Sister's earlier comments about the state Bertrand was in forced their way into his thoughts. Again he came out from their screen to find a nurse.

'How long do you think she'll sleep?'

'She had a disturbed night so we gave her light medication. Come back in an hour.'

Jean forced himself to ask where to find Intensive Care, then set off for Ward 30, through the maze of passageways, barely noting the directions. Twice he became lost. Past reading had come into his mind; some points which, last autumn, he had dismissed as irrelevant. A premature baby might not develop properly – there could be malfunctions. The baby might not even survive birth. He burned with anger against that egotistical man. Lifting his head to take air and suppress his feelings, he saw the sign for Ward 28. Not far to go now to the child-murderer.

Outside Intensive Care, he gave his name curtly. The young man on duty was not surprised.

'You understand the seriousness of the injuries?'

'Yes,' Jean replied, his tone betraying impatience that Bertrand was alive at all.

'As well as a broken leg, broken ribs and other minor fractures, the skull is fractured. There's a danger of bleeding in the brain; we're keeping this under close watch. We've carried out a tracheostomy for his breathing and we'll x-ray the spine as soon as possible. Severe falls with head injury mean that neck fracture is also likely. Once he's stabilised we'll carry out the x-ray. Any movement at the moment could be fatal.'

Fury could not resist this onslaught. Jean nodded more calmly.

'You may stay as long as you wish.'

He nodded again and pushed at the swing door. Inside, the beds were arranged in two rows, facing each other. Most of the mounds on them were still but one tossed restlessly and a nurse by its side pulled the curtain closed. The other curtains were pulled back and Jean could see nurses quietly attending to drips, and to machines which wheezed and thumped rhythmically. There was an atmosphere of tense tranquillity. Jean felt

219

that any sudden movement from him would send shock waves rippling through the air to strike dead any of the fragile bodies around him. None of the nurses paid any attention to him as he stood and looked for his ex-partner. How could one bundle of tubes be distinguished from another? But Jean walked towards the still figure whose proportions reminded him of the man he had spent much of his life with. He stood at the end of the bed, looking at the name on the card, engulfed in sadness. Impossible to imagine it would end like this. Bertrand was on his back with a tube emerging from his throat. It was connected to one of the asthmatic machines and prevented from tearing his neck by straps tied around the board he lay on. His head was bandaged on the right side. The dressing was perfectly white and arranged with a perfect neatness, which only served to accentuate how damaged the man under it was. The left eye was black and swollen, the cheek black too and scratched under large bruises. His eyes were closed and his lips and nostrils were clearly playing no part at all in the rise and fall of the blanket which moved in time with the automatic pace of the machine. There were two drips, one a red substance and one clear. A nurse came over. She smiled briefly at Jean, then checked the saline drip and the blood transfusion. After this, she lifted each of Bertrand's eyelids, shone a small light in and studied what she saw. She turned and spoke quietly:

'It might help if you speak to him. There's a chance a familiar voice could wake him.'

The way Bertrand looked was so totally unexpected that Jean found it hard to equate this dummy with a man who might respond to a voice. Bertrand was putting on a very good imitation of death. He lay on its very edge. One thing the nurse did not realise, of course, was that Jean's voice might be the last Bertrand wished to hear and the one to send him fully into the next world. That would be best. Once the nurse had gone he moved closer and spoke as loudly as he dared:

'Can you hear me, Bertrand?'

Could he – that lost soul? He spoke again, more quietly for the sake of the others in the ward.

'Can you hear me?' The words hung foolishly in the air.

A little saliva was trickling out of the side of Bertrand's mouth. Jean could not bear to watch the liquid dribbling over his face and picked up a towel from the cabinet. As he wiped the moisture away he could feel the warmth that made the difference between life and death.

'Why did you do it?' The question was hoarsely whispered and he paused, half-afraid Bertrand might reply. He did not, so Jean went on, more insistently. 'Why? Why destroy all our lives?'

The blanket continued with its rise and fall. This was the only response and, having no more to say, Jean went to look at the report hanging at the foot of the bed. It was incomprehensible so he sat again in the chair by the bed, watching for movement. The first nurse had spoken of spine injury. Might Bertrand be paralysed? If he recovered consciousness would Jean come back and nurse him? Or would he abandon him? Either version of the future was equally impossible. Bertrand had, indeed, destroyed all their lives. Better not to think; better to respond to the moment only. One of the nurses was seated at the desk. Jean went over and mentioned the dribbling.

'Thank you,' she replied quietly. 'We can do something about that.' Jean went back to the bed, soon followed by the nurse who pulled out another tube attached to the wall and placed its metal end in Bertrand's mouth. A gentle sucking noise followed. Then she removed the tube, re-attached it to the wall, and returned to the desk. Bertrand was totally de-humanised. There was nothing left but this shell. Jean sat with it and the background sighing and thumping of the ventilator. No one came to wheel Bertrand away for x-rays. After an hour had passed Jean got up and left.

Perhaps the reason his legs were trembling was that he hadn't eaten that morning. He took a brief detour, appreciating the low hubbub in the visitors' canteen. On eventually pushing open the doors to Ward 6, there were the more welcome sounds of life. Amy, though, was not in her bed. Robotically, he sought out someone in uniform.

When the mild sedative had worn off, Amy woke to find the curtain closed round the bed and a midwife and a nurse considering her notes.

'Your husband was in,' the nurse said as she stirred. 'He'll be back soon.'

'Thank you,' she said, grateful not to be alone in this place, and too sleepy to think of where Jean might have gone. She did not know Bertrand was at the other end of the building. To the staff it even seemed she had forgotten the events of last night as she happily took from them a weak cup of coffee. The pleasant-looking midwife came forward.

'We're going to see where the baby has got to.'

A simple examination followed. The midwife was pleased.

'The right way round – head down and on its way into the vagina.'

The baby's heart beat and her own pulse throbbed at their intended speeds and her blood pressure had come down to normal. But the waters still had not broken and there had been no further contractions.

'Just to be sure, we're going to take you to another department. We have a new machine we're very proud of. It can tell us more of what is – or is not – going on.'

They were on their way back when Jean returned to Ward 6. He could not make much sense of the brief message he was given except for the fact that Amy had been moved to another department. He sat down and held back the tears. An emergency. He always missed the crises – punishment for having abandoned her. Events now had their own momentum in which he did not figure at all. The baby was dead and all he could do was stew in his guilt-ridden loneliness.

'Hello Jean.'

Amy had returned in the wheelchair, overjoyed to find him there and it was the nurse who noticed his withdrawn look.

'You'll be glad to know, Monsieur Estienne, that all is well with your wife and the baby.'

She saw the hope rekindle and turned back to Amy.

'If the waters don't break in the next twenty-four hours, we'll discharge you.'

Jean leaped at this.

'If it's safe, that would be best, wouldn't it darling? We can go back to Laon.'

For the baby, of course, this would be best, but Laon was not a place Amy could enthuse about and she was glad the nurse had more to say.

'A useful way to pass the time would be to have a bath – not too hot, just to relax you. Perhaps your husband would help.'

As she leaned on him Amy felt Jean's distress. For her, at the moment, it was easy to do as she was told and put all recent events, Bertrand and René, out of her mind. She had someone else to concentrate on and tried to bring Jean in from the cold.

'Hello, lover.'

'Hello.' He tried to smile. 'Are you in pain?'

'No. Everything's going to be all right.'

He helped her undress and supported her down the steps into the warm water of the sunken bath, with her injured arm resting on the side.

'Is that painful?' he asked again, anxiously.

'No – just a little throbbing.'

'Would you like a wash?'

'Love one.'

Jean reached for the soap and began the tender ministration. Her belly had grown so much since he'd last seen it. He should not have left Laon. He made amends by gently washing its smooth curve.

'You've been shaved.'

'Yes – too soon maybe.'

As the nurse had promised, the warmth was relaxing. Jean blinked. To keep awake he kept talking.

'Can you feel anything happening?'

'Not a thing.'

'And there's no pain?' he asked for the third time.

'Nothing at all.' Amy yawned as she spoke.

'Don't go to sleep,' he protested and his voice sounded distant to him. His ears kept submerging under waves of drowsiness. The heaviness in his body could not be resisted and Jean keeled over on the tiles. Amy, helpless in the bath, had no option but to press the emergency buzzer. The nurse who came in immediately diagnosed emotional exhaustion and treated it lightly. There was no point drawing Amy's attention to the patient in Ward 30.

'Not the first time that's happened.'

After some coffee, Jean was sent home.

'We'll contact you immediately if there's any change.'

Passing the main reception desk again Jean caught

the end of a conversation between a nurse and a young policewoman.

'I'm afraid it isn't possible for you to see either patient. One is in Intensive Care and the other may go into labour at any moment. I'll find someone to give you information.'

He hurried past. The awfulness was everywhere, waiting. And he was still dead tired. Once in the car, he pushed the seat back and, thankfully, slept for some time.

The château was weird without Bertrand or his mother – not even the dog. There was no comfort in the silence. To escape it, Jean swung the television out from its niche and cooked a simple supper against its babble. He had turned on what he thought might be a serious channel and discovered another news feature on space travel: the crew of Apollo 13 were preparing for launch. The commentator's excited speculations – how long would it be before human beings were walking on Mars? – burst in on Jean's sensitised mind. Weightless bodies floating in a decompression chamber took on another meaning. Bertrand was quite literally between heaven and earth. And Amy and himself had been pulled off their feet, juggled in some cosmic free fall. How long would this last? And how would they land? It was too much to hope they could escape back to Laon as though nothing had happened. These were events they would never forget. And the police were involved. Soon it would be the newspapers. The probing would not spare any of them. And the baby? 'What baby?' replied his depression.

Jean cleared the table and went outside, out of habit, as the place to settle after dinner needs. He passed his old studio with a shudder. He would never work there again. The evening was still and quiet – very beautiful

– the kind that once had brought him his happiest thoughts. Now, though, he was brought face to face with another change, the crumbled lavatory. There wasn't even a privy. Absorbed in misery, he wandered along the moat, the self-pity repeating in his mind. Standing exposed, urinating into the moat, a laugh broke out of him. It swelled over the fields. Each time it subsided the absurdity struck again. 'There wasn't even a privy!' His cackling bordered on hysteria, and anyone hearing him would have thought he had cracked under the strain. Sitting crouched, gasping inanely, he looked across the yard to the good old home that Ivrez had been over the years. He saw doors that needed repairing, the guttering along the roof that they'd always meant to improve – and, of course, the terrible lack of sanitation. Jean's travels had enlarged his mind. 'A change of approach is needed here,' he thought. Investment is needed to make the place a bit more in line with the modern world. Then he checked himself. He was planning as though Bertrand were dead.

Amy was enjoying a light supper. It would have been more delicious shared with Jean but at least the curtain round the bed was pulled open. There was friendly chat in the ward and Amy hid her concerns. Her waters had broken so she was on track for the birth. Everyone around her was cheerful, supportive. The optimism that was beaming down on her was infectious. Then the nurse came in with fruit salads and more light-hearted quips. Amy toyed with some unfamiliar yellow berries among the grapes.

'They are mirabelles, from down south.'

'Fruit often has a pregnant look doesn't it – round, bulging...'

'...bursting with seed,' agreed the nurse, picking up the used dishes. 'You speak very good French.'

'Thank you.'

'You must have lived here for years.'

'Eight months, but quite a lot has happened.'

The compliment comforted her but the laugh that followed resulted, inevitably, in one more trip to the loo.

'I really feel very fit,' Amy said as she leaned on the offered arm. 'I've done nothing but sleep all afternoon.'

Then she gasped. The baby had stood up and punched her in the spine. The nurse was interested.

'Where was it?'

'In the back.'

'Ah, we could be in business.'

With Jean's return, the night that followed became their strangest tryst ever. There were times when Amy needed holding under the elbows as she crouched stretching down, to give space for the contractions to do their work. There were quiet intervals with time to talk, though this was difficult as there was so much neither wished to talk about. As much as possible Amy snatched moments of sleep, which she was told would help her later on. Sometimes words of encouragement were needed when a more urgent contraction arrived and Amy rocked patiently with it on all fours. Urine was tested and she was given barley sugar. As the hours went by Jean and Amy were increasingly conscious of and fascinated by this small creature's journey out towards the open world. Sometimes Jean was brushed aside as gloved hands thrust their way into the cavities to keep track of events. No breakfast was allowed but, not long after its aroma tantalised them, a series of muscular tidal waves took Amy over and demanded total attention. Her plan to give birth upright was obviously impossible.

227

But at least, since the child was smaller than a full-term baby, the final labour was not as difficult as it could have been. Lying on her back she could not see a thing, but felt the relief as the head was guided clear and emerged beyond the bony structures. Another push and the body followed, with a downy covering over the skin. The sight gave Jean one more throb of fear. Did this mean it was malformed?

'Don't worry,' said the nurse, 'it's normal for pre-term babies,' and fear could be forgotten at last when the lungs produced a cry.

The infant was cleaned, wrapped in warm towels and placed in the mother's arms. It was a boy. He was not chubby at all and the lack of fat gave him a curiously adult look, though the small facial features showed he still had some way to develop. After a few minutes with them he was whisked away to the warmth of the incubator.

24

There was anger in the village.

'First that girl seduces Jean, then she kills his partner' ... 'How could a slip of a girl, eight months pregnant, kill a great fellow like that?'

Comments like these ricocheted between those who saw their livelihoods threatened. Nor could they understand the sudden collapse of the friendship. After all, Jean had been quite content before last summer. Why should he suddenly go for a girl – a stranger at that – and bring about such a disaster? As usual, most of this was discussed in the Post Office and Monique listened from behind the counter, frustrated that she could not put them right on the facts. Nor could she put the police right in their enquiries.

The interview room had been set up at the back of the hotel – the only available space in the village – and Inspector Gérard Dupré, not a local man, set about the enquiries. Monique received her summons with more than a few qualms. It would have been bad enough to have been found out in a passionate, ongoing affair. She could not allow a dead old one, which had ended with her being discarded, to be wafted around like a bad smell.

'How well did you know Bertrand Barenton?'

'Not well at all.'

'I believe you went to see him a couple of times this winter.'

'Just once, and it was to see Madame Estienne.'

'But you saw both men quite recently.'

Monique paused to consider her safety.

'Yes, that's right.'

'Were they still friends?'

'So it seemed.'

'Did Jean appear uneasy?'

'No, he was very relaxed.'

'What did you talk about?'

This time she did not pause: 'Local gossip – bringing him up to date.'

'Were you a special friend?'

'No.'

'Then why bother to go?'

'I was very curious.'

Her smile was confiding, suggesting that the complexity of these men's lives would have been enough to tempt anyone's curiosity. Luckily for her, the police had plenty of evidence of Jean's virility; they did not need to pry too closely and Gérard Dupré found that he just did not want to.

'And what about Bertrand? Did he join in the gossip?'

'No – he was listening, but as though from a distance. But then he always was a bit moody. It was nothing unusual.'

'He said nothing to make you think him capable of murder?'

How could she put it, without feeling that she was blackening his character? But yes, she had felt him capable of violence. 'Well, as I was leaving ... he suggested ... he said he wanted to frighten her ... away.'

'Why tell you?'

'He seemed to want to confide in someone. Perhaps I just happened to be there.'

Policeman's instinct sensed this was not all, but Gérard left it at that. The crime of passion, which had backfired, was quite straightforward. No one else was implicated.

*   *   *

Bertrand had still not wakened and he was moved to a neurosurgical ward which Jean refused to visit. There was nothing he could do, he protested, and it was hard enough listening to nurses' reports about Bertrand while thinking all the time that his state was solely the result of the terrible thing he had done. The baby would need the incubator for about a month and, for a few days, Jean was staying with acquaintances in Auxerre.

'What name would you like for him?' Amy asked.

He smiled wrily.

'Nearly all French men are called Jean. Jean-something.'

'Yes,' she said non-committally, and he sensed that she had no great attachment to the name. It came to his mind that, anyway, he had no family traditions to hand down.

'What names have you thought of?'

'Édouard, maybe. Or is it too flowery? There's "Michel" – that goes with anything. What name would *you* like?'

It seemed to Jean that either of the two she'd already mentioned would crystallise the identity of the new personality. Eventually, after all, it would be the child who would make the name, not the other way round. A month ago he would have left the decision to her. Now, he felt that this was the wrong thing to do.

'I prefer Édouard. It's a good name for a painter.'

'Yes, it is,' she smiled warmly, glad that this was a joint venture and adding, light-heartedly, 'He can shorten it to Eddie if he decides to be a decorator.'

After the intravenous feed, Amy held his face to her breast, as instructed, and squeezed out a little milk for him to get the scent of it, and of her. His mouth opened and he tried to suck. Holding him and talking to him occupied all of Amy's time for as long as he remained

231

comfortable outside the incubator. It was, though, less easy now for her to block out recent events. She might be engrossed in encouraging Eddie when a flashback of the quarry, sensations of being dragged over grass, would come back to her. Jean's nightmare, too, played at the edges of his visits. Eddie was progressing well, yet when he was returned to his bed and became again a wired-up little man in his special unit, it reminded Jean of the man at the other side of the hospital. It was as though he were living in light and darkness at the same time.

Bertrand's condition was grave but not hopeless. The x-rays confirmed a fracture in the neck, yet tests on his reflexes showed there was no paralysis. The spinal cord was intact and it was the damage under the skull which threatened his life. Twenty-four hours after his arrival he became restless and, when the small light was shone into his eyes, it was found that the left pupil was larger than the right, and increasingly slow to react, while the pupil of the right did contract. The fracture had caused bleeding, which was affecting the left eye. With a protective collar round his neck, it was possible to drill small holes in his skull and drain away the blood – a fragile hope, yet all that was possible. Bertrand weathered the operation and his condition improved. It was possible for him to breathe without the ventilator. He did not wake but he became quiet. The appearance of his face suggested local nerve damage, which might, in time, recover. Finite boundaries began to be placed round his condition and a prognosis was possible. If he woke he would eventually be discharged, either home or, if there were substantial brain damage, into life-long care. His coma had now lasted ten days and the longer he was unconscious the more likely it was that, when he woke, they would find that the damage was irreversible.

The report drove Jean entirely away from the hospital and back to work, tackling the assembly of the sculpture for Mr Perrachan. Amy and Eddie would be out in three weeks and then they could clear off for good. Three weeks was all he needed, and once the commission was delivered he would receive a year's income. Bertrand deserved to be abandoned.

'We'll be able to go back to Laon,' he said to Amy over the phone. 'Rent a house – bring Mother.'

'Yes,' she said non-committally, 'and Semilly would be nearer your work.'

Jean hired a portaloo, had it hidden in the moat behind the outdoor studio, which he did not unlock and worked round the clock to finish their means of escape.

By the end of the second week, the gossip in the Post Office at Ivrez had become more resigned.

'They built that place out of nothing. Put so much into it.'

'Fifteen years – feels like they've always been here.'

'We've done well out of them.'

'But it was a difficult relationship. Jean always looked imprisoned. Until this last time he came back.'

Monique attended to their letters and dropped in the occasional remark. They did not need her opinion and as the days went by the subject mattered less and less to her. Gérard Dupré was a charming man – all the village had taken to him. She had spoken to him several times on an equal footing, forwarding his messages from the Post Office, and now he was in the habit of having lunch with her and her father. No one was surprised when they were seen out together. They made a handsome couple.

'It's an ill-wind...' was the new line of gossip.

Marcia Chabot heard it from the mother of Pierre, the boy who dug her garden at weekends. She, too, felt the relief that the recent past could, for a moment, be obliterated by good news.

25

In the last quarter of her life Marcia was in a position to choose for herself which corners of existence she should devote her time to, perhaps even to reshape a little. She and Alice were from the same generation and opposite poles of experience. Before the recent disaster their friendship had brought each a new perspective on life and Marcia was the only person in the world who knew of Alice's early experiences. Now, the unfolding of events in Auxerre came to their attention in daily bulletins which never got easier for Alice to hear, even though the social filter tried to suggest practical answers. What would become of Bertrand, alive but brain dead? Ivrez could be sold and the money put in trust so that, if he woke, he could afford special care for the rest of his vegetative life. It was terrible, just terrible. She would have to stay near him and visit him, even if he never woke. Visit him daily – make up for her son's betrayal. Bertrand, she decided, was more of a son to her now than Jean who had finished 'the bank' as she thought of it and was up in Laon discussing its installation. When he returned she would have to move back with him, for the time being, to the gallery while he arranged its sale. But she would not leave the village. She would stay where she was known for herself rather than as her son's appendage. Each time she visited the village stores – which she was able to do now on foot – she made a point of talking about Bertrand's need of her.

This recovering strength was also applied to straightening

the wilderness of Marcia's extensive garden, this morning in charge of Pierre who was cutting the grass from around the fruit trees. Easter was past and the sun was giving out real heat at last. Alice realised its strength as the hour moved on to midday – time to prepare lunch before Marcia's return from town. An exchange of hand waves passed between her and Pierre and she returned to the house.

Cold lunch did not take long to arrange. She straightened up, cast an approving glance through the large windows at the re-emerging garden, and opened the door to the hall to read the paper in the living room. Sounds came to her that told her Marcia was back. She was talking, on the phone perhaps. Then came something unmistakable. A baby cried. Alice closed the door and, looking for an escape, went back to the window.

Amy helped Eddie find the teat again and he was soon quiet.

'He takes the breast well,' she said, as pleased as if he were running the four-minute mile. Each sign that he was developing normally brought overwhelming happiness.

'Yes, he's a normal baby,' Marcia said, reassuringly level-headed. His features, too, were normal: the usual snub nose and button chin. Although not plump, he had gained weight and grown to the appropriate size. All babies have blue eyes but Amy, of course, saw Jean in their thoughtful expression. Feeding over, including an iron-and-vitamin syrup, she put him back in the carry-cot. It had to be done.

'Time for introductions. I'll follow in a few minutes.'

'All right, my dear. I'll leave the kitchen door open, so you'll know which one it is.'

Alice had begun to make herself useful again, cleaning the sink, when Marcia came in, carrying an unmistakably modern cot, its plastic cover brightly decorated with pictures of rabbits and bears. She made a space for it on the table.

'Well, Alice, we have someone for you.'

'My ears work when I need them, you know.' She did not turn round.

'Good. So you heard Édouard calling for his lunch?'

'Édouard – that's fancy.'

'No fancier than Estienne. Call him Eddie.'

Alice washed her hands and turned reluctantly toward the garish cot. She couldn't abide plastic and its presence in front of her confirmed her opinion that Jean's woman was a pernicious influence. Still, she did what Marcia demanded, walked towards it and leant over. Eddie fixed his blue eyes on the new face, gazed shortsightedly for a few seconds and yawned. In those seconds Alice's life ticked into a new century. Then she looked up at Marcia watching.

'Aye, they have a way with them. Are the groceries in the car?'

'Yes, they are, but don't you trouble.'

To escape inquisition though, and accidental embarrassment in the hall, she went via the garden door to fetch some of the packages. Soon after, Amy came into the kitchen.

'She's fled,' said Marcia. 'But she's happy.'

'That's good,' Amy replied cautiously, wondering whether Marcia had the right interpretation. 'You'll need the table for lunch. Could I put the cot over here?'

'Yes, my dear. He'll be comfortable there.' Amy cleared away a few books and moved the bed containing the now sleeping infant to a table at the side of the room. Alice came in with the bags. Glancing quickly at her,

237

Amy was pleased to see how well she looked. She was about to speak when she noticed Pierre standing by the door, startled by the new company. He sat on the step and took off his caked shoes.

'I won't need lunch today Madame Chabot,' he called awkwardly over his shoulder. 'Mum wants me to pick something up from the village.'

'Oh, that's all right, Pierre,' Marcia said, slightly surprised. 'Will you be back this afternoon?'

'Yes, I should think so,' he said shyly, aware that this was not a private conversation, and hurried to get his ordinary shoes on. 'Grass is nearly cut now.'

'Oh, that's good. You've been a great help.'

He blushed at the public praise, so Marcia turned away.

'Let's sit down,' and Pierre slipped away, down the path.

'Has he gone because of me?' Amy asked.

'A boy that age hasn't time for any strange woman,' Marcia replied, adding dismissively, 'He doesn't know who you are.' Amy got up, feeling she was, thankfully – like her son – just another ordinary person, and helped Marcia and Alice to the water they might need with the wine.

'Hello, Madame Estienne,' she said gently, 'What do you think of Eddie?'

'Babies are all much the same, don't you think?'

In the pause that followed Alice felt social pressures and, contrary to her rebuff, suddenly pushed cheese towards her daughter-in-law. Their eyes met without hostility.

'Well, well. Call him Eddie,' Alice went on. 'That's what they call Édipe now, at the farm.'

This was normal conversation. Amy picked up on it quickly.

238

'Is he settled?'

'Yes, chasing rabbits – seems fine. Bertrand hadn't paid much attention to him, you know, the last months, and the children love him.'

No blame against Amy was implied for Bertrand neglecting his dog. Alice was more pleased over having a grandchild than she chose to say. Bertrand's state was appalling, Amy thought, and it was even more appalling that, if he recovered – even partially – the police might charge him with attempted murder. She and Jean would be called upon to testify. All this would have to be faced eventually but here, for the moment, they were enjoying less turbulent waters. While Bertrand lay in his deep sleep the world continued its ruthless process of change and reshaping.

As it happened Pierre had seen the cot. He had guessed who the stranger was and could not sit down with the enemy of the village. Marcia too, he thought, would lose friends if she kept up these eccentric whims. But he did not tell his mother when he reached home. He had his own preoccupations. As he peddled away his concerns were with quite another woman. Monique had been a star in his firmament all his sixteen-year-old life. For two years his spare time jobs had included faithfully running errands for her shop. Now she was going to leave and he could not persuade himself that she would come back.

26

The morning was as ordinary as any other. Breakfast was over; so, too, the doctors' rounds – routine activity in the hospital continued at a slower pace. A nurse came into a side ward and noticed that the air was stale so she opened the window a little, then checked the patient's saline drip. She wrote up the notes on his condition and saw, too, that some flowers were past their best. As she went to remove them the man in the bed began to notice her blurred figure moving, moth-like, to and fro across the room. Her outline was hazy.

He had no idea who he was or where he was – his half-focused eyes simply followed the silent movement of this white outline. It was tiring. He closed his eyes and tried to remember. As he did, a sensation came to him: falling – a terrible fall – hurting. He groaned and suddenly the figure in white was bent over him.

When he woke again the room was empty. He had a hazy view of the metal end to his bed – a squarish shape with bars, and the whiteness beyond. So alien. Could he be...? His half-conscious mind could not quite grasp the concept of death. He tried to turn his head and came up against useless muscles. He groaned again and gave up.

Over the next few days, Bertrand became aware that his face was twisted on the right side as though he had had a stroke, though this revealed itself to him each time as a stiffness. He also realised that something was wrong with his sight. He remembered the fall but not the reason

240

for it, nor anything that had happened that evening. And he had no idea who he was. Efforts to remember tired him. Without material already there in the memory there were no building blocks; he could not begin to think. All effort was unbearably tiring and, each time, he fell into a half sleep until the nourishment fed into his veins prompted him awake again. From time to time he was aware of tall, white-robed figures turning him over, massaging his neck. The massage sent him to sleep again until they turned him again onto his back, took hold of some other part of him, which barely seemed to belong to him any more, stretching and bending it before putting the leg or arm back under the sheet.

A smaller white figure spoke. Her voice came to him as though through water and he stared helplessly back. He didn't have the strength, the knowledge any more, or the will, to reply. He was propped up and substances were put into his mouth. Some of it he was able to swallow, with effort. Enthusiastic noises came to him through the water barrier.

'Yes, Bertrand, it is difficult but you will get better.'

Better! The word struck him with some meaning. It suggested impossible happiness. Tears rolled down his cheeks. Without the ability to speak, he drifted instead back to the peace of unconsciousness. When he woke again, he found part of him was being moved forwards – nurses were lifting his hand onto a sheet. It was white paper on a board they had put on the bed. The texture was familiar and he brought what was left of his sight down onto it. He succeeded in dragging his large, now clumsy, hand over the surface. Cool and smooth – it brought pleasant sensations. The nurses next placed a brush in his hand. By accident it came into contact with the paper and he tried a waving, stroking movement. Then something deep in his brain told him the gesture was useless and he thrust both to the floor.

Downstairs, the phone rang. Jean could hear but suspected what it was and stayed in the gallery, sifting through the old, unsold paintings to see if any of his were worth salvaging. Not really – he was secure enough now to admit that only working in three dimensions fired his imagination. He could burn this adolescent rubbish. Bertrand's old work, though, he put to one side. When eventually he went downstairs, he knew what to expect.

'That was the hospital.'

'Yes.'

'Again.'

Yes, he knew. The whole business was nauseous. How could he see him? The longer time passed, the more devastated was he by the knowledge that Bertrand had tried to kill Amy and the unborn child. This man was not the person he knew: it was some vile stranger dying there or, what was worse, coming back to life.

'Success is making you ruthless,' his mother went on. 'It's rubbing off from the people you're with.'

'They're all artists!'

'Your new friends. The men with money.'

She'd never met Monsieur Perrachan but Jean had talked enthusiastically about his deal. Now, he was outraged by her selective memory. She might be pleased about the grandchild, now staying with its mother in Veuillans, but her loyalty to Bertrand remained stubbornly strong and Jean was stung by the injustice.

'Do you realise what Bertrand tried to do?'

'I said your leaving would be the end of him – and so it is.'

242

'It didn't have to be,' he shouted.

'If you don't go,' she concluded, 'I will.'

She was sending him back to the abyss. At the hospital next day there was a squeal of brakes as another driver narrowly missed him when he thrust the car door open and lunged across the road. Numbly, he arrived at the main doors and continued with his automaton progress. This journey was just a terrible repeat of the first. He reached the side ward and tried to relax, avoiding looking through its small window. He had no choice but to go in so there was no point learning more to deter him. Eventually, he made himself push at the swing door.

Bertrand was awake and vacant eyed. He looked awful. Jean hung back in the doorway, adapting to the sight of the gaunt figure – cheeks sunken, skin waxy, the outline of his shoulder bones appearing through the pyjama top. A faint sweet odour hung in the room. Fear was Jean's only emotion. He dreaded the claims the ruins of this man might have on his sympathy, the responsibility of all those years together. Bertrand was manipulative. What impossible promise might he wring out of him now with the blackmail of his ruin? He wouldn't remember his crime, of course, but if he had any understanding left he would play on any weakness. Jean steeled himself to look firm: more than that, above it all. Bertrand turned his head listlessly and looked into the new person's resolute eyes.

After a few moments his vacant look turned to one of interest. The blurred figure had a shape and a gaze that were familiar. Bertrand laid his head back on the pillow and, without a forced attempt to remember, images returned: a château, a gallery, paintings, forms – and a love. The oppressive emptiness in his head lifted a little and his face relaxed into a twisted smile of relief. Jean stood and watched this returning consciousness, hating his power to help. He looked at the twisted expression of Bertrand's smile. Was it bitterness or just the way his face was now? A guttural noise came out of the patient's mouth. The sound was sickening but Jean guessed that Bertrand was saying 'hello.' As he watched, Bertrand's expression became anxious. Something had spoiled it. A slim young man had ruined it. No, it was a woman. He had wanted her and she had been his destruction. A horrible understanding came clear in his mind. With frightening clarity he realised that what he was now was all he would ever be, ever again in this life. But Jean was talking now. He was being practical.

'I see you're getting better, Bertrand.'

In striving for detachment, Jean found the words mocking to his ears. He could not tell whether Bertrand heard him so went on without a pause.

'You needn't have any worries. I'm selling Ivrez. There'll be all the money you need.'

There was no reason to go into details and, as he looked at Bertrand's disfigured face, some kindness escaped from him.

'There's been a lot of praise for your work.'

Bertrand did not hear this. He was concentrating as best he could to fathom the sensation of his loss of everything; a loss so profound, so irretrievable that he drowned in it. This man, he knew, had won.

'Did you hear me, Bertrand? You'll have all the money you need.'

He caught the word 'money'. Fragments of memory came to him: rooms full of people, smiling faces, applause and night-time rides in a bright red car. All over. All over for ever. Everything over for ever. He turned away. Jean took it as his cue and moved towards the door. But then waited. This conversation was not over. As Bertrand's look fell towards the window a blurred image of a table in front of it appeared, with the blurred image of a simple glass tumbler on it full of water. The sight was so ordinary it distracted him from his thoughts and brought a peaceful space into them. There, he found the answer. He turned his face again, looking directly at Jean for some time and Jean read the expression in Bertrand's eyes with unexpected affection. It seemed he was cancelling all debts. It seemed, Jean read with relief, that Bertrand did not want to see him any more. Did he remember? Did he know what he had done? Was he acknowledging his responsibility? As Jean wondered and held the look of his old friend he was taken back to the time they first met. So much that was good had happened. He would like to say that, but it was not possible. Not even relevant. There was no room for sentiment. This was good-bye. Jean nodded and left the room. 'Life was a poor thing anyway': the thought came to Bertrand. The man who'd come in was fit, but Bertrand had seen the skeleton beneath the skin.

It was some days later when, as usual, two white bird-like figures entered his room. His fragile consciousness followed them as they approached the bed. It seemed to him they were flying: gentle, dove-like creatures, now lifting his head. There were pains – odd since no part of him seemed connected any more. The creatures arranged the pillows and offered him food on a spoon, which he did not respond to. They murmured to him for a while, then the white birds flew away. The room was very quiet. Now there was work to do; work in patience, in withdrawing, and waiting. He felt himself moving along a conveyor belt towards something inevitable. Not too unpleasant and, anyway, inevitable. His mind went over the scattered fragments he could recall: metal

245

and fire, the smart red car, applause, destruction. This bed was his grave, which he would leave. He would achieve great things. His attention shifted to the sunlight strengthening through the window, catching on something coloured outside and casting a white pool inside on the lino. So bright and cheerful, so inviting, it absorbed him into its happiness. He would move across the room and into it. After a few minutes another figure came in; she walked quietly through the room and dropped the blind, cutting off the pool. After this brutality she left. But it made no difference at all.

Jean was finishing his painstaking work, fusing a thin coating of gold leaf in precise amounts along the frame of the elegant, oval wheel. It demanded that he sit very still and his muscles threatened cramp. When he reached the next spoke he stood up and stretched. The room had become warm. The summer sun had got round to this north-facing window. As he strolled over to open it, a sweet emotion came to him. Even the scent of flowers, though there were none outside. Most of all, came the conviction that all was well with Bertrand.

He had died. An embarrassment was gone. No one would miss him.

POSTSCRIPT

1972

Between Cannes and Nice the curve of the coastline is long and meandering, ladling up sun when other corners of the Mediterranean are cold-shouldered by mist or stubborn knots of cloud. In front of tall hotels rubber-capped heads are already bobbing in the sea and promenades are dotted with strollers on their way to, or returning from, the same exercise. Behind this playground for the elderly the coast gives way to Alpine slopes, their crags softened by poplars, cypresses, and palms. White houses lean against orange trees; terraces of vegetables cascade down hillsides, linking house with house. A heat-haze has begun to rise, absorbing the colours of land and sky, and starts to float as a blue-green wash down to the cobalt sea.

If you were in the glider circling leisurely in the rising air you would become aware of a group of people on one of the stony outcrops to the north. You would become aware of them because of the bright colours of the dresses and the hats. You might hear the chink of glasses, and note the talk was not high-pitched, therefore they had only had one glass of the excellent champagne. The famous Côte d'Azur light intensifies the colours and falls too on one couple dressed, curiously, in black. Silence would seem to follow as the voice of the man giving the speech would not reach you, but the applause after it would. And you might watch the crowd as it then began to climb a hillside path through the pines towards a distinctive building at the top. The track steepens and the company breaks into smaller units, some pausing to catch their breath while taking in, through the trees behind them, the view sweeping down to the sea. The group in front reaches the top and passes Miro's waterspout; but you would not see this colourful gargoyle, only the sun glinting on its falling water.

'...it shows how just a few years can be enough to do a lifetime's work.'

'And lasting long beyond that.'

Amy is talking easily with the gallery owner but she is glad they have reached an open spot where the sun can penetrate. She pauses to put her camera away and allows the two women in black to pass with a brief nod of recognition to one of them, then catches sight of Jean down the hill below, and waves. The two women continue on ahead. They reach a low gate at the top leading into a courtyard. Inside is a group of light-hearted sculptures: a man-chair, a senile car, a man-abstract with pitchfork balanced on the wall and about to topple into the trees. The two women pass them with a smile of pleased familiarity. They pass briefly through an entrance hall and out again onto the front lawn where Pepin the Giant by their old neighbour, Jean Arp, stands. They continue leisurely, talking confidingly, as they open the entrance gate, disturbing brown and yellow butterflies sunning themselves on it.

'Madeleine – leaving already?'

'To discuss business with my mother,' she replies graciously. 'Come and join us.' The older woman smiles in agreement.

Conversation with the tall man with well-chiselled, very masculine face and hair in the new long fashion continues

250

a few moments before the women step into their limousine and speed downhill.

Jean waves back and waits until the sound of voices fades completely. He has much to think about. In the copse of cypress behind him are works he has so far refused to look at. When Jacques had broken his way into the studio, in defiance of the 'lost' key, Jean had remained in the kitchen deep in the paperwork of the gallery's sale. When the lorry arrived to transport Bertrand's last work, Jean had chosen to be elsewhere. But it was easier now that Eddie was a healthy two-year old and Jean and Amy doing well. The horrors were part of another man's life and Jean is curious about this unexpected legacy – Bertrand honoured with a display here in this ground-breaking gallery, the Museum of the Open Air, the only one of its kind in France. When the only sounds are the thrushes singing Jean walks into the dappled shade to re-engage with older shadows.

Nothing here reminds him of that private viewing two years ago. Here, the pieces pushing up through the angular branches of the trees are figures over two metres high and his first thought is wonder at how Bertrand had ever got them inside the studio. Of course, they'd been kept horizontally which was why he'd never even noticed them. They are breathtaking, elongated and wraith-like, neither male nor female. The first has small arms emerging from the hips – bony hands tightly clasped in front. The face is a hollow cry. The second has only one leg into which the spine curves. The head is twisted round to the left beyond what is humanly possible. This is a tortured amputee but, in the open air, Jean can see that both are expressions of grief rather than of malice. They would now stand permanently here. Smaller figures

251

hide in the bushes: foetal forms of aggression and hurt but highly inventive. They were taking the art world by storm. Gone were the coy metaphors – this was un-adulterated pain.

No one was to blame of course. Bertrand had created his own demise. That was what was recorded here. Extra-ordinarily stupid he'd been to tempt fate. What a brainstorm to over-ride years of calculated self-preservation. What long-buried deep desires had been there? And how odd that, for Jean, the result is still the only fulfilment he could imagine. Two years on and he and Amy are still happy. Jean had changed in many ways. He had even become a first-rate businessman, persuading Jacques to persuade the State to buy the gallery at Ivrez, and make it a Regional Arts Centre. And it had been Jean's idea for Amy not to sell the London flat – it was proving a useful base for their expanding life-style. It would be an insult to Bertrand not to enjoy his own success after the price Bertrand had paid for it. Most surprising is the way Jean has embraced a contemporary image. Gone is the self-effacement, the old clothes. Jean's prosperity shows in the sharply cut, fawn leather jacket, his good humour in the spring in his step. His embracing of the modern has even allowed him to try out, for this special occasion, the new, flared trousers. His past remains only in the interesting lines of his face. He has stopped running his hands through his hair, also grown longer, but the benefits of past years have left a healthy gleam – even though it is thinning a little as he approaches his thirty-ninth birthday. To those who look at him with shock after Bertrand's death he turns a steely resolution. He tests public accusations against that last meeting and the charges disintegrate. Once Amy had accepted the invitation the three had been caught by currents beyond them. Yet these works of Bertrand's are powerful. If it

252

had been his intention to have a final say then he had succeeded. They are original and unforgettable in ways that Jean would never achieve and he would have to live with that. He makes his way out of the copse and starts on the upward climb, wondering whether the glider overhead is part of the celebration.

Madeleine Védrine and her mother, though, had found the exhibition slightly distasteful, not the kind of genius they warmed to – and would their calves ever recover? The whole episode had been curious – 'the wrong-angled triangle', René had quipped. Once settled in the stylish Café Onze their talk picks up again on the more interesting topic of the future of the vineyard since the death of Madeleine's father – an unreasoning man, whom she had avoided since marrying René, devout in the forms of his faith: outward form, inherited structures, inherited behaviour – only these had mattered. It was hardly surprising that, during the war, he had also developed fascist leanings and no surprise at all that the man Madeleine had chosen to marry had no convictions whatsoever. Now that the tyrant is gone Madeleine is renewing ties with her mother whose close eye on the vineyard – repairing her husband's social brutalities – makes her more than ready to see what she herself can do. Madeleine shares her feeling of achievement. Once back in Paris she had dropped other of her family reservations. It was still early days but she confides a possibility to her mother. Despite this good news and the summer warmth, both had chosen what was in keeping with family circumstances and both look very smart in black. They had kept to outward forms; the dead man would rest content.

The door of the restaurant opens and Alain Degré

comes towards them. How clever of him to have found them so easily. He has with him another man whom Madeleine vaguely remembers, picking out the right name at the last minute as she introduces to her Mother Hébert Chapu from the Semilly studio. She had always thought this man very strange and very unhappy – even alarmingly depressive. Today he is much less dishevelled, both in his clothes and his face. Both men are wearing rings on their middle fingers. This means nothing to her mother of course but, on seeing the rings, Madeleine experiences a moment of crystallised time, conscious of still-spreading ripples of social change and guessing that Hébert's newfound confidence has much to do with the recent publication of two novels, Job's Dream and The Great Love. Both are explicit homosexual broadsides and they have been well reviewed. They are even fashionable. Hébert sees the flash of understanding in Madeleine's eyes and a glint of appreciation appears in his own. It is true. He is getting used to a feeling that he is, for the first time in his life, 'socially visible' – his private title for Alain's recent portrait of him – and his lopsided smile has lost some of its cynicism.

'Bertrand was born out of his time,' he says confidingly to her.

'That could be true,' she replies with the same cool intimacy.

'But, at least he has made his name,' adds Alain. 'That's all any of us can ask. Or,' he went on, turning to Madeleine's mother, 'I could be consoling myself with that thought.'

'Yes,' she replies, oblivious of his real meaning, 'we'll never know.'

'I'm surprised René didn't find a reason to come down,' Hébert adds, wondering about the facts behind Madeleine's own life.

'No,' Madeleine says, happy to continue this meeting of minds, 'he's much too involved with l'Orangerie.'

They had known of his own frustrations and, like her, would understand that in his own way René also felt much more of a man now back in Paris where the real life was and with the job he wanted – even his wife carrying his child, though these men knew nothing of that of course and would not be interested if they did. Alain nods sympathetically and both conceal what they really think about René. They know something she does not – the obligatory mistresses strung about around Paris.

Amy sits on the low wall of one of the gallery courtyards watching a curly-headed toddler run and fall about with other toddlers. He is enjoying himself too much to notice her and his involvement with the game gives her equal pangs of pleasure and pain. An eighteen-year-old girl rolls a large, soft sausage-shape over the mat and the infants tumble, squealing, onto it. Apart from a slight look of fragility Eddie is no different from the others. When he wakes in the morning his grey eyes are always merry. When he falls over he cries a couple of bursts, as though that is the right thing to do, then picks himself up. Amy is glad to see that, among other children, he forgets to cry. She has no need at all to be concerned and sits, wondering where Eddie's curls could have come from. They contain more of those mysteries which still surround the loves of her life. For there are moments when John Barton's image slips into the picture. Not only is there the small matter of the same name but John also had curly hair. The baby sometimes seems born of them both and the name, 'Eddie', breaks this completely. He is his own person and too small to carry her baggage. Small, but very active, she can see as a chasing game begins. And how very south-of-France it is that the infants run about around a priceless piece by Miro. Relieved of responsibility, she takes advantage of the quiet time to make notes on her photographs of Bertrand's exhibition.

'The figures are effigies,' she writes, 'spectres from another world.' It had been unnerving revisiting his death, reminded again of the closeness of her own. She concentrates objectively. The sculptures are Bertrand's spectres, she thinks, not her own. It would be better not to include much about his private despair, nothing to create a connection between him and herself. It was true that it had been his ghoulish expression of love that had galvanised her feelings for Jean but it would be some years before she could admit to this. What is in her mind at the moment is the need for this, her second collection of photographs on the work of contemporary artists, to be out by the end of the year.

Jean approaches from the path, delaying his arrival so as to enjoy the sight of her tranquility as she sits, smart in her light suede dress, its short skirt revealing shapely legs. She is aware of his gaze and decides to enjoy it rather than look up. When he reaches her she has not quite finished her work.

'Was it an ordeal?' she asks, glad that her notes make the question an incidental one.

'No, not really. They're amazing. He'll be remembered. He might even think it was all worth it.'

'Yes, maybe,' and she waits until Jean is gathering up Eddie before casting an eye over the expression on his face. There is just a shade of jealousy. As they reach the car park they can see Jacques already getting into his own. Amy turns questioningly to Jean.

'We've arranged to meet in Vence.'

Neither need mention Jean's own work being displayed there, so different from what they've just seen – so full of life. First, though, is the short journey back to St Paul. Jean parks outside its walls, watching again while Amy's elegant form carries Eddie into thick stone shadows under the deep archway. Steep gunnels honeycomb this village; houses sit huddled one on another, making use of every inch of space, their rough-cut, white stone reflecting light the way that coral does. Eventually, Amy reaches a small courtyard with a fountain. She places Eddie on his two feet and they climb the few stairs to their own rented corner. After watching them go Jean heads on, up the hill.

The glider, too, is floating north. It has passed the marbled chalk of St Paul, housing the bones of Chagall. Carried by currents strengthening against the hills it circles high over the steepening road – a recent black gash cutting a serpentine route up through the deep pines to where Vence nestles below jagged white rocks, the last outpost before the Alps. From the Chapelle du Rosaire beyond the town, a group of morning visitors are emerging from their devotion to Matisse and are climbing into their coach to return for lunch in the town square. The slopes below the road resonate with the sound of woodpeckers and the buzzing of swarms of bees, as drills and electric saws claim more places in the sun for incomers.

Jacques has parked in Ash Tree Place, a high point in Vence's medieval defences. Behind the tree, the château houses Jean's installation which Jacques has organised along with Bertrand's because the even-handedness gives him a kick and, sitting beside his daughter's swimming-pool, the time to acquire a suntan. Now the ground floor of Château Villeneuve looks anything but medieval. The walls are lined and the floor padded. Mechanical figures beckon you inside, pull faces and blow raspberries. They invite you to dress up as clowns to the fanfare of an electric guitar. By magic, ten year olds behind red and white masks drop their good behaviour and run, dance, shout, wave their arms about as if their disguise has become their real selves. The word 'inter-active' has recently been invented. The interior of this first room is a vast cube with different colours of light transmitted down thousands of nylon threads hanging from the ceiling. The effect is like running through water. The second holds a large billiard table built of bric-à-brac. Bouncy balls are fired by giant levers. Around the walls watch cartoon silhouettes of smart folk, umbrellas singing to the sound of real drops of water falling on them. In a third you run on clouds, panels of soft blues and reds alternating with more strident gold and silver. They lead to a central bouncy bed which glows like the heart of sunshine and, finally, through a corridor of deconstructing marionettes that children can operate, you enter an *Alice-in-Wonderland* world: giant rhubarb, strawberries and cauliflowers of rubber – a dense forest for hide-and-seek. Jean's total environment has impressed the critics. 'It liberates and creates a dialogue between child and art.' Jacques walks round, absorbing the effect it is having on the present stream. He feels invigorated enough to open another door leading out of the enchanted world and into the more mundane one of the usual paperwork.

Jean follows up round the hairpin bends. His exhibition will be moving to Auxerre at the end of the week. And there is business to do at the Ivrez Gallery or, as it is now called, the Barenton Centre. He still hates the name. It erases his own and negates all his years of work there. It was the only one possible in the circumstances but it still ensured Bertrand's memory at the expense of his own – and it was Jean, not Bertrand, who had lost a finger rebuilding the roof. Struggling with resentment he'd originally suggested a neutral 'Ivrez Centre' or 'Loiret Centre'; barren alternatives, depersonalised, reflecting the meanness of his thinking. The Barenton Centre it had to be. After all, it had been Jean's idea to go, so it was up to him to accept the logical omission. Then he had found that agreeing to the name set him free all over again. When jealous pangs sometimes hit him they do at least keep his adrenalin flowing. While in Ivrez he will stay with his mother, installed in her small house. She has had her way and, in one last piece of mischievousness, Monique has invited her and Marcia to her wedding with Gérard Dupré. This way Jean will hear of the happy ending.

Jacques finds a bar and takes his coffee to a pavement table to wait – a free man who enjoys mulling over the past. The Moore exhibition had been an extraordinary climax and near disaster. Never would he forget walking into Rodin's garden that Monday morning, where Moore's fourteen-foot bronze 'Reclining figure – arch leg' dominated the terrace. The strong sunshine had brought out the orange-gold tones of the bronze. It had also played across the words 'This is' on one half and 'ridiculous' on the other, painted by a vandal in large white letters. The man's bigotry was passionate. It had impelled him to climb a ten-foot wall in the night with his paint-pot to express this point of view. Thankfully, the paint cleaned off easily. Equally thankfully the French press could be relied on not to make public any blot on the nation's honour. No overseas gallery would have trusted them again. And much else besides would have been ruined: getting Britain to warm to Europe after de Gaulle's departure, breaking down European prejudice against a great artist, salvaging Jacques' own reputation so as to leave on a high note. All that had found its way to the public and across the channel had been the critics' ecstatic praise. Jacques recalls his favourite: 'Moore has an ambition to speak of the great things in life. His work is creative in a large sense, communicating the power of creation. Innovators are the fashion, with their bags of tricks and gimmickry.' He dismisses thoughts that Jean is one; Jean is sincere in what he does and knows that he plays with the ephemeral.

The newly installed President had been pleased and Jacques had shared the glory. Using money released by cancelling one of de Gaulle's megalomaniac ideas, the State had bought the Gare d'Orsay. There would be no future break-ins there. It is no bad thing too, thinks Jacques, that even Paul was chastened. Two years on and there are more surprises. Bertrand has stepped up to be measured with the Greats: 'a man of modern anguish, born out of his time.' Alain is right about this, Jacques thinks. There have been such advances in surgery that, today, Bertrand might have made a good recovery.

Jean-Claude sees Jacques and holds up the traffic, as everyone does up here, to shout a few words signalling that he will park by the Ash Tree. Getting out, he notices again the glider that he fancies is following him. Up there is sunshine and stillness, suspended between sky and earth – lovely, but not for him. The bustle of the world is where his happiness lies. Even though he sees a visitor drop a plastic bag Jean waits till she is out of sight before putting it in the bin without rancour. He could base an artwork on the way it blows in the wind.

Once Eddie is asleep Amy finishes her work, then picks up the bulky letter that arrived that morning. It is from Sarah and the longest communication from her for several months.

'As you probably know, Stephen now lives in Grenoble. We have left our financial problems behind. Stephen is beginning to bring in enough to live on – there's a touch of success in the air. The house, too, hasn't been bad as a base, and the children are really happy. But there was something we didn't think about. Stephen and I brought ourselves with us. We simply haven't changed and the marriage was already over before we left. We both feel better since admitting this. In a way I admire Stephen for going off on his own. His French is so terrible. But he's not going back to Britain. He has charm of course. French women seem to like him. So he's found himself a French woman in Grenoble.'

Generous, Amy thinks, for Sarah not to feel dumped with two children.

'She's even helping him get another old car! I don't feel dumped though because I've been making discoveries of my own. You remember the leaflet you sent about Bertrand's commemoration. (Sorry I can't be there.) But did you notice that two of the exhibitions on there this year will be by women.

261

Two out of six – that's nearly half! Wonderful – impossible, I'm sure, a couple of years ago. So encouraging to us all. So I'm not going back to Britain either. I'll be going to University here. I'll need to take a language exam but that'll be fine and I've decided to move to Grenoble too. It's large enough for S & I to avoid each other but the boys will be able to see him and the boys are so happy it would be awful to drag them back north. S has agreed I shall keep the money from selling this house. And I'll get a good grant – Europe's wonderful for that sort of thing – the mayor here has been v. helpful. I feel really optimistic about the future! I even have a good friend in Grenoble, the daughter of our neighbours.

Lots of love, Sarah.
(Will phone when you get back to Paris.)'

This time it's Sarah who's the teenager, thinks Amy, and I'm the sober matron. Curious that I found my partner and they broke up. Sarah needn't worry about money though. Jean and I have more than enough. Amy still has enough of the old anxiety about Eddie's survival to check on the sleeping boy. He's fine. On her way back she passes a mirror and has a look at her matronly reflection. An exaggeration, but she has lost that heart-rending beauty of a couple of years ago. There is a calmer look about her, a confident air that men respect rather than instantly lust after. She is not at all sorry to see that bewildered soul depart.

Dusk approaches and Jacques' car follows Jean's back down to St Paul. Arrangements for the transfer to Auxerre are complete. As their cars glide down the switchback road both men are aware of how many new buildings are going up down in the valley – some good, some not. Jacques has recently read of the sale of the marshes outside Marseille to a company of oil importers. The mayor of the region had tried to rouse farmers and local businessmen to join him in buying up the *marais* themselves for the region, but the thought of money coming into their pockets had won over the thought of money leaving them. The modern world was still striding forward as confidently as ever, thought Jacques, interested in these human quirks.

What the man hanging around above them all day thinks of it is impossible to know. It is dusk. The glider has disappeared.